JUST A LITTLE JUNK

STYLO FANTÔME

Published by BattleAxe Productions
Copyright © 2017
Stylo Fantôme

ISBN-13: 978-1546736110
ISBN-10: 1546736115

Critique Partner: Ratula Roy

Editing Aides:
Barbara Shane Hoover
Ratula Roy

Cover Design:
Najla Qamber Designs
www.najlaqamberdesigns.com
Copyright © 2017

Interior Design: Champagne Formats

DEDICATION

To anyone who watches way too many movies.

10:00 A.M.

DAY ONE

What. The. Fuck.

She slammed her car trunk shut. Took a couple quick breaths, then popped it back open.

What the fuck!

Slammed it shut once more. Then slowly, very slowly, opened it again.

Yup. She wasn't seeing things.

There was definitely a dead body in her trunk.

What in the actual fuck!

...NINE HOURS EARLIER...

"I love this song!"

Jodi Morgan was drunk. And not just a little drunk, but A LOT drunk. Well into wasted territory. She tottered back and forth on her heels, somewhat swaying to the bass music that was filling the club. Her drink sloshed around in its glass, most of it splattering on the floor.

"Whooaaa, honey, careful now," her new friend chuckled as he steered her back towards a table.

"*You* be careful now," she snorted, then cracked up laughing at her own joke.

Friday night. She'd been avoiding work for most of the week, but come Sunday, she'd have to go back. So she and some coworkers had gone downtown to a bar, a last hurrah before Jo had to return to real life.

One bar had led to another bar, though, which then led to an Applebee's, which in turn led to a dance club. At least, she was pretty sure it was a dance club. She was on her eighth vodka sour—she could've been on the moon and she wouldn't have realized it.

"Can I get you another?" the guy asked, pointing at her mostly empty drink. She shrugged and handed him the glass.

"Why not?"

While her errand boy scampered off to fetch her more alcohol, she let her eyes wander around the room. Where had her friends gone? She was pretty sure she'd come with friends, but she didn't see any of the other girls anywhere. She sat up straight and squinted her eyes, trying to focus as she looked over the people on the dance floor. There was a brunette who might have been Kim, and a blonde who looked sort of like Michelle, and then *rawr*, some gorgeous tall drink of water who was just begging for her to come and slurp him up. She smiled to herself and managed to stand up, but then the drink of water turned to face her.

What are the chances!?

"Hey! Going somewhere?"

The guy who'd been following her around for most of the night was back at her side, a fresh drink in his hand. She glared at the dance floor for a second longer before taking the glass from him. She

2

chugged down its entire contents, then slammed the cup onto the table next to her before grabbing his wrist.

"Yeah. Let's dance."

She pulled what's-his-face out onto the floor, shoving and elbowing bodies out of the way. When she was in perfect viewing distance of her real prey, she came to an abrupt stop. New guy slammed into her back and she immediately started dancing, swaying her hips in a circle and grinding her butt against his crotch.

"Whoa, you got some moves," the man chuckled, and she felt his hands come to rest on her hips. She slowly turned around to face him.

"You have no idea."

For the rest of the song, she did her best imitation of a music video ho. Jo usually wasn't too big on the clubbing scene—she had rhythm, she could dance, she just didn't do it very often. That night, though, it was like she was auditioning to become a stripper, and new guy was her stripper pole.

"How you feeling?" he asked when the song finally wound down and the DJ began yelling something out over a megaphone.

"Hot," she replied, peeking over his shoulder, trying to see if her dance moves had any effect on their neighbor. But the other guy was gone, she couldn't see him anywhere.

"You sure are," her dance partner chuckled. "Let me get you another drink."

As he walked away, she waved her hands in front of her face, trying to create a breeze. The act of moving her arms and standing upright proved to be a little bit too much to handle, though, and she stumbled to the side. Jo could feel herself falling over, but before she could go down, an arm wrapped around her waist and propped her upright.

"Whoa there, someone's having a good time."

She just barely managed to conceal her excitement behind a look of feigned nonchalance. She didn't even bother looking at her knight in shining armor, she just went about smoothing out her dress. Or trying to—her fingers and brain weren't communicating very well with each other.

"I was. I *am*," she corrected herself quickly. "What are you doing here?"

"Looking for you."

"Didn't have anything better to do tonight? So sad."

"What's your problem?"

"*You* are, you stupid … water drink."

He burst out laughing.

"I'm sorry—what did you just call me?"

Jo opened her mouth to cuttingly explain herself, then realized even she didn't have a clue what she'd meant by that insult.

"I don't really know," she finally replied, then she squealed as her ankle abruptly rolled, throwing her to the side. The arm around her waist squeezed tight, holding her in place.

"Oh, Jojo, can't leave you alone for a minute," his deep voice laughed. She finally lifted her eyes to look her savior in the face.

"I hate it when you call me that, *Archie*," she drew out the nickname she knew he couldn't stand.

"Ah, see? Mine was preemptive—I knew you were gonna call me that."

Archer Calhoun. It was one thing to see him dancing from a distance, looking all sexy and smirky and … tall water drink-y. It was quite another to have him pressed up against her with his arm around her waist. It felt like her entire body was melting. He was so tall, she had to tilt her head back, back, sooooo far back, she just let it fall till she was staring at the ceiling.

"I called you like eighty times," she blurted out in a loud voice. He laughed again, and the melting sensation moved to her organs.

"Yeah, I saw all the missed calls. I was at work, my phone was off. Thanks for all the voicemails."

"I was trying to invite you to come out with us. Your job is so lame."

"Hey, it pays the bills. And I'm here now, aren't I?"

"Yeah. Yeah, hey, how'd you find us?" Jo asked, suddenly catching onto the fact he'd magically ended up in the same club as them.

"Called what's her name, your coworker. The redhead with the big ass. She said she'd left you all down here, and that *you* were two drinks away from being on your face," he chuckled.

"Yeah," she laughed as well. "And that was probably like three drinks ago."

"I can tell. C'mon, let's go sit down," Archer said as he held her tight and started walking.

"You can't tell me what to do," she informed him, but she clung to his side as he headed off the dance floor.

He sat her down first before taking a chair across the table from her. He continued smiling at her—no wait, *smirking*, she was positive it was a smirk—as he sipped at a drink in an old fashioned glass.

"I'm not that drunk," Jo suddenly decided to defend herself. Archer snorted.

"Really? Then what other reason could you have for working some random dude like a stripper pole?"

Yessssss, he was totally watching!

"Uh, cause maybe I want to strip for him? Why were you watching, anyway? *Jealous?*" she asked, grabbing a full drink that was sitting on the table and picking it up. He quickly snatched it out of her hand.

"Always jealous, Jojo. Hot dress, by the way," he said, then she watched as his eyes slowly dipped down to her body and traveled over her figure.

"Thanks, I borrowed it from your mom," she replied, smiling big at him. He barked out a laugh.

"Nice. But c'mon, this isn't you. Slutty dancing, picking up random guys? What's up?" he pressed. She bristled at his choice of words.

"Okay, my dancing was sexy, NOT slutty, and I am *not* drunk," she insisted. "Just because *you* drink like a pussy doesn't mean the rest of us can't handle our alcohol."

It was a challenge, and it didn't go unnoticed. He'd been holding a drink the whole time he'd been talking to her, and now finished it in one shot. She rolled her eyes, which only made him pick up the drink he'd taken away from her only moments before and he chugged the whole thing down.

"One time," he started talking as soon as he'd finished. "*One time* I puke in your car, and you will never let me forget it."

"Because only a bitch pukes after drinking three beers," she reminded him.

"I had food poisoning!" he laughed at her.

"Whatever. You handle your alcohol like a bitch."

"Takes one to know one, Jojo. So, tell me about your new friend. Seems like a real awesome dude. Gonna take him home?"

It was in their nature to rib each other, an integral part of their friendship. Archer did it because he thought it was all in good fun, but Jo did it because he drove her insane. He thought they were just friends, but he was so much more than that to her. Something different. Something she couldn't quite define. He was her best friend. Her neighbor. Her older-brother's-high-school-best-friend-slash-partner-in-crime-slash-the-dude-she-wanted-to-bang-so-hard-it-made-her-grind-her-teeth-at-night.

But the alcohol was clouding her brain, not to mention her judgement, and suddenly it wasn't good natured teasing. She wanted him to really see her. Wanted him to acknowledge the fact that not only was she the best friend he'd ever had, but probably the sexiest one, too. Wanted him to lose some of those oh-so-cool vibes he always had coming off him in waves.

Jo slowly stood up and pressed one hand flat on the table top, keeping her balance as she leaned forward and grabbed a beer that was sitting next to him. While still leaning over, she lifted the bottle to her lips and stretched her neck, slowly taking in the fizzy liquid. She was very aware of her position and the fantastic view he now had of her rack, and what her stance was doing for said rack. When she finally sat the bottle down, he was still staring at her tits.

"If you'll excuse me," she said in a loud voice. When his eyes met hers, she gave him a tight smile. "I have to go find my stripper pole."

"I'm sorry ... what?" Archer was caught off guard. She waved her hand at him and began stumbling away from the table.

"Sorry, water glass, things to do, people to sleep with, all that jazz," she informed him. He gaped at her for another second, then when she almost face planted into a railing, he jumped up and hurried after her.

"Jo, you're not sleeping with that dude," he told her as he stood her upright once again.

"Pfffft, yes I so am," she laughed.

"You can't, Jo. He's ... you're way too drunk to do this," he insisted.

"*You're* too drunk."

"No I'm—" and because the gods seemed to be smiling on her that night, he interrupted himself with a hiccup. They stared at each other for a second, then both burst out laughing.

"You're drunk," she repeated herself. He nodded.

"Maybe a little, but I stopped drinking once I saw you two on the dance floor and ... and noticed how drunk *you* were. C'mon, let me take you home before you do something you'll regret. I'll tuck you in bed and put on your favorite movie. Hell, I'll even watch it with you."

Tempting. Archer hated watching her favorite movie. But at the same time, she didn't want to go home and curl up in front of the TV. She wanted to go home and have hot, nasty, crazy, heart attack inducing sex with him. But he treated her like she was his little sister or something.

Not sexy at all. I should just go home and have hot nasty sex with myself, and then watch my movie. Fuck these boys.

"*There you are!* I've been looking all over for you!"

Jo blinked her eyes at the man who'd walked up next to them.

7

She didn't recognize him at first, but then she saw the vodka sour in his hand and she remembered. Her stripper pole slash errand boy. She smiled big and took the drink from him.

"Sorry, you worked me up into a sweat out there! I had to take a breather," she laughed, stepping away from Archer so she was standing between the men, both of whom were now staring at each other in a super uncomfortable manner.

"Hi, I'm Bernard," her new friend introduced himself, holding out his hand. Archer smiled, and she couldn't be sure, but it looked a little strained. He didn't shake hands.

"I'm Jojo's friend," was all he said in response, and now she was positive he was strained.

Straining? Straineded? Stained? Shit, maybe I am too drunk ...

"Jojo," the man, Bernard, laughed. "Cute name."

"Oh, he's the only one who calls me that," Jo was quick to inter-ject. "He's like ... like ... like my kid brother, always coming up with cute pet names."

"Kid brother!?" Archer exclaimed. She smiled broadly. He was two years older than her.

"Ah, gotcha, so you two are like brother and sister," Bernard said.

"Basically."

"Not even remotely," Archer said at the same time as Jo spoke.

"Sounds fun. Wanna go dance again, Jo?" Bernard asked. She sneaked a peek at Archer's face, and was a little surprised to find that he looked beyond strained. He looked *angry*, and he was staring at her dance partner like he wanted to punch him in the face.

Hmmm, this is new! Let's play with this.

"I dunno, I'm still so worn out," she sighed, pressing up against Bernard's side. She was impressed with herself—the whole room seemed to be tilting on its axis, yet she still managed to remain up-right. She shook her head, then instantly regretted it. She knew she'd had a lot to drink, knew she was drunk, but she felt strange. More dizzy than just drunk spinny.

"Wanna go sit down, baby?" he asked, and she felt her gag reflex kick into gear. She hated men who did baby talk. And men who gave pet names before they even knew a chick. Hated sleazy men who hit on her in bars and were oblivious to the fact she was just using them to make another man jealous.

But then she saw the way Archer was looking at her new friend Bernard. So intense, so serious. She was always trying to get Archer to notice her as a sexual entity. Maybe it was time to take it to the next level and really put on a show for him.

"I'd love that," she breathed. As Bernard slid his arm around her waist, she winked at Archer. She watched as the muscles in his neck went tight with anger.

"Hey," he said as she walked off. "Be careful."

"Oh, I'll take good care of your *friend*," Bernard replied before she could open her mouth.

"I wasn't fucking talking to you, and if anything happens to her, I'll break both your legs," Archer stated in a loud voice. Jo was stunned and she gaped at him as he turned his gaze to her. "I'll be keeping an eye on you, Jojo. Don't do anything stupid."

"You guys must be close for him to be so jealous," Bernard was chuckling as he led her away.

But Jo wasn't really listening to him. She was glancing behind her and frowning as she watched Archer disappear into the crowd. So much for "keeping an eye" on her. She sighed and looked away, sitting down at a table Bernard had set aside for them. There was a fresh vodka sour sitting there, so she gulped it down. She was dizzy and dehydrated, and her brain felt like it was wrapped in a wet towel.

"Jesus, those drinks were strong," she grumbled, bringing a hand to her head as he sat down across from her. The room wasn't just tilting anymore, but spinning and possibly melting. She also couldn't feel her face. Or her feet. It felt like her tongue was swelling in her mouth.

What is going on?

"Relax, sweetie. I'm going to show you a better time than Archer ever could," Bernard assured her, and then he was kissing her, his own tongue battling hers for space in her mouth.

Seriously, Jo? He's not even that cute. What a fuckshow. I hope I puke on him before I pass out.

She never got the chance, though. While his tongue was still searching for her tonsils, she started falling back in her chair. She was completely blacked out before she even hit the backrest.

10:15 A.M.

DAY ONE

"Please be here, please be here, please be here."

Jo shifted her weight from foot to foot, almost like she was doing a potty dance.

Probably because I'm about to piss myself.

"Archer! Please be here!" she shouted, banging on his door for the millionth time.

"Be quiet down there, you're scaring my cats!"

Jo turned to see that two doors down, an old woman was sticking her head out into the hall. Mrs. Copernicus—building tattletale and general bitch. She had a thick wooden cane and wasn't afraid to crack it across shins. Jo glared.

"Oh, just go back inside!" she snarled, not in any kind of mood to deal with bitchy neighbors.

"Screw you!" the old woman snapped right back. Jo's jaw dropped.

"You know what? Today is not the day, Satan! So just turn the fuck around, or I'll come down there and make you eat your stupid little hat!" she yelled.

"Just try it, ya floozy, and I'll ram this walking stick up your ass!" Mrs. Copernicus warned her, brandishing her cane.

"Just try it, old lady!"

"Slut!"

"Bitch!"

"Hussy!"

"Goblin!"

"I'm gonna call the police!" the other woman finally threatened. Jo put her hands on her hips.

"Do it! And be sure to tell them some old woman is about to get her ass beat!" she shouted.

"I'll have you evicted so fast, you won't even—"

Suddenly, the door Jo was standing in front of was ripped open.

"Shut the fuck up, both of you!" Archer shouted, stomping into the hall, forcing Jo to back out of the way.

"She started it! She said she was gonna—" Mrs. Copernicus began yelling.

"Me? You old fucking bat, you're the one who—" Jo jumped right in.

"*Enough!*" Archer roared. "I have a fucking headache the size of the San Andreas fault! Mrs. Copernicus, you're not gonna beat anyone with your cane, and you're not gonna call the cops because then they'll find out you have fifty billion cats. Just go back inside, I'll shut Jo up."

There was some grumbling and definitely some more name calling, but Mrs. Copernicus finally crawled back into her hole.

"Archer," Jo breathed his name. "You have to come outside, I—"

"What the fuck? Jesus, Jojo, I'm hungover as fuck, and you're out here banging on my door and screaming at neighbors!" he groaned as he turned away from her. She snorted as he started walking back into his apartment.

"She's not a neighbor, she's a troll that got evicted from its bridge. Please, Archer, this is important, I need you to—" she tried again as she trailed after him, but he held up a hand.

"Coffee. Not another word until coffee, or I swear to christ, I will let Mrs. Copernicus beat you to death."

Normally, that would've been like a challenge to her, but the tone in his voice made her keep her mouth shut. Luckily, he had a full pot of coffee already made. She watched as he dumped some into a mug, then threw the cup into the microwave.

While the contraption dinged through the seconds, Archer yawned and raked his fingers through his hair, and for the first time since he'd opened the door, Jo realized she'd woken him up. He was wearing a pair of pants—Carharts, if she wasn't mistaken. His work clothes. Probably the first thing he'd stumbled across, they weren't even zipped or buttoned up. No shirt, clearly unshaven, and his hair looked insane. Under normal circumstances, all that usually equaled a package so sexy she'd have trouble concentrating on anything else. However, her little trunk situation had her kind of distracted.

"Okay," she began the moment his lips touched the cup. "Please, I know you're hungover and tired and cranky, but *please*, please come outside with me and look at something."

"I don't want to go outside. Let's have breakfast first," he suggested after a long pause, his voice hoarse and scratchy.

"No breakfast. I need your help."

"I'll change your tire later."

"It's not a flat tire. Come outside."

"I really don't want to—"

"Just come outside."

"Jo, if it's another dead raccoon, I will make you wear it as a hat."

"*JUST FUCKING COME OUTSIDE!*"

His headache was bad enough that he didn't want to endure another shriek from her, so after he'd pulled on a t-shirt and some shoes, Archer allowed her to yank him out the door. He cringed when they stepped into the bright sunlight—it was right around ten and the crisp morning air made everything clear and shiny. As they walked across the lot, his glare stayed in place, and he rubbed at the back of his neck.

"You wanted to show me your car?" he asked. "C'mon, Jo, I have to go to work, I don't have time for this. Go inside and get some sleep and I'll—"

"We've been friends a long time, yeah?" she started, interrupting him.

"I guess so."

"You guess so!?"

"Well, I was friends with Andy in school—do I count that for us?" he asked, referring to her older brother. She rolled her eyes.

"Jesus christ, Archer. Look, we're friends. I consider you a good friend. My *best* friend. So I'm trusting you not to judge me, okay?"

"Awww, best friends, Jojo? I'm touched!"

"I swear to all that is holy, I will cut off your nuts and turn them into key chains."

"Okay, okay, Bestie, chill out. Your seriously need to calm down. Maybe a little hair of the dog? Wanna go back inside and have a beer?"

She ignored him and nervously started playing with her hair, dragging the long brunette locks up into a ponytail.

"So I went out last night, with some friends from work. Just to like blow off some steam. But I kinda drank a lot, and I don't really—" she began babbling when he interrupted her by laughing.

"Kinda? Jo, you were so fucked up, I was surprised you were able to stand."

"You were there!?" she exclaimed.

"I was," Archer shook his head and chuckled. "You don't remember?"

"Clearly I don't!" she was almost shouting. She didn't remember him being there *at all*. She barely remembered the club, and had no idea how she'd gotten home.

"We had a full blown conversation. You had this guy you were

14

working over on the dance floor, then you and I had some drinks. Then Creeper dancing dude showed back up and you got all weird and you walked off while sucking on his neck. Was super gross," he explained to her.

"I … he … you …"

Jo felt all the air rush out of her body and she fell back against her trunk. It was a gorgeous, bright day already, but she didn't take any notice of it. A busy road was nearby, but she couldn't hear it. All she could hear was her own heart beat.

"C'mon, Jojo, it's not the worst thing ever. At least you didn't go home with him," Archer pointed out. That statement surprised her.

"How do you know?" she asked, glancing at him. He was silent for a second, glancing between her and the car.

"Because we came home together. How do you think your car got here? I drove us," he told her.

"You drove?"

"Yeah. Bad idea, I was a little drunk. In fact, I might still be a little drunk. Can we please go back to bed? We can discuss your car tomorrow," he offered.

"But if I came home with you … the guy you saw me dancing with, did you see him later? Before we left?" she asked.

"No, I lost track of you for a while. I found you after closing, sitting on the ground outside the club, snoring," Archer explained. She dropped her face into her hands.

"*Oh god!* Oh god oh god oh god," she moaned.

"Seriously, Jojo. It's just a one-night stand. We've all done it," he assured her. She snorted and rolled her eyes.

"No, *I* didn't. Or at least I don't think I did. Fuck, I don't know what I did. What am I going to do?" she shouted, standing up and pacing in front of the trunk.

"Shit, calm down. I'll take you to the free clinic, we can get you tested, I'm sure it's fine!" he kept going. She stopped moving and glared at him.

"Oh yeah? Does this look fine to you!?" she snapped, and with that, she popped open her trunk.

She wasn't sure what she'd been expecting. Maybe for him to jump back, or yell, or start accusing her of murder. She'd certainly do one of those things, or all of them, if someone showed her a dead body. Archer, though, he stood completely still and stared wide eyed into her trunk. But when she looked closer, she saw that his tan was fading away and he was going pale right in front of her.

"Oh god," he breathed, staring down.

"Yeah," Jo sighed, rubbing her hand across her forehead. "Think the free clinic will take care of this?"

"What the ..." Archer gasped as he leaned into the trunk. "Is that ... holy shit, Jo. What is he doing in your trunk?"

"Taking a nap. I was hoping you could kiss him awake."

"Why is he sleeping in your—"

"THERE'S A GODDAMN DEAD BODY IN MY TRUNK!" she screamed, slapping him in the chest. "WHAT THE FUCK AM I GOING TO DO!?"

"Okay. Okay, calm down. First thing is definitely calming down," he insisted, and he rested a heavy hand on her shoulder.

"How did this happen? Did I kill him?" she asked.

"Are you sure he's dead?" Archer checked. She glared at him.

"Not positive, but the massive pool of congealed blood underneath him makes me think he has to be," she replied.

"Okay. Okay, okay, okay."

"Stop saying okay."

"Okay."

She hit him in the chest again.

"Archer, I'm serious," she groaned. "I know I should call the police, but ... did I do this?"

She was horrified as she felt her lips start to quiver. Her eyes start to water. She almost never cried, and she certainly didn't want to cry in front of Archer. But it couldn't be helped. Besides, if a person couldn't cry over a random dead body in their trunk, that they may or may not have killed, then what could a person cry over?

"Oh, hey, Jojo. C'mon, you didn't do this," he assured her.

"How do you know that?" she cried, wiping at tears. "I mean, I was with him. It's my car. God, I did this, didn't I?"

"No, no, no," he moaned, and then he was pulling her into him. They'd known each other for over ten years, and for the last five they had been extremely close, but they didn't touch a whole lot. She was his friend's little sister—off limits. He was her brother's sexy out-of-her-league friend—untouchable. But none of that mattered in that moment, and she fell into his chest. Cried into his shirt as she wrapped her arms around his middle.

"I don't want to go to prison," she sniffled.

"I know you, Jo. Better than anyone else, and you could never do something like this," he whispered, his arms going around her shoulders. "You couldn't hurt a fly, let alone stuff a dead body in your trunk."

"Then how did he get in there? It had to have happened before you took me home, and you said I was alone outside," she pointed out.

"Doesn't matter. You didn't do this, I know it. And we'll figure this out. But first," he sighed and rubbed his hands up and down her back. "Let's go inside, drink a shit ton of coffee, eat some greasy food, and then tackle this."

"But shouldn't we call the cops?" Jo asked, pulling away enough to look up at him. She was a little startled to find him already staring down at her.

"Yeah, we should …" he let his voice trail off, and he glanced back at her car.

"But we're not?"

"No. Not a good idea. Let's just go inside," he urged, then he reached out with one arm and closed the trunk.

Jo moved to step away from him, but he kept an arm around her shoulders, anchoring her to his side. It was nice, being so close to him. She sniffled and leaned into him, letting him help her into the building and up the stairs.

They went back to his place instead of hers. They lived in a shitty building, in a shitty part of town—neither of them were exactly rolling in the dough. But he made more money than her, so he had the bigger apartment, and usually more food in his fridge.

"So why aren't we calling the police?" Jo asked about five minutes later. She was sitting at the island in his kitchen, and she cupped a warm mug in her hands—it was full of coffee and a healthy amount of brandy. Both had done wonders to steady her nerves and cure her hangover.

"Well, a couple reasons," Archer spoke slowly, leaning his elbows against the island across from her. "First being—it does look pretty bad. You were the last one to be with him when he was alive, and now he's dead in your trunk. Maybe we should see what we can remember and piece together before we involve the law."

"Okay, with you so far," Jo nodded her head while he spoke.

"Second of all—is your car even registered? Insured? Emissions tested? Smog certified?" he checked. She coughed and shook her head.

"No."

"Which one?"

"Most of them."

"How many times have I bugged you about that shit?"

"Well, it's too late now, isn't it?"

They stared at each other for a second, then Archer just shook his head and they both sipped at their drinks.

"And third of all—remember that party the other week?" he asked. She nodded.

"Yeah, you passed out in my kitchen," she reminded him.

"Yeah. I also may or may not have hidden an ounce of coke in your bathroom," he said in a quick voice.

"Are you shitting me?" Jo gasped, sitting upright. He winced and rubbed at the back of his neck.

"Sorry. I was a little drunk, a little stoned. I … some guy talked me into buying, and then I just … I panicked. Paranoid, thought someone would find out or whatever. So I was like *'hey, no one would ever suspect cute little Jodi of having hard drugs, I'll hide it here'*—but then I sort of … forgot," he explained.

Normally, Archer calling her cute would've sent her over the moon. That day, however, she wasn't exactly in the mood.

"You bought and hid drugs in my apartment," she groaned. "I can't believe you! I don't even do coke!"

"Hey, neither do I. It was just … a really good deal."

"Oh, I'm so glad, Archer. So frickin' happy."

"We're getting off track here," he sighed. "So we can't call the cops because you look kind of guilty, and you would become someone's bitch so fast in prison."

"I would not …" she started to argue, but then she thought about it. "Yeah. Yeah, it wouldn't be pretty. And even if I didn't look guilty, we can't have officers wandering around here till we get rid of your little drug habit."

"Hardly a habit, Jojo. It was a … drunken impulse purchase."

"Impulse purchase, jesus. This is my life," she dropped her forehead to the counter top.

"Why don't we just dump the car?" he suggested. She lifted her head and sighed.

"Awesome idea, Archer. Dump the car and just hang out for a couple days, waiting for the police to find it. I love the suspense of it all, not knowing exactly when I'll go to jail."

"C'mon, Jo. I doubt you even registered the car, did you? And even if you did, you probably did it wrong. They won't be able to trace the car back to you!"

She frowned. Buying drugs and hiding them in her apartment was bad enough, but hearing him talk so comfortably about dumping her car somewhere, knowing there was some random stranger dead in the back of it … it all made Jo feel uncomfortable. A feeling she'd never experienced before with Archer.

"Yes, but even then, what? The cops show up at the original owner's house? We just let them take the fall? Or wait for them to point the police in my direction, anyway? And what about the poor guy in my trunk? I mean, I don't want him in there, but don't you … I'm sorry, Archer. I just can't. He's got to have a family or something somewhere. Could you really just … *leave him* in the middle of nowhere? No. However he got there, whatever happened, it's at least partially my fault. It's *my* car. Either we do this ourselves, or we call the cops."

There was a long pause, and for a second, Jo was worried he would argue with her. She wasn't sure how well she would handle it. But then he took a deep breath and stood upright.

"Okay!" he yelled, clapping his hands together so loud it startled her. "We're going to figure this out. We can do this."

"You really think so?" Jo asked, resting her head in her hands and watching as he walked around the island and came to a stop next to her.

"Yeah. We'll come up with a plan. We'll retrace your steps last night, ask around, figure some stuff out."

"What about your job?"

"A dead body is a little more important than work, Jo. I'm gonna take a shower and then we can dedicate the whole day to this. It'll be okay," he assured her, reaching out and rubbing her shoulder.

"I'm sorry I dragged you into this," she said, looking up at him. "You don't have to do anything, you know. I know missing work is hard."

He was a stringer on a construction team—not really an employee, but a friend of a friend who worked for the company. He got paid under the table, worked at random locations, usually pretty far away, and regularly put in ten hours or more a day. It worked for him, he seemed to like the come-and-go nature of his job, but she worried that if he didn't show up, he might lose his spot on the crew.

"Hey, if you can't share a dead body with your friend, who can you?" he asked, and she actually laughed.

Her life was mostly likely over as she knew it, and she was probably going to end up in jail before the weekend was over, but she had to laugh when he laughed. It was just the way it had always been between them. Her basking in his overwhelming presence.

"But hey," he said as he moved towards his bathroom. "What were you doing in your trunk at ten in the morning, anyway?"

Jo's laughter fell away and she stared hard at him for a second, trying to read his features. Why would he ask that? Did he think she'd done it? Did Archer really think she was capable of doing something like that?

*Do **I** think I'm capable of something like that?*

"My work outfit," she started, then she had to clear her throat. "That costume I have to wear? I've gotta go to work tomorrow and I remembered it was in the trunk. It has to be hand washed, I wanted to get it over with and give it plenty of time to dry. Now I'm kinda wishing I'd just slept in."

He nodded, staring off into the distance. As she watched, he lifted his hand to the back of his neck and rubbed at it nervously.

"Yeah. I'm kinda wishing that, too," he mumbled, and Jo felt the waterworks getting ready to start again. Then he sighed and looked at her, his smile back in place. "But hey—let's look at this as another crazy Archer-and-Jo-Adventure. Maybe we won't get arrested at the end of this one!"

Before she could argue that this was in no way like any of their previous "adventures", he stepped into the bathroom and slammed the door shut.

11:03 A.M.

DAY ONE

Jo stared at her toilet tank, her hands on her hips. A nervous, defensive pose she assumed often. Archer stood next to her, his bottom lip caught between his teeth, his right hand rubbing the back of his neck—his own nervous tic.

"I still can't believe you hid it in here," Jo grumbled. Archer leaned back and glanced out the bathroom door.

"You sure she's gone?" he asked, referring to her roommate Mandy.

Jo's full time job as a waitress at a strip club was barely enough to pay her cell phone bill, let alone cover rent. But at the ripe old age of seventeen, when it had become obvious that she wouldn't be going to college like all the other shiny pretty girls at Burbank High School, she had decided to forge her own path.

Apparently, that path led to a shitty part of Van Nuys. She'd met Mandy at the casting call—er, she meant, *interview*—for the strip club waitress job. Mandy's uncle managed an apartment complex, said he would cut her a deal. It was still too much for the girl to afford, but splitting it with a roommate would put it just under budget.

Jo had known instantly her and Mandy would never be besties, but she'd needed a place to live. She had to get away from home. Being from one of the poorest families in Burbank had never been a joy, but on top of that, she'd also come to the realization that if she ever wanted happiness, she'd have to go find it somewhere else.

She'd fallen in love with Archer the first time she'd ever met him. She'd been thirteen and her older brother had just made varsity basketball. A big deal in their household. About two weeks after the announcement, he'd come home with a friend from the team—Archer Calhoun. If her family had been one of the poorest, Archer's was probably *the* poorest.

She didn't care about any of that, though. All she saw was a great smile on top of long legs, hazel eyes under shaggy light brown hair. He was funny, and he was nice, and he always made her feel comfortable. She'd been an awkward tween, all legs and no body. Andrew Morgan, the sports star, and his gawky little sister. No one had ever really paid attention to her, until Archer.

Sure, he'd been two years older than her, but the age difference hadn't mattered to Jo. And as they grew older, her crush grew, as well. She used to fantasize about him coming into her room, or asking her to a dance. Being homecoming king to her queen. Dumping his current girlfriend in the crowded cafeteria by loudly proclaiming it was Jo he'd really been in love with the whole time.

Of course, none of that ever happened. Her brother graduated with a 3.9 grade point average, and an even better average on the basketball court—he went to UCLA on a full scholarship. Archer's playing hadn't been half as good, and his grades had been even worse—he went on to work in his step-dad's garage.

Jo's own grades had been nothing to brag about, and though she'd eventually grown out of the awkward stage and had filled out pretty nicely, nothing much else changed by the time she'd graduated. Her brother was gone, she was a disappointment to her parents, and Archer was banging some chick from the Marinello School of Beauty.

Fuck that. Because of her birthday, she'd graduated at seventeen, so she got a fake I.D. and she looked for jobs in neighboring towns. Far enough away she wouldn't have to see him, but close enough for her to visit home whenever she needed to borrow money from her parents.

It had been good, at first. Spreading her wings and whatnot. Her job was shit—at least the strippers had the stage between them and the seedy guys who frequented the club. It mostly paid the rent, though, and she made pretty good friends with some of the dancers and other servers. She even met a guy at a Chili's one night and went on to date him for almost her whole first year away from home.

Everything changed after that, though. Her brother came home for the summer, and he and Archer visited her over her birthday weekend. Andy had always been a sort of do-gooder, so it was Archer and Jo who wound up shutting down the bar. He slept on her couch, then the next morning a big group of them all went to breakfast.

That was it. She could feel the change coming before it even happened. Van Nuys neighborhood was only about twenty or thirty minutes away from Burbank. He started driving over on the weekends to party with her and her friends. She dumped her boyfriend. Though she still had a crush on Archer, it wasn't as bad as it had been in high school. It was easier being around him. Fun, even.

About two months after her birthday, the apartment at the end of her hall came up for rent. She casually mentioned it to him one day. A couple weeks later, he was all moved in, using the excuse that the rent was good and that Andy had asked him to keep an eye on Jo.

Pffft. If anything, Archer was a bad influence on her. Her jealousy made her competitive, so it was often a pissing contest between them. Who could drink more, who could get more numbers during a night out, who could bag the best looking person in the room.

... who could make who jealous at a night club and then get black out wasted and then possibly kill a man and dump him in their trunk ...

Archer fucking Calhoun. Since he'd moved into the building,

he'd been slowly driving her insane. And now that she found herself staring at her own toilet for a solid five minutes, she wondered if he'd finally pushed her over the edge into irreversibly crazy.

"Okay," she took a deep breath. "We can do this. I mean, remember our trip to Vegas? You sold all that weed to pay for the weekend."

"Selling some dirt pot to a tourist is a little different from trying to unload an ounce of coke, Jo," Archer warned her. She threw up her hands.

"Like you would know how hard it is to sell coke. We need money, Archer."

"This is a bad idea."

"You're totally right—but my car is almost empty. We can't take your bike. I have negative two dollars in my bank account, and it's the middle of the month, you haven't gotten paid yet," she said, though she looked at him hopefully, as if maybe he'd magically gotten his paycheck early. He frowned and looked away from her.

"Yeah, pretty much broke."

"So that means we either start selling our clothes for a couple bucks, or we get rid of this fucking coke," she stated.

"Right. Okay, you're right," he agreed. "I know some guys, we could unload it quick. Plus, we should get it out of here, just in case the police do get involved."

"Sounds good," Jo nodded, and as she turned to walk out of the bathroom, Archer leaned over the toilet tank. They'd removed the lid and just inside there had been a plastic baggy floating. He plucked it out of the water and shook it off as he trailed behind her.

While he sat on the couch and made a phone call, Jo scoured the house for loose change. Stole a couple bucks from Mandy's piggy bank, then grabbed a couple pairs of her jeans, as well. To sell in case they couldn't unload the drugs and needed more money later.

When she went back into the kitchen, Archer was talking animatedly to someone, using ridiculous code words. She felt like she was going to burst apart at the seams, or break down into tears, so she had to keep busy. She fried up a bunch of bacon, then ate so much she started to feel sick. She used the rest to make them sandwiches. A little snack to bring along on their "adventure".

"Are you planning on having a picnic?" Archer asked, walking up as she shoved four sandwiches and a bunch of diet cokes into a plastic bag.

"I'm saving us money. What did you find out?" she replied.

"There's some daytime rave happening today, out near the airport. I can find a buyer there," he said.

"Awesome. We can get rid of the drugs. You haven't hidden anything else around here, have you?" she checked. He held up his hands.

"Promise."

"Good. Okay. Okay ... maybe we should make a list?" she suggested. He nodded his head.

"A list is good," he agreed, and he walked over and grabbed a magnetized pad off her fridge.

"What should we do first?" she asked, chewing on her thumb nail.

"It's like what, ten o'clock? I say let's go back to the club, start at the beginning," he suggested, scribbling it all down as he said it.

"*Ug*, that's all the way back downtown," she groaned. He glanced at her.

"Would you rather the police do it?"

"Right, downtown first."

"We'll ask around, see if anyone there saw us last night. Did you know the guy's name?" Archer asked, watching her carefully. She frowned.

"I don't know. Terry? Tom? Something?"

"You were gonna bang the dude and you didn't even know his name?"

"Hey! You are not one to judge, and you know it."

"Whatever, ho-bag," he chuckled, then went back to writing. "We just need to ask the right questions. Look around. Google some shit. Something will turn up."

"You sound so confident," she sighed, staring down at his handwriting.

"Because I am. It'll be okay. We'll get to the bottom of this," he assured her.

"What happens if we get to the bottom of this and I'm not innocent?" she asked. He stopped writing and looked up again. She hadn't realized how close they were to each other and she was startled to see his eyes had taken on a mossy green hue, with brown flecks around his pupils.

You have a dead body in your trunk, stop thinking about how hot Archer is.

"You're innocent, Jo. And even if you weren't …" he let his voice trail off and it took her a second to realize he was staring at her mouth. She took a shaky breath.

"If I'm not?" she urged him.

"Then we'll deal with it," he replied, his gaze sliding away from her.

"You would do that for me? Bury a body?" she checked.

"Jo, if you haven't figured out yet that I'd do just about anything for you, then you're even stupider than you look," he snorted at her, then he turned away with a laugh. She was still reeling from his words as he headed towards the door, so she scrambled to grab the bag with their food and rushed after him.

Jodi was generally a good driver—obeyed speed limits, braked for yellow lights, never cut anyone off. But with a body in the trunk, she'd turned into a Sunday driver. An old one, possibly with gout. She was gripping the steering wheel so hard at ten and two, her hands ached. She was doing eight miles under the speed limit and sweat was breaking out along her hair line.

"I am not cut out for this," she panted. Archer snorted and she glanced over at him. He was sunk low in his seat, gnawing at one of his thumb nails.

"Not even a little. Just chill out and we'll be downtown in no time," he assured her. She grimaced and glanced in her rear view mirror.

"See, moments like this are why you should own a real car," she suggested, and he burst out laughing.

"So I should trade in my motorcycle—a.k.a. the pussy magnet—for some four door sedan, just in case you wind up with another body in your trunk," he double checked.

"Well, 'magnet' is being a bit generous, but otherwise, yeah."

"You're a laugh, Jojo. A goddamn riot. And why'd you take the 170 to 101 south?" he questioned her navigating.

"Because it's faster," she replied, grinding her teeth together.

"Traffic is shit right now."

"I just like this way better, okay?"

"Should've taken the 405," he said, tapping at his phone for a moment before holding up a picture of a map. "Could've saved us five minutes."

"Just stop," she snapped loudly, startling him.

"What?"

"I know what you're doing," she stated. "You think busting my balls will distract me. Well, it won't, it's just annoying me and making me even more paranoid."

"Hey, I'm just trying to help with the directions, that's all," he replied, dropping his phone and holding up his hands.

"Sure. Fine. Whatever. I'm good on directions," she said through clenched teeth. He was silent for all of four seconds.

"But really, you also should've stayed on 134 east."

She let out an angry shriek and suddenly yanked the car out of its lane. The vehicle behind them honked, but she ignored it and came to a stop on the shoulder. She put on the emergency lights before turning in her seat to face Archer.

"I'm goddamn serious," she said, pointing a finger in his face. "*This* is serious. There's a fucking dead guy in my trunk! *A dead guy*. What does it take for you to be serious, just for like five fucking minutes!?"

"Chill, Jo. I didn't mean—"

"I appreciate your help, Archer, I really do. But if I hear your mouth one more time before we get down there, I swear to christ, I will punch you in the nuts until you piss blood."

"Damn, dude," he mumbled. They stared hard at each for a second, and she thought that just maybe she had gotten through to him. Then he took a deep breath and smiled. "But you have to admit, it's totally working—you're not freaking out about going to jail anymore."

"Because at this point, jail would be a blessing. It would mean I'd be getting away from *you*," she told him.

"Such a sweet talker, Jo. It was probably your mouth that led to him being dead in your trunk," he chuckled, and she gasped.

"Jesus, Archer! Too soon!" she yelled, slapping him upside the head.

"No such thing," he argued through his laughter, smacking her hands away as she continued slapping him.

"You are the worst. The absolute worst. I'm gonna turn this car around and figure this out on my own, because at this rate, there will be two dead bodies back there!"

"Ouch. *Too soon*," he mocked her.

"That's it, I—"

They both turned into statues as a car slowly rolled up behind them. Normally, she would figure it was just a concerned motorist, stopping to offer assistance. This time, however, the flashing red and blue lights made her think it might be a different kind of motorist.

"Oh shit!" she hissed, ducking in her seat. "Oh shit, oh shit, *oh shit!*"

"Calm," Archer insisted, peeking between his headrest and the seat, trying to look out the back of the car. "He's just getting out, he's talking into his radio. We need to think of something."

"Like what? Donate to the policemens foundation!?" she snapped.

"Shit, he's looking at the trunk," he mumbled, and Jo felt all the color drain out of her face.

"Oh god. I'm gonna go to jail," she breathed.

"No wait, I think he's looking at … a tail light? Goddammit, Jo, is your fucking tail light out?" Archer growled. She chomped on her bottom lip.

"Um … I don't know?" she offered. She honestly couldn't remember. She'd changed it a couple months ago, she was pretty sure.

"Christ, he's walking up here. He's gonna ask why we're stopped in the emergency lane. Just go with me, okay? We'll be fine," he assured her, his hand landing heavily on her shoulder. She turned in her seat, twisting so she was facing him again.

"Alright. What are you going to say?" she asked. He grimaced at her.

"It's not so much what I'm going to say …"

"Huh?"

Jo let out a yelp as the hand on her shoulder abruptly jerked her forward. She didn't have time to think as his lips covered hers, couldn't even process what was happening when his tongue slid into her mouth. She was yanked out of her seat and she halfway fell onto him, her butt resting against the gear shift at an awkward angle.

"How is this a plan!?" she gasped when he moved to kiss along her jawline. All the times she'd fantasized about kissing Archer, and none of them had ever involved the police.

"Just go with it. Act like you like this," he insisted, and she let out another yelp when his free hand cupped her breast.

"What the fu—"

He wasn't screwing around with the next kiss. The hand on her shoulder moved to the back of her head, curling into her hair and pulling at the strands. His tongue felt like it was everywhere, memorizing the interior of her mouth, all while his other hand moved to slide under her shirt. Just as she was about to pass out from oxygen deprivation, he pulled away enough to whisper in her ear.

"Touch me," his voice was barely above a breath. "Five minutes, Jo. Pretend you want me for just five minutes."

*Uh, **sold**.*

She dove into the next kiss, her tongue going to war with his as her hands scratched their way up his chest. She managed to turn onto her hip so she was fully sitting in his lap.

She was all but giving him a lap dance, her hands in fists and clutching his t-shirt, when there was an abrupt knock on the roof of the car. She was startled out of their "act" and jumped, pulling away to look outside.

"Cut it out!" a state trooper barked, leaning into the open window. Jo went to wiggle out of Archer's lap, but he wrapped his arms tightly around her waist.

"Sorry, officer," he said, and she was shocked to hear a twangy accent come out of his mouth. "I just can't help myself around her. I mean, could you?"

Jo felt herself blush and she wiped at her lips, glancing nervously between the cop and Archer.

"It's illegal to pull over to the shoulder unless it's an emergency," the officer informed them.

"We're so sorry, we—" Jo began babbling when Archer pinched her side.

"Oh, it was an emergency, Officer," he said in that ridiculous accent. "You see, I'm out here on leave, I'm stationed over in Arkansas. We just got married over there in Vegas, and we're on our way to see my mama-in-law, and well, my sweet little bride just informed me that we got a little critter coming our way."

Jo almost gasped, but she managed to swallow it down. She

31

turned to stare at Archer, to give him the "are you fucking crazy!?" look they often shared with each other, but he was gazing up at her as if he was completely head over heels in love with her. She froze as he reached up a hand and brushed some stray locks of hair behind her ear.

"Congratulations," the officer sighed, then he glanced up the freeway. "But you can't stop here, and you've got a brake light out."

"Really?" Archer groaned. "I been tellin' her and tellin' her— that's just plain dangerous."

"It is," the trooper agreed. "You might have a loose wire back there. Want me to take a look?"

Jo was pretty sure her heart actually stopped. Luckily, Archer didn't miss a beat.

"Aw, that's okay, I'll take a look when we get home. She's got all this junk back there in her trunk, it's a mess."

She barked out a laugh, then slapped both hands over her mouth. Archer held completely still and the cop stared at her for a second. Finally, though, he let out a deep sigh and looked back at his squad car.

"I'm gonna let you go with a warning, okay? But get that light fixed, or you *will* get a ticket. Now get on the road and don't stop until you reach your destination. Understand?"

"Completely, sir. You have a blessed day, ya hear?" Archer said, smiling big at the trooper. Jo almost started laughing again and was able to conceal it behind a fake cough.

"Alright. Get moving."

Jo slid back into her seat, smiling shyly at the trooper. He was glaring at her from behind his aviators, she could just tell. She waited for him to change his mind and demand her license and insurance.

Her license, which was expired, and her insurance, which didn't exist.

But he didn't say anything else, just nodded sternly and walked to his car. Jo stared at him in her side view for so long, Archer had to prompt her to move. She slowly pulled into the lane and held her breath when the trooper's car fell in line behind her. They stayed silent for about five minutes, until the officer took off down an exit.

"Holy shit," she let out a deep breath.

"Holy shit is right. Do you always kiss like that? I've been missing out for years," Archer teased. She let out a frustrated yell and took one hand off the wheel so she could hit him with it.

"Fuck off! Do you think this is funny? We could be in jail right now!" she yelled at him.

"I know, but we're not, because I saved us. You need to relax, Jojo. *Relax.* You're never gonna make it through the day like this, you'll have a heart attack," he warned her, and she felt his hand on the back of her neck, lightly massaging the tense muscles there.

She took another deep breath and concentrated on driving. She wasn't really annoyed with him for turning everything into a joke— it's what he did, it was how Archer coped with life. She was used to it, and even appreciated it because it usually worked at calming her down.

No, she was upset because for ten years, she had been fantasizing about kissing Archer Calhoun. Dreaming about it, *wishing* for it. He would kiss her under a full moon and realize she was everything he'd ever wanted in life, blah blah blah.

Never once had any of those fantasies involved a dead body, the police, or being on the 101 in broad daylight.

She supposed she should be thankful for small favors. Archer had never shown the slightest interest in her, sexually. Without their current fucked up situation, she probably never would've gotten a kiss from him.

Still. A small part of her felt cheated.

This is seriously what you're upset about, when your one night stand is decomposing in the back of your car.

A couple miles ahead, there was a nasty accident shutting down all the lanes going into L.A., and it wound up being almost a full hour before they got downtown. It was practically noon when they finally found a parking spot a couple blocks down from the seedy nightclub. When they moved out of the car and started heading down the street, she felt around her back pocket and pulled out a wallet.

"There was nothing in there," Archer sighed, rubbing a hand over his face. He had searched the body before they'd left their apartments, looking for any kind of identification. The man's wallet had been in his jacket pocket, with money still inside it, but all the credit cards, the ID, any sort of identifying information had been missing.

"Just double checking," she said, then she put the wallet away again. "He must have said his name to me. I mean, sure, I was wasted, but I've been wasted before, and I wouldn't just sleep with some dude without at least knowing his name."

"That's what I thought."

As they turned into the parking lot for the club, she racked her brain. Tried to go back over the night. She could remember going to the club. Her and a couple friends, dancing around like idiots. Getting some frat boy to buy them a round. She was really trying, but the night was so blurry. She'd never gotten drunk like that before, usually she could at least remember up until a certain point. This time, though, everything was blurry. Like she'd been wearing goggles and ear muffs for the evening.

"I think …" she struggled to clear her mind. "I remember you. Did we dance?"

"No. You were falling over, I grabbed you."

"Something about … water glasses?"

He burst out laughing.

"I forgot that part. You kept calling me a drink of water, or something. You must have been hammered," he snorted. She came to a stop and plunked her hands on her hips.

"It's like this guy doesn't really exist," she growled, staring hard at the ground. "Did I meet him after you?"

"No," Archer replied, moving to stand in front of her. "You'd been dancing with him for a while—you'd turned him into your own personal cocktail waitress."

"Great. Good to know I've still got it. Jesus, how much did I drink last night?" she moaned.

"Don't beat yourself up," he insisted, and she felt his hands on her hips as well, just above her own. "Remember my birthday last year?"

"Yeah."

"Well, I still don't, yet I've got this wicked scar on my eyebrow to remind me it happened, and that it must have been fucked up. We all do dumb shit and get wasted sometimes," he assured her. She finally looked up at him and he was giving her that perfect grin of his, the one that always made her smile.

"You passed out in the bathroom, nailed the counter on your way down," she told him. He chuckled and wiggled her hips from side to side, making her dance in place.

"See? This is why we're a good team. We help each other, and together we'll figure this out," he said.

"You're so confident and chipper, it's almost annoying."

"*'Almost'* being the key word."

"*Calhoun!*"

Someone shouted Archer's last name, and they both whipped their heads towards the sound. A large man was lumbering down the street, munching away on a foot long sub sandwich. Archer gave her hips a quick squeeze, sending electrical pulses up her spine, then he pulled away.

"Hey, Big Eddy, what's going on?" Archer laughed, slapping his hand into the other man's. They shook for a second before stepping apart.

"Not a whole lot, getting ready to cover some party. You looked like you were having a good time last night," Big Eddy grunted. He was speaking to Archer, but looking at Jo. She cleared her throat and dropped her hands to her sides. Tried to not look suspicious.

"Too good a time," Archer laughed. "That's why we're here. Actually, I'm glad *you're* here, you could totally help us out."

Jo was lost. Who was this dude, and how could he help them?

"Anything, bro, but first maybe introduce me to your girlfriend," Big Eddy suggested. Both of them laughed.

"Sure. Jojo, this is Big Eddy—bouncer extraordinaire. Eddy, this is Jodi," Archer introduced her. She was a little surprised when Archer didn't correct the girlfriend word, but didn't say anything. Just smiled and shook the other man's hand.

"Nice to finally meet the chick who tamed Archer frickin' Calhoun," he said, crushing her fingers. She pulled away, confused.

"Excuse me?"

"Your man here," he said, taking another bite of sandwich.

"You think I tamed him?" Jo asked, glancing between the two men.

"Yeah. Never thought I'd see the day, but then I came outside last night to see yous two making out. The way you were kissing him, I knew you were more than some random hook up," he explained.

"The way I …" she let her voice trail off as she turned to stare at her best friend. He stayed facing the bouncer, smiling big and acting oblivious. She knew better, though, and she smirked as he reached up and rubbed at the back of his neck.

"Crazy night!" Archer burst out laughing. "Yeah, super crazy. Actually got so crazy, we had a party at my place."

"Party, huh? And didn't invite ol' Eddy?" Big Eddy asked, eyeballing them both.

"Ah, c'mon, I'm way out in the valley. Besides, you were working. I was drunk, a ton of random people showed up. That's what I wanted to ask you about—some dude left his wallet at my place," Archer told him. Jo stayed silent, desperately trying to guess if there really had been a party—she didn't remember kissing him, or driving home, so there could've been a kegger for all she knew. But when he said wallet, she finally caught on.

"What's that got to do with me?" Eddy asked around a mouthful of sandwich.

"Oh, he was some dude we met here at the club," Archer explained. "But we didn't really know him. He left his wallet, but it doesn't have much in it, no ID or cards or nothing. We were hoping maybe you saw us with him, and could give us like a phone number, maybe even an address?"

"Man, I see lots of people. I saw her come in with a group of chicks," Big Eddy said, gesturing to Jo. "Saw you come in with that blonde."

Jo glared at Archer. He kept looking forward.

"C'mon. Jo took him out to our car, before, uh … I came outside. We're trying to figure out where he lives. You know, so we can return the wallet," Archer stressed. Eddy sighed and glanced at Jo again.

"Alright, alright. Yeah, I saw your girl here with the dude. Didn't want to say nothing cause I thought she was stepping out on you," he explained.

"I wouldn't step out!" she snapped.

"Really? Cause you was on the dude like a rash."

"We're into that," Archer said quickly. "Threesome city at our place. Can you help us or what?"

"Kinky. I like it," Eddy said, and he looked at Jo with a new appreciation in his eyes. She sneered at him.

"You have no idea. The guy, wallet, would like to return it," Archer insisted.

"Yeah, yeah. He's been coming here for a while. Uh … Bernard something," Eddy said, scratching his head.

"Bernard!" Jo shouted, clapping her hands together as a memory burst through the fog in her brain. Archer winced at her outburst, but she ignored him "Yes, Bernard! His name was Bernard!"

"Yeah, like I said," Eddy growled. "Bernard. Tryin' to think of his last name. He comes early, before things pop off. Shoots the shit with Howie, the girls, me. Has a lot of money."

"If he has a lot of money, why does he come to this shit hole?" Jo asked, tired of Eddy's attitude.

"Cool it, Jojo," Archer urged.

"Yeah, *Jojo*, cool your jets. This place may be a shit hole, but two blocks south, and you can buy just about any drug you can think of. I think that's why he comes here. Sells his shit, flaunts his money. Krakow, I think. Bernard Krakow. Lives out in the valley, too. Always talking about these chicks he bangs, from some strip joint. That's all I know. Drugs and strippers, yo. Bernard Krakow," Eddy laid it all out.

"Did he ever say where, exactly, in the valley?" Archer asked.

"Nah, man."

"Well, thanks. Can you ask around the other bouncers, or whoever? See if you can find his address? I just want to get him his shit, you know?" Archer asked in what Jo recognized as his I'm-a-stand-up-and-trustworthy-guy voice.

"Yeah, sure I'll do that. Man, you're a good guy, Archer."

"I try."

"Can we go?" Jo asked, folding her arms across her chest.

"You know," Eddy started, running his eyes over her form. "I like a chick with attitude. Threesomes, huh?"

She resisted the urge to gag.

"Sorry, dude. One threesome a month, that's the rules. We gotta go," Archer said quickly, wrapping an arm around her waist and pulling her backwards towards the car.

"Nice talkin' to you, man. See you next weekend?" Eddy asked.

"Maybe, we'll see how this week goes. Thanks again!" Archer waved before turning them around.

"Threesomes?" Jo hissed, elbowing him in the side.

"I had to think quick, I thought I did well," he whispered back.

"And what kiss? I did not kiss you, I would remember that!" she insisted.

"Jojo, you don't even remember the guy you treated like a stripper pole."

"Why didn't you tell me?"

"Because ..." his voice trailed off, and when she glanced up at him, she saw that he was looking straight ahead, avoiding her gaze.

"Because ... what?" she demanded. He took a deep breath and opened his mouth, but they were interrupted.

"Hey, yo!" Eddy called out, and Archer whirled around. "I remember somethin'!"

"Phone number?" Archer yelled back, his voice full of eagerness.

"Nah! But the strip joint, where he gets his bang buddies! You want the name?"

"Oh, thank god," Jo breathed.

"Yeah, what is it?" Archer shouted.

"Bunny Love!"

Archer's jaw dropped. Jo's face turned white. Big Eddy waved goodbye with his sandwich and headed back towards the club.

"Did he ..." Jo gasped, panting for air. She felt like she couldn't breathe. "Did he say ..."

"What is going on?" Archer asked, turning to face her.

"I have no fucking clue," she replied. He gripped her shoulders and forced her to face him.

"The random dude you tried to have a one night stand with, the one who is currently turning into a puddle in your trunk, also just happens to frequent the same strip club *you work at*. What are the chances of it being a coincidence?"

"If I was a betting gal," she said, staring up at him. "I'd say slim to none."

12:28 P.M.

DAY ONE

They went back to Van Nuys.

All they had was a name and a hang out spot—not a lot, but it would have to do. They googled the dude's name while they drove, but nothing solid turned up, so Archer wanted to head right to Jo's work place. Start asking around there, see if anyone knew anything about a creepy guy named Bernard.

Jo vetoed that idea, in favor of first getting rid of the cocaine Archer had stashed under his seat. Not only did they need money—they were out of food and her car was on empty—but it was also just making her more nervous. A dead body was bad enough, but driving around with enough coke to qualify as trafficking? She was positive her hair was going to be white by the end of the day.

So she took control of their "adventure" and decided they would sell the drugs first.

"How are we going to do this?" she mumbled, leaning against her steering wheel and staring out the windshield.

"Just walk in and … do it," he said simply. She rolled her eyes.

"Archer, you know I normally love your laid back, go with the flow, don't worry be happy attitude, but today … today I think you need a little more bite, okay?" she asked, glancing over at him. He had reclined the passenger seat almost all the way back, looking like he was ready to take a nap.

"I've got lots of bite, baby. Look, we're just going to go in and act normal. Remember to smile, you frown all the time."

"I do not!"

"You're frowning right now."

"*Because there's a dead body in my trunk!*"

"Blah blah blah. After a couple minutes of blending in, we'll go find this dude Reggie. He's the one who organized this rave. We'll make him an offer, really low ball him, then we continue on with our day," he told her.

"I have a dead guy in my car, who may or may not have been stalking me, and now I'm about sell enough drugs to put me in jail for like three years," she whispered to herself.

"Three years until they find the body. Then it'll be like, pffft, possibly life?" Archer guessed. She turned to glare at him.

"You're not helping, I hope you know. In fact, you just make everything worse."

"Awwww, c'mon, Jojo. If it makes you feel better, I'll probably go to jail, too. Now c'mon, let's get in there and sell some drugs!"

Before she could say anything else, Archer practically leapt out of the car. She watched as he strolled across the parking lot, his long legs moving him quickly across the ground. She gave him a hard time, but really, she was so grateful she wasn't alone. If he hadn't been there, she would probably still be crying in her apartment. Maybe they weren't handling it in the best way possible, but they were handling it.

She finally got out of the vehicle and jogged after him. They were heading towards a warehouse of some sort. Barren, crumbling apart in a few places. Birds flew around exposed rafters in one corner.

It looked like no one had been there in years, and when they walked through a broken doorway, the whole place just appeared empty and dirty. Yet from somewhere within the labyrinth of rooms, they could hear a beat. Pumping bass. As they worked their way towards the sounds, they started to hear people. Laughter, shouting, a couple moans.

"Have you ever met this Reggie guy before?" Jo whispered, staying close to Archer's side. She'd never been to a rave before, and she wasn't exactly in the mood to party. Her nerves were hanging on by a thread.

"Once, at a rave a year or so ago," Archer said back. "But people I know have partied with him a lot. He's ... kind of weird."

"How so?"

"Just ... weird. He's been on the party scene for a long time. Maybe too long. Done a few too many drugs."

"Then should we really be selling him more?" she asked. He snorted.

"Do you want to go through this weekend carrying an ounce of coke, or not? This was your idea, technically. We can go back outside if you want."

"No. A druggy weirdo, got it. I'm ready. I can do this," she hyped herself up as they came to a stop in front of a large door.

"You sure? It's gonna be crazy in there," he warned her, his hand on the knob. She nodded her head.

"Totally sure. Let's sell some drugs."

The music had been loud before, but when Archer opened the door, she thought the sound was going to knock her over. The bass was disrupting her heartbeat. He looked like he was laughing at her, but she couldn't hear it. She just moved forward when he put a hand on her lower back and pushed.

There were no real lights in the big space, just a bunch of Christmas lights wrapped around support beams, and of course glow sticks. Glow sticks EVERYWHERE. There were also people covered in all sorts of LED lights, and foam light sticks were being waved around throughout the crowd. Together, it all created a sort of technicolor ambient glow.

And of course there were all the people! Bodies packed tightly together, all of them moving. Some to the beat, some not to the beat, but everyone smiling and having a good time. There was a lot of skin showing, and even more sweat. She saw two girls and guy making out in one corner, and when she turned away, she saw a daisy chain of people giving each other massages on the floor.

"Hey!" some girl walked up and shouted at them. "You guys want your faces painted?"

Jo stared at her for a moment. The chick had her hair in pigtails, gold glitter coating her lips, and a flower painted around one eye. She held a paintbrush in one hand and an actual palette in the other.

"No thanks, we're good!" Archer yelled back. The girl smiled, kissed Jo on the cheek, then skipped off.

"I don't think I like raves," Jo said, and Archer just laughed and moved her along.

She didn't really get it. Maybe because she was from humble beginnings, or liked punk music more than techno, but she preferred a good old fashioned bar or night club. She couldn't hear anything anyone was saying, it smelled overwhelmingly like cheap perfume and B.O., and worst of all, there didn't seem to be any alcohol. Large garbage bins full of ice and water were everywhere, there were some sodas floating around, but no booze. What kind of party could it be without alcohol!? Someone offered her a Fanta, and when she grudgingly went to accept it, Archer grabbed her hand.

"*Do not* drink anything here," he instructed, leaning in so close to her ear, she could feel his lips against her skin.

"Why?" she asked.

"Because it's probably laced with all sorts of shit."

"What kind of party is this!?"

"Everyone is here to like ex-out and dance and PLUR and all that bullshit—if you're here, it's assumed you're into it all," he told her.

"Are you speaking another language?" she asked. "I understood almost none of that."

"You're so innocent, it's adorable. C'mon, let's go find this dude."

After asking around for a bit, they were led behind the makeshift DJ booth to another door. Some girl in gigantic fuzzy boots and a bikini led the way inside, babbling on and on about something, even though no one could hear her over the music. They went down a hallway, then entered an abandoned office.

The first thing Jo noticed were the walls—someone had covered them all in egg crate mattresses. When she looked over her shoulder, she saw that even the inside of the door was coated in them. When the door was shut, all that padding very effectively blocked a lot of the music.

The second thing she noticed was the man sitting against the back wall, and how absolutely ridiculous he looked. Like he was auditioning for a Panic! at the Disco cover band. He wore a top hat at a jaunty angle and had black eyeliner on his left eye. Not only on the lids, but also curling around the side of his socket in an intricate design. He was sitting down, yet she could tell his jacket was long, almost to his knees, and double breasted. He'd completed the look by tucking his pants into a pair of combat boots.

"Where did I go wrong in my life?" she whispered to herself, and from beside her Archer coughed out a laugh.

"Probably right about when you decided cutting class and getting stoned in high school was more fun than actually going," he replied, and she gasped.

"How did you know I used to do that?"

He wasn't given the chance to answer, though. Bikini girl had finished talking to the circus master and the strange man clapped his hands together.

"Butterfly tells me you wanted to speak," he said in a very obviously fake British accent.

"Butterfly?" Jo couldn't help it, she burst out laughing. Everyone stared at her and she cut it off with a cough.

"Peace," Butterfly said, smiling big before sashaying out of the room.

"Hey, Reggie," Archer said, waving his hand. "Remember me? We met like ... last March? At that thing out in Riverside?"

"Yes, yes, yes, of course," the weird guy, Reggie, said. "Archer! Known as Sagittarius to the other zodiac signs. Orion in the constellations. Katniss in the Hunger Games."

It was so hard for Jo to hold in her laughter that time, she thought she was going to have an aneurysm.

"Uh, yeah. Sure. Arrows, whatever. So, cool rave you got going here," Archer steamrolled right through the weirdness.

"Yes, thank you. We strive to provide a good time," Reggie said, nodding his head in what she guessed he thought was a regal gesture.

"I noticed that, and we were hoping to maybe make it a better time," Archer offered.

"Really? And what, exactly, did you have in mind?"

"Uh, could we talk about it in private?"

Everyone looked at the corner. Two girls were sitting together, their legs intertwined. Neither of them were wearing tops and they were painting their breasts with what looked like shoe polish.

That's gonna be a bitch to get off.

"Trust me, we're in private. What have you got for me?" Reggie asked, and his British accent was magically gone.

"One ounce of the purest cocaine you're gonna find this side of the Rio Grande, at the cheapest price," Archer stated. Jo was impressed—he actually sounded like he knew what he was doing.

"He comes bearing gifts!" Reggie belted out, throwing his hands up. "But why, one must wonder."

"We need the money," Archer said simply. "You probably want a little pick me up when this rave enters its eleventh hour. Let's help each other out."

"Alright. How cheap is cheap?"

"Six hundred dollars."

"You said cheap, not full price. I'll give you two hundred."

"Ha! Whatever you've had today must be amazing. Five hundred," Archer countered.

"Three hundred, and not a penny more," Reggie stated.

"Four hundred. You know you'll never get a price that good ever again, and this is good shit. Take it or leave it," Archer said, standing up tall and pushing his shoulders back.

"Hmmm, four hundred is very steep, considering I hadn't planned on buying anything at all," Reggie sighed.

There was a long silence. Jo glanced between the two of them, but the men just stared at each other. Finally, Archer nodded his head and turned to her.

"Right, we're out of here. Skid Row, here we come."

He grabbed her arm and started hauling her towards the door, but a loud gonging noise stopped them. They whirled around to find Reggie banging what looked like a staff—a scepter?—against the ground. Archer folded his arms across his chest and narrowed his eyes, and again, Jo was impressed. She was used to goofy Archer, so it was easy to forget he was actually fairly intimidating. Tall, lots of muscles, stern face. She folded her arms, as well, and tried to imitate his glare.

"Such eager beavers!" Reggie laughed, his fake accent back again. "Four hundred dollars, and we drink to our partnership. Marigold!"

One of the girls in the corner extracted herself and walked across the room to a large roll top desk. Jo noticed Archer's eyes were glued to the woman's chest, so she smacked him in the arm.

"Sorry," he snorted, as if she'd just woken him up. "Yeah, uh, Reggie, not much of a partnership, and we're good on drinks. We'll just take the money."

"I insist! A toast."

Marigold turned back from the desk, holding a tray in her hands. When she walked up to them, Jo saw that there was a stack of cash in the center of it, and three large glasses of what looked like orange juice on either side of the money.

"Seriously, we're not thirsty," Jo held up her hand.

"The beauty speaks, be still my heart! But alas, you will offend me if you don't partake in my toast," Reggie insisted.

"Look, dude, we just want the cash," Archer stated, and he pulled the baggy of cocaine out of his pocket. He threw it on the tray and went to grab the money, but then the cane thingy banged on the floor again. Marigold whirled around, putting the tray out of reach.

"Let me put it this way—you have shown up at my rave uninvited," Reggie said through clenched teeth as he climbed to his feet. "You have brought drugs with you. Drugs I neither requested nor needed, yet you are insisting I buy them. You haggled over the price, and now insist on turning your back on my hospitality so you can leave post haste. I must say, doesn't that all sound a little … suspicious?"

While he'd spoken, the other girl in the corner had stood up, and Marigold had turned back around. Everyone was staring at them with wide eyes, and it made Jo's skin crawl. She felt like at any moment, one of them was going to mutate into a zombie and gnaw on her skull. Or maybe her face. What drug was it that made people eat faces? Was it ecstasy? The way Jo's day was going, it probably was ecstasy.

I don't want to get my face eaten off. Not today.

"Alright!" she shouted, startling everyone. "Whatever, fine, we'll drink the fucking orange juice, okay?"

She leaned forward and grabbed one of the glasses, toasted it in the air, then took a big gulp of the fruit juice. She noticed Archer wincing, but he eventually grabbed the other glass. He took a small sip, and Reggie finally smiled. He picked up the last glass and held it aloft.

"To a new friendship, and a lovely afternoon."

They all took another drink, with Jo chugging the last of her juice. It tasted totally normal to her, no vodka, no bitterness from pills or anything like that, so she hoped for the best. She didn't want to stay there any longer than necessary.

"This is just juice, right?" Archer asked, nodding at Reggie's glass.

"Of course. I never partake when I'm in charge of the festivities," the strange man replied, then he sipped at his juice and rolled it around in his mouth, making sucking sounds like he was a sommelier tasting a fine wine. Archer rolled his eyes, then finished off his own glass.

They made awkward chit chat for a while. Marigold kindly offered to paint Jo's breasts, which Archer heartily encouraged, but she politely declined. Reggie read them a poem he'd written, then told them all about the new kitten he'd just adopted. Its name? Wheatgrass.

Of fucking course it is.

It felt like they were in that room forever. The dust and smell of shoe polish was making Jo's nose itch, and as each attempt to leave was rebuffed, she could tell Archer was becoming more and more agitated. Finally, after about half an hour, he held up a hand in the middle of another poem.

"That's awesome," Archer said. "Goddamn amazing. They'll be talking about your work for eons. But we seriously, *really*, need to go."

"It was nice doing business with you, Man of the Bow and Arrows," Reggie dipped into a deep bow. "And fair lady, thank you for providing an inspiring view. I hope you'll stay for a while, enjoy the music and love. Remember, anyone can dance at night—it takes true bravery to dance in the light of day."

Jo was out the door before the weirdo had even finished speaking. Archer shouted goodbyes, then slammed the door behind them before anyone could say anything else. They walked down the hall a couple feet, then paused before the door to the rave. They glanced at each other, then burst out laughing.

"What the fuck was that?" she asked.

"I have no fucking clue. I thought he'd never shut up! But hey, we got a couple hundred bucks out of it," Archer pointed out. She laughed even harder, bending in half and holding her sides.

"Four hundred dollars. We can get gas, and I can even pay back the bartender at work—he loaned me money the other week and will not shut up about it. And hey, we'll still have enough money for Domino's tonight."

"Domino's sounds so good right now. Domino's, and like a huge slushy," he sighed, and she was surprised to feel his hand on her back, lightly scratching up and down.

"A slushy, huh," she chuckled as she slowly stood upright. "You sure you don't want orange juice?"

"What was that? Who has OJ on hand to offer to their drug dealing guests?" Archer asked.

"No idea, but I haven't been a drug dealer for very long, maybe it's standard. You don't, uh … you don't think anything was in it, do you?" she asked, remembering his warning from earlier about accepting drinks at the rave.

"No. He said there wasn't, and besides, if there had been, we'd be feeling it already," he assured her. She rolled her head from side to side, trying to judge whether or not she felt anything. Everything seemed normal, no hint of a high or foggy brain or drunkeness.

"You think so?"

"Yeah."

"You're right. I feel great."

"You look great. *I* look great. We're totally fine."

"Totally, totally fine."

"I can't feel my face!"

Jo danced in a circle and rubbed her hands over her dance partner's face. The other woman giggled and laughed.

"Feels fine to me!" Jo yelled back.

A man came in between them, waving his arms like crazy. She shouted and clapped her hands for him. As the song wound down, he leaned in and kissed her. Before he pulled away, he placed a glow stick necklace around her throat, and another smaller one around her head.

"This place is amazing!" she laughed as he danced away.

She couldn't describe the feelings running through her body. Like she was a live wire, but also calm. Like she could feel everything as it was happening to her, every single sensation. The music was speaking to her soul, running through her veins and moving her muscles. Why didn't she listen to techno more often!? It was life changing!

It was like being in love. She was in love with the day. In love with raves, and dancing, and every single person in that room. All the beautiful lights that were floating around, she swore she could feel them moving over her body. Like silk against her skin. The room was pulsing with energy, she could actually see it. Waves, rippling out from the DJ booth. Giving everyone in the room life.

"This is amazing," she gasped, coming to a stop. "I'm in love!"

Everyone around her cheered and she turned in a circle, looking at all her new friends. Archer was nowhere to be seen and she felt like he needed to be there. He needed to share that moment with her, had to experience her epiphany.

She barreled through the crowd, slipping and sliding against writhing bodies. Normally, she hated touching people she didn't know, but for some reason she didn't mind anymore. She enjoyed it right then, loved feeling their energy and their love washing over her.

"Archer!" she squealed when she finally saw him. He was sitting at the end of a long, ratty couch that was full of people. He was talking very animatedly to a man sitting next to him, his hands waving in the air, water flying out of the bottle he was holding. She yelled his name again and he finally looked at her.

"Jojo! Guys, guys, everyone—this is her!" he yelled back, gesturing from the group of people on the couch to her. Everyone cheered.

"*Jojo!*"

She hurried forward, but tripped over something and toppled onto the woman sitting at the foot of the couch. Everyone laughed, so Jo laughed, too. She proceeded to crawl down the length of the sofa, over all the people, and everyone just kept laughing and helped her along.

"Oh my god, did you see that? I just crawled like a mile," she gasped when she finally reached Archer. She squeezed into the non-existent space between him and the man next to him, halfway sitting on his lap.

"You're amazing, thank you for doing that," he told her, wrapping an around her shoulders and hugging her close.

"Why have we never been to a rave before? This is literally—*literally*—the best day of my life," she said.

"I've been to a rave before," he pointed out.

"Well, you should've invited me! I could have had the best day a lot sooner!" she laughed, hitting him in the chest. Before she could hit him again, he grabbed her hand and pressed it down over his heart.

"I promise, I will invite you next time."

"Are they always like this?"

"No," he shook his head, then he took a long chug from his water bottle.

"Why is this one different?" she asked.

"Because we're high as fuck," he replied, and she burst out laughing again.

"High on life! High on love! I love this place. I love these people," she told him, gesturing to the dancing crowd in front of them. "And I love you, Archer. I really do."

"You're fucking beautiful, Jojo," he laughed.

She wanted to tell him that he was beautiful. That she had

thought he was beautiful ten years ago, and now he'd graduated into full blown Greek god status. That she wanted to memorize his heart beat and become an actual adult for him and be the reason he got up in the morning. She would try, goddammit, she would try her hardest. Because he deserved so many great things.

Before she could say any of that, though, someone else crash landed on the couch. Her dancing friend from earlier, the man who'd given her the glow stick jewelry. She shrieked as Archer's water bottle flew through the air, soaking her shirt in an instant. Then she laughed as dancing guy started doing a back stroke on top of them.

"C'mon, up up up," Archer said as he jumped off the sofa. She managed to wiggle out from under the couch crasher and she knelt on the arm rest.

"Where are we going?" she asked.

"For a ride, hop on."

She chuckled as he turned his back to her and she climbed onto the piggyback he was offering. After he had his arms locked around her thighs, he galloped off, skirting the crowd.

"I feel like we're forgetting something," she yelled.

"What did you say?" he asked.

"I think we're forgetting something!"

"I can't hear you, it's too loud!"

"What?"

She burst out laughing, which turned into screams when he spun them in a tight circle. The glowing lights kaleidoscoped in front of her eyes, making starbursts and patterns in her brain.

"Seriously, what?" Archer yelled when he stopped spinning. She hugged him tightly and leaned close to his ear.

"It's too loud! My brain can only hear music!" she told him.

"Ah! Hold on!"

They wound their way through the crowd. She was given several more glowing necklaces, and Archer received a kiss on the cheek from a girl wearing green lipstick, before they reached the other side of the room. He skipped down a long hallway, causing Jo to lurch up and down on his back. She was apoplectic with laughter when they came upon an open doorway, and he turned inside it. They could still hear the music, but the distance and multiple walls cut the sound in half, easily.

"My heart," she gasped when Archer finally let her down. "I don't think it knows how to beat without the music."

He leaned down and pressed his ear to the top of her chest.

"Still beating. Sounds fine. What were you saying?" he asked, standing upright again.

"I think … I forgot what I was saying," she said, glancing around the room. There was a desk on one side, and across from it was a mattress with what looked like a drop cloth on it. Graffiti covered all the walls, making her feel like she was actually inside a painting.

"Maybe if you think about what you forgot, you'll remember what you were forgetting," he suggested.

"You're so smart, Archer. I just—"

She was going to launch into her love and beauty speech, but they were interrupted once again. A group of five or six girls in matching fur bikinis burst into the room, all giggling and laughing.

"Can we chill in here with you?" several of them yelled.

"No, no, no, no chill in here, sorry," Archer explained, ushering them back out the door.

"The opposite of chill," Jo agreed, hurrying to the other side and grabbing the door knob. "You should try the other hall. Ask for the guy with the top hat."

"Top hat?" one of the girls asked.

"Yeah. He's the ring leader. Have fun!"

Before they could ask anymore questions, Arched backed out of the way and Jo swung the door shut. It slammed closed, and both of them braced themselves against it, as if to hold fast against a marauding group of raving fur babies. The girls didn't try to break in, though, and they listened as the group cackled and giggled their way further down the hall.

"How come you don't ever wear a fur bikini?" Archer asked, turning to face her.

"Oh, I do. All the time. You're just never around," she laughed. His eyes wandered down to her chest and she followed his gaze. She hadn't realized it, but her white tank top had been rendered almost completely sheer from the water he'd doused her in. Her black bra was completely visible.

"That is so unfair, Jojo. If I owned fur underwear, I'd wear it in front of you," he offered, and she laughed harder.

"Please, god, don't ever, ever do that," she begged.

"You would love it."

He started laughing as well and they stood still for a moment, looking at each other and laughing. Smiling. Being in the moment and loving every single atom that was in the air. Happiness. That's what she was feeling. Pure, unfiltered, raw happiness. That's what Archer made her feel, every time she was with him.

"You make me happy, Archer," she told him, smiling big.

He stared at her for a moment longer, and she could feel her heart beating in between her ears. Would swear she could actually see his pulse beating in his pupils. She licked her lips and held her breath and waited for time to start moving again.

It was like he fell into her. The same sensation as standing under a waterfall, he just crashed over her. His lips touched hers and all other feelings were erased. He was the oxygen in the room, the blood in her veins, the beat in her heart.

He also literally fell on her, all of his weight slamming against her and pressing her into the door. She moaned into his mouth, working her tongue against his as she ran her hands under the back of his shirt. His hands were on her head, his fingers pressing hard into her skull.

"God," he groaned as she kissed her way across the side of his face. "Did you always taste this good?"

"Yes."

"It's like … jesus, it's like skittles and sunshine."

"Thank you."

"And your skin. I can feel what you're feeling," he gasped, dragging his fingertips down her neck. When his right hand reached her tank top, he shoved at the material, pushing the strap over her shoulder.

"Archer."

"Yeah?"

"Shut up," she growled, and she bit down on his bottom lip.

It seemed to wake him up. His hands moved to her ass and he squeezed hard, lifting at the same time. She wrapped her legs around his waist and giggled as he carried her across the room. Jo was skinny and lanky, but tall—around five foot nine—and had lots of tits and ass. She knew she was cumbersome, but he carried her like she was a feather.

As they shuffled across the room, she managed to pull off her wet tank top. His face immediately went to her chest, his tongue working its way across her right breast. They rammed into the old desk, and though it creaked and moaned like it wanted to collapse, it didn't. It held her weight as he sat her on it and went about taking off his own shirt.

"Oh my god, this is amazing," she sighed, trailing her fingertips over his abs. She marveled at his body. At a work of art honed by years worked in hard labor. "I want to worship you."

"You have no idea how often I've thought about this," he breathed, cupping her breasts and kissing the top of each one.

"My breasts?" she asked as she worked to take off his belt.

"Yes."

"How often?"

"In the shower," he groaned, sliding both his hands up her chest. "In the mornings. Any time I'm with you. During lunch."

"Jesus, Archer. Why didn't you ever say anything? My breasts think about you *all the time."*

"Because," he whispered, his hands coming to rest around the bottom of her neck. "You're too perfect. I couldn't ruin you."

Any other time, and she would've been blown away by that statement. She felt like a failure about ninety percent of the time—how could he think she was perfect? How could they have gone so long without telling each other how they felt? Why hadn't they been doing this years ago?

But right that moment, she had finally ripped his belt free from his pants and was millimeters away from the one part of him she hadn't ever been properly introduced to—she was not going to spoil the moment with a silly thing like her heart.

He hissed through his teeth when she shoved her hand down his pants. When she wrapped her fingers around the base of his dick, his own hands squeezed tight around her throat for a moment.

"Holy shit, Archer," she gasped, looking down between them. "You have seriously been holding out on me."

"Jojo."

"Yeah?"

"Now it's your turn to shut up."

All the sweetness and cute words were gone. His tongue was back in her mouth, moving in time with the hand she had on his cock. He let go of her neck, pulling off her glow stick jewelry as he moved. The lights scattered across the room, creating pools of neon green and electric blue around them.

"Wait, wait, wait," she panted, pulling back from him. He didn't stop, though, just continued licking and biting along the side of her neck.

"I'm warning you, if you stop," he growled, "I will *literally* die."

"We have to move," she insisted. She really didn't want to, but she pulled her hand away from him and put it against his chest, shoving him away.

"What the fuck are you doing?" he demanded as she hopped

down from the desk.

"Too slow," she grunted, unbuttoning her pants. "I need to be naked with you."

He didn't need anymore encouragement. She was surprised as he abruptly spun her around, then gasped when he shoved her over. She was bent in half over the desk with one of his hands in the center of her back, forcing her flat. He kept her like that for a second, then moved both his hands to her waist. Her pants were pushed over her hips and shoved down her legs. She hopped up and down on each foot, toeing off her shoes so he could pull the material free from her.

"You have the most incredible body," he whispered, and she moaned as he kissed his way up the back of her thigh.

"Oh my god," she sighed, letting her head drop forward. He wasn't having it, though, and she felt him coil her ponytail into his fist and jerk back. She was forced to stand upright and he pressed himself up against her from behind.

"I feel like everything is in fast forward," he breathed, wrapping an arm around her waist and walking them backwards.

"It is. Everything is spinning. Colors, everywhere," she groaned.

Her feet got caught in something and they tripped, falling hard onto the mattress. They rolled around, arms and legs everywhere, but finally he was on top of her, settling his weight between her thighs.

"No going back from this, Jojo," he warned her. She nodded her head and used her feet to work his pants down his legs.

"I was already gone," she explained while he wiggled his hands under her back, unhooking her bra.

"You'll be a part of me," he said, kissing his way down her stomach while she tossed the lace and cotton across the room.

"I've always been a part of you. You just never noticed."

"Always. You wear too much underwear," he complained, biting at the top of her panties.

"You didn't wear any," she pointed out, smoothing her feet up and down the backs of his thighs.

"Good thing, too. I'm getting rid of this," he said, moving onto his knees and pulling her underwear over her hips. Her legs were too long and awkward, though, he had trouble getting the material down them. Finally, he let out a shout and started yanking. She laughed as he finally jerked them free of her feet and then laid back down on top of her.

"I cannot believe this is happening," she groaned, rubbing her hands across his shoulder blades.

"I can't believe how good your body feels," he replied, and it felt like his hands were everywhere. Pressing down on her breasts, smoothing over her stomach. He leaned away again, propping himself up on one arm. She tried to follow him, to put her elbows under herself, but he pressed her flat and bent his head down, kissing her deeply.

"Archer," she whispered when he let her go. "Please, I want—"

She choked on the last word and she swore her eyes actually crossed as she felt him slide a finger inside her. No warning, no working up to it, just *bam*. Archer Calhoun and his body parts, making themselves at home inside of her.

Awesome *weekend*.

She moaned and writhed around underneath him, raking her nails down his chest. Crying out when he clamped his teeth around a nipple, groaning as he dragged his tongue along the length of her neck. All the while, his hand kept moving against her, another finger joining the first as it pumped in and out of her. She was panting and begging, her hands hooked onto his shoulders, when he started kissing the side of her face.

"You are so amazing, Jojo," he sighed, dragging his teeth against her jaw. "So fucking sweet."

"More," she gasped, turning to look at him. "I want more. I want all of you."

She meant that in more ways than one. In all the ways it could possibly be meant. She wanted to be young and stupid with him forever, to just live in that moment and never leave that room.

But then he was moving between her legs and her hand was back around his dick, guiding him home. They both shuddered and groaned when he made contact, and he lowered his head so he could watch as his cock disappeared inside of her.

"*Fuck,* Jo," he growled, dropping his forehead to her breastbone. "Goddamn. You feel ... *fucking perfect.*"

She wanted to respond, but she couldn't even breathe, let alone find her words. She wasn't some innocent virgin, but she also hadn't slept with a lot of people, and not anyone in the last six months. Her body didn't quite know how to respond to the suddenly almost-too-big presence that had been introduced. She squirmed around, trying to adjust to his size, trying to make room.

Then he pulled his hips back and she was table to take a deep breath, but it ended in a cry as he slammed into her. They both moaned swear words and he did it again. And again and again, picking up speed with each thrust. Her body eventually got used to his size, but his intensity shocked her.

"Oh my god, Archer," she gasped, arching her back. He took the opportunity to trap a nipple between his lips and he sucked hard. "This is ... you are ... I can't ..."

He'd actually fucked her vocabulary away. A couple more minutes, and she'd be reduced to only grunts and moans.

"I love this," he moved to whisper in her ear. One of his hands was in the hair on the back of her head, pulling tight enough to sting. "I love hearing you moan my name. Love seeing you naked under me. Panting, begging. Fuck, do it again."

"I don't know—" she started, then groaned when he yanked hard on her hair, forcing her head back.

"*Beg me.*"

He bit down on the side of her neck, where it met her shoulder, making her cry out again. Her whole body felt like it was burning up. Like all the glowing colors in the room were racing into her veins and setting her on fire. An explosion was imminent, she could tell.

"*Please,* Archer," she begged, clawing her nails down his back and making him hiss again. "Harder. Faster. Everything. Do this again. Always."

She was speaking gibberish, but he still managed to comply, slamming into her even harder. He forced the air from her lungs with each thrust, made her shriek every time he pulled back. He finally let go of her hair and moved his hand to her thigh, scratching and squeezing before tugging at her leg. He pulled and pushed until it was flush with her chest, the back of her thigh resting against his shoulder.

It allowed his dick to reach places inside her even she hadn't known existed. Her eyes rolled so far back in her head, she swore she could look into the past, present, *and* future.

"Fuck, babe, I'm gonna come," he warned her, his hand sliding down her leg and smacking her on the ass.

"God, yes. Me, too. Me, too," she assured him.

"Jesus, the lights. Everywhere, and the music. Can you feel it?" he moaned.

"I feel it. I feel all of it."

"Come with me, please," he begged. "Do it, Jojo. Come for me."

"Archer ..." she cried his name. "I'm ... god, please, yes ... I'm ... I'm ..."

"Fuck, I can feel it. Do it, do it, do it," he chanted.

"Oh my god, Archer. *Oh my god.*"

She screamed as the orgasm ripped through her body. The room exploded in light, then strobed all around her. Pulsed in time to her orgasm, intensifying it. She sobbed and wrapped her arms around his shoulders, holding on as he dove into her once, twice, a third time hard enough to shove their bodies up the mattress, then he growled. She shuddered and struggled to breathe, locked in the orgasm, coming even as he came inside her, both of them spurning each other on.

"I'm gonna die," he whispered, all of his muscles locking up, his fingers digging into her leg. "I'm dead, I'm dead, *I died.*"

"Me, too," she panted, her arms dropping heavily to the mattress.

"Did you see that? The strobe light?" he asked before collapsing on top of her.

"Yeah," she breathed. "Yeah, I saw it."

"You did that," he told her, kissing along the edge of her ear. "All you. You're light and air and magic."

"I am?" she asked, staring at the ceiling. Waves of color were radiating out from a broken light fixture.

"You're everything," he said.

"I never knew," she replied. He chuckled, and then she felt his teeth on her earlobe.

"Give me a couple minutes, and I'll prove it to you again," he whispered, moving his hips in a lazy circle. She moaned deep in her throat and managed to nod.

"I would like that. I would like that, a lot."

2:00 P.M.

DAY ONE

Archer stared at the ceiling.

Fuck.

He couldn't believe he'd let that happen. He glanced to his right, where Jo was fast asleep, laying on her stomach.

Fuck fuck fuck!

He'd known they were high—he'd done ecstasy before, he wasn't an idiot. He'd even recognized that it was either very strong ecstasy, or a shit ton of it. He'd also known Jo had never done that drug before; she may have liked to party and drink and hit the occasional bong, but really, she was a good girl. She didn't do drugs. So of course the MDMA had hit her hard and she'd been totally unprepared for it, and totally unaware of it.

FUCK.

She'd been staring up at him with those big blue eyes. Like doll eyes, he'd always thought. She had a smile that was worth a million bucks, always showing all her perfect pearly white teeth, and whenever she turned it on him, it almost undid him. And that day, that moment, that amount of drugs in his system ... he had finally come undone. Kissing her had been necessary, an act required of him by destiny. By god.

Jesus, it had felt so right. Like candy and cake and the best champagne and pure unadulterated *sex*. Talk about an instant hard on. Combined with the fucking amazing body she was rocking, which she just had to press against him, and he'd been a goner.

Of course Archer liked Jo. They were pals, buddies, best friends, all that jazz. He'd always liked her. And he wasn't blind, so he'd been attracted to her for years. It hadn't been the drugs talking—he fantasized about her all the time. *Dreamed* about her.

Years ago, he'd made a promise to her brother. Jodi was off limits to a horn dog like Archer Calhoun. Of course, things changed. Andy had ditched everyone once he'd realized he was a hot shit college student, and Archer and Jo were just lame "townies" working dead end jobs. Suddenly things shifted and Archer was less her brother's friend, and more her friend. He grew to be closer to her than he'd ever been to her brother.

A relationship was the natural next step. His mom had asked him about it, his dad harassed him about it, their mutual friends cracked jokes about it. They were always hanging out together, always teasing each other. Why didn't they just fuck and get it over with already? He was hot, she was hot, they were hot for each other, it was simple math. What was the fucking problem?

Archer groaned and pressed his hands over his eyes.

Nothing was ever simple in his life. He'd had to fight for everything. Fight his step-dad, just to survive. Fight in school, just to get by. His mom was manic-depressive and an alcoholic, so from a young age, he'd had to help take care of her. He couldn't remember ever not having some sort of job, and working nights fucked with staying awake in class, which in turn fucked up his grades, which of course had fucked up his future. He'd locked himself into a worthless future, and that realization had caused him to make some bad decisions in his life.

He glanced back at Jo again. She was laying on her stomach, her head turned away from him. Her long brown hair had come loose from its ponytail and was spreading across the mattress, almost brushing against his arm. She had her arms tucked under her chest and he listened as she breathed deeply in her sleep.

She'd grabbed his t-shirt at some point and had attempted to use it as a blanket. He was a lot bigger than her, it covered her from her hips to her calves. Her smooth back was exposed to him, and he reached out a hand, gently placing his palm on her skin.

So different. She was so different from him. Her skin was soft and creamy, completely unblemished. He was rough and tan, a couple tattoos marking different milestones on his body. She was all laughter and happiness, just skipping her way through life. He was always hiding behind his smiles and jokes.

Bad, bad, bad. He pulled his hand away before she felt him and woke up. This was all bad. He'd never slept with Jo before because he was bad for her. She was still young, she would eventually figure her shit out and she'd settle down with a real man. With a good guy. With someone who would take care of her.

He didn't like it, thinking of another man touching her. It always killed him whenever she had a boyfriend or slept with anyone. Long before that night, he'd felt like a small part of her had belonged to him. Now it would be so much harder—he felt like *all* of her belonged to him. Every inch, every smile, every look.

"Sorry, Jojo," he whispered, resisting the urge to touch her again. "I wish I could be good enough for you."

"Archer," she mumbled his name in her sleep, and he smiled to himself. Remembered a couple hours earlier when she'd been proclaiming that she loved everything. That she loved *him*.

I hope not, Jo. For your sake, I really hope not.

2:58 P.M.

DAY ONE

Jo sat bolt upright with a gasp. She glanced around, wondering where the fuck she was, then realized she was naked. She squealed as she scrambled to grab the blanket that was wrapped around her legs, only to discover it wasn't a blanket. It was a large t-shirt. She unfurled it and pressed it against her chest, then took a couple deep breaths.

Calm down. Calm down, you know where you are. Just chill out.

She was in a room that was covered in graffiti. She could hear music coming from somewhere, and a lot of voices. A couple of dying glow sticks were scattered about the floor. As she stared at a blue one, she groaned and remembered everything. She was at that stupid rave. They'd sold the coke to the weirdo in the hat, and then she'd danced for almost an hour straight. After dancing, Archer had piggybacked her into that room, and she'd been smiling at him, and then …

… and then we had the most incredible sex I've ever had in my life.

"Oh my god," she gasped again. "We were so fucking stoned!"

She whipped her head around and found him next to her. Buck naked, sleeping on his stomach, half off the mattress. She slapped her hand over her mouth and stared down at him.

Holy shit. *Holy shit.* She had fucked Archer Calhoun. Well, really, *he* had fucked *her*, but semantics. It had happened. It had finally happened.

And yet, she kind of wanted to cry. She sniffled and tried to hold it together as she slowly stood up. She dropped the t-shirt to the ground and tip toed around, collecting her different pieces of clothing and putting them on as she moved.

She'd always dreamed of sleeping with Archer. Making love, having sex, banging, fucking, any of the above. But she'd always fantasized it being a mutual thing. She wanted him to want her as much as she wanted him. Instead, though, he'd been completely ripped on a drug that inspired intense feelings of love and affection, and she'd just happened to be there. It probably could've been anybody—he'd never shown an interest in her before, not really.

It was unfair. It had been amazing sex, and she didn't really regret it, but she was still upset. Like something had been taken away from her. It was just like the kiss in front of the police officer. An amazing moment that ultimately hadn't meant anything to the person she'd shared it with.

Just be glad it happened, period. Now at least you have that memory with him.

She was focusing on that when the object of her thoughts started moaning on the mattress.

"What time is it?" he asked in a hoarse voice. He rolled over onto his back and stretched. Her tongue became glued to the roof of her mouth for a second. He was so fucking gorgeous, and he'd been inside her. She was embarrassed to admit it, but just seeing him in all his glory had her ready to beg him to do it all over again.

Please, sir, I'd like some more …

"Uh," she finally shook herself out of it and turned away. "Fuck, it's almost three."

"Shit. We better get moving. Good thing it's not too hot

today—did we park in the shade?" he asked from behind her.

"Oh shit," she groaned, remembering their purpose for being there. "I hope so. How is this my life?"

"Don't worry. We have the rest of the day, we're doing alright," Archer pointed out, and she listened as he moved around and put on some clothes. She had everything on but her tank top, which she couldn't find.

"We are not alright," she sighed, finally turning around. He had just put on his shoes and was moving to stand upright, his t-shirt in his hands.

"Seriously, you're going to have a break down if you keep being so negative," he warned her.

"I'm sorry if I'm being negative," she laughed, finally walking over to him. "Maybe it's because I'm going to go to jail for life. Or maybe because I'll probably have a heart attack before that can happen. Oh! Or if I'm really lucky, I'll die of blood poisoning from tainted ecstasy."

"You're just a ray of sunshine, Jojo," he chuckled, then he lifted his arms to put on his shirt.

She didn't say anything, just glanced at the large tattoo covering his rib cage down his right side. It was some sort of large tree, done all in black, with the roots dangling down to his hip. He'd never told her the meaning behind it, had gotten it before he'd moved to Van Nuys.

He also had one on the inside of his right bicep, a geometric bow-and-arrow she'd sketched for him, and his last tattoo was just above his pelvis. It was almost unnoticeable, the top of it barely peeking above the edge of his pants. He'd gotten it one night while black out drunk, had no memory of getting it, and often talked about covering it up. It was just four words, in Old English font.

To Infinity And Beyond

"I can't believe you still have this," she said, and without thinking about it, she reached out and slid her finger along his skin, running it over the tops of the letters. His muscles jumped and contracted under her touch.

"Yeah, well, it's your fault I have it at all. Always making me watch that fucking movie," he grumbled, then he slid his shirt into place, breaking her contact with him. She took a step back.

"No one forces you to watch my favorite movie," she pointed out.

"Yes, *you* do. All the time," he reminded her, combing his hands through his hair. "I probably got the tat some night after fucking watching it at your place."

The good humor that normally coated his words was gone. He actually sounded a little pissed off. She frowned.

"Okay, now you're the one who needs to calm down. Just get it covered up," she said.

"Can *you* cover up? Or are you planning on walking around all night with your tits on display?" he snapped, gesturing to her chest.

She felt like she'd been slapped. Her jaw dropped for a second, then she turned around and stomped away. Ignored him when he said her name. She looked around and finally found her top in a corner. It was dusty, but she just shook it out and pulled it on.

"Jo," he sighed, walking up behind her. She hurried away, making a beeline for the door. "C'mon, I'm—"

"If we go now," she cut him off. "We can get to my work before the shift change. I don't recognize the guy, he must not come in when I'm there."

"Jojo, I think we should—" he kept trying to talk.

"Should get out of here, you're right. We need to go," she barreled through him. She reached out and grabbed the doorknob, ready to whip open the door and stride off down the hall. But when she pulled, the knob fell off in her hand and then dropped to the floor. It rolled across the room before banging loudly into the desk.

"Jo," Archer said softly, and she felt his hand on her shoulder. He slowly turned her so she was facing him. "I'm sorry."

"For what? It's just a knob. *You* have to figure out how to get us out of here," she said, staring at the frosted glass in the door. He reached out and put his finger under her chin, then forced her to look up at him.

"That's not what I'm sorry about, and you know it," he said. She stared at him and chewed on her bottom lip for a second.

"You don't have to be sorry," she whispered. He groaned and pulled her into a hug.

"I knew better," he said. "I even told you not to drink anything. I should've known better."

"This isn't your fault," she told him, wrapping her arms around him and hugging him back.

"I didn't want to do anything to hurt you."

"You didn't. I swear, you didn't."

"We were fucked up," he said, and she frowned.

"Yeah … we were pretty high," she replied.

"And we've done a lot of stupid shit while high," he reminded her.

"We have," she agreed.

"And this time, we just did some stupid shit together," he said.

She held still for a moment. The best sex of her life, with someone she'd quite possibly been in love with since she was thirteen, and it was "stupid shit" to him?

"Um …" she couldn't formulate a response.

"But you're okay, right?"

"Sure?"

"I didn't hurt you?"

She didn't like where this line of conversation was going. Sure, she'd been high out of her mind, but she'd also been present. She'd known exactly who she'd been doing all that stuff with, every second. Yet he was acting like she was some innocent bystander who hadn't known any better. She pulled away from him.

"No, Archer. I'm a big girl, I'm *fine*," she stressed, holding her arms out at her sides.

"Good. Cause I'd hate to lose my best friend over some dumb shit we did while we were on drugs."

"Yeah. That would be *awful*. Can we open this fucking door now?" she snapped, turning away from him and clawing at their exit.

"What, are you mad again?" he asked, sounding surprised.

"Peachy fucking keen. Door, Calhoun. Open it," she insisted, pounding her hand on the glass, hoping someone outside would hear.

"You sound mad, Jojo," he told her.

"I'm not. I'm claustrophobic. Get me out of here."

"You're not claustrophobic. Tell me what—"

She let out a shout and gave the door a savage kick. Much to her surprise, it worked. Where she kicked it, the frame splintered and dropped away from the wall. The strike plate and latch were completely exposed, she was able to simply press it down with her finger and the door fell open. She hurried through it and all but jogged down the hallway.

He caught up to her in the huge expanse before the exit, the area they'd walked through three hours earlier, when they'd been looking for the rave. Now they were finally leaving a little richer, somewhat wiser, and a lot more disappointed in life.

"Cmon, Jo, don't be mad at me. I hate it when you're mad at me!" he groaned, matching her step for step as they went outside.

"I'm *never* mad at you!" she snapped, increasing her pace. It didn't make much of a difference—Archer was like six foot three, with long legs. He easily kept up with her.

"Is it because of the sex?" he asked, and she took a deep breath, willing away a blush.

"No, Archer."

"Don't worry, it was pretty good."

"Pretty good!?" she yelled, whirling around on him.

"Yeah. If that's what you're upset about," he said, rubbing at the back of his neck. She held up her hands.

"Let me get this straight—you think I'm upset because I think I wasn't good in bed?" she double checked.

"Don't worry about it," he said while nodding. "We were stoned, it was crazy, who knew what was going on."

"Are you saying I wasn't good!?" she gasped.

"No," he said quickly. "I'm just saying don't feel bad about anything that happened in there."

"Jesus, Archer, you're a real fucking piece of work!" she yelled, shoving him in the chest.

"Thanks. And I'm sure the next guy you sleep with, it'll be awesome. You'll be sober, you'll be present, you'll be totally into it," he prattled off.

Jo couldn't handle it. She'd been up since ten in the morning, she had a body decomposing in her car, said body was possibly a stalker, she'd gotten drugged at a rave, and she'd fucked her life long crush—who had then described the incident as "*pretty good*". She had officially reached the end of her tether.

So she didn't feel at all bad when she shrieked and punched him in the throat.

3:32 P.M.

DAY 1

"You are being *such* a baby about it," Jo said, glancing over at Archer. He refused to look at her, just glared out the windshield as she drove them down the street.

"You hit me in the goddamn throat!" he croaked out, rubbing at his neck. She shrugged.

"You deserved it."

"I was *joking*, Jo!"

"Does it seem funny now?"

"I am never sleeping with you again," he grumbled.

"Is that a threat, or a promise?" she snapped.

"You'll be begging me before the week is out," he predicted. She guffawed as she cranked the steering wheel, turning into a parking lot.

"Hold your breath for that to happen, okay?" she suggested.

"Please. You loved it," he told her.

"It was *pretty good*."

"Hey!" he yelled as she climbed out of the car. "How come you get to joke about it, but I can't?"

JUST A LITTLE JUNK

"Because *I'm* not joking," she said back, then she slammed her door.

She felt pretty good about herself as she walked away from him, but her mood quickly crashed as she came around to the back of the car. She stood still and stared down at her vehicle. It was easy to sort of play it off when they were driving around and doing stuff and getting stoned at raves, but now that she had to open her trunk, she wasn't sure she was able to.

"You okay?" Archer asked, appearing at her side.

"Fine," she breathed, then cleared her throat. "My, uh ... my uniform is in there."

"Why do you need your uniform?" he asked. "We're just going in to ask some questions, right?"

"If I go in there, the regulars will recognize me and ask for something, or another waitress will see me and get pissed because I've missed the last four days, or a floor manager will see me and give me shit for not being in uniform while in the club. Trust me—there's a reason why I never go into work when I'm not actually working. Besides, it'll look weird if I'm here on my day off, wandering around, asking everyone questions. This way, I can move around freely, have a reason to be talking to everyone. Just a chick at work, being friendly and chatty."

"I'll just go in alone. Act like a regular customer, say I'm asking about my buddy who'd lost his wallet," he suggested.

"Yeah, but you can't go into the back, not by yourself. And the dancers and waitresses won't tell you anything, we get a lot of weirdos asking a lot of weird questions. You'll just blend in."

"Are you calling me a weirdo?"

"Yes. Yes I am. Now let's get this over with and get my outfit."

"Will it be okay?" he asked, glancing at the trunk. She nodded.

"It's in a sealed plastic bag," she said. "Under the tarp he's on top of."

"Why do you have a tarp in there, anyway?"

"To protect my shit from all the people I murder!" she hissed, hitting him in the stomach. "Why do you think? Because this car doesn't seal for shit and when it rains, I have to cover the top!"

"You've become so violent lately," he grumbled, rubbing at the spot she hit.

"Thanks to *you*. I probably have an ulcer now."

Without warning, Archer reached out and hit the button to pop the trunk. Jo was unprepared for it. She gasped and turned away, squeezing her eyes shut tight. Scared she would smell it, she also covered her mouth and nose with her hand.

"Have you ever seen a dead body before?" Archer asked. She managed to shake her head.

"No, not until this morning," she said. There was a pause, then his hand was on her shoulder, squeezing.

"Okay. It's okay. It doesn't really smell, not much," he assured her. "Want me to get your stuff?"

"Yes," she sighed in relief. "Yes, please. It should be on the left somewhere—a bunch of like gold lamé in a bag."

There was some shuffling noise. A distinct *thunk* that if she had to guess what it was, it sounded like a foot hitting the bottom of the trunk. She gagged and put her other hand over her mouth, as well.

"Got it," Archer said, and as soon as the trunk slammed shut, she turned around.

"Thank you," she said, holding out her hand. He didn't hand over the bag, though.

"It's ... it's got blood on it," he warned her. She grimaced, but took it from him anyway.

"Whatever, I'll just ..." her voice trailed off as some dots connected in her brain. She held up the bag and stared at it, at the smear of blood down the side.

"Just what?" Archer asked.

"Blood," she said, glancing at her trunk. "He's bleeding, that's why he's on that tarp. Whoever put him in there knew he was bleeding, that's why they spread the tarp out and draped it over him."

"Yeah … so?"

"You moved him—did you see how he was killed?" Jo asked. He frowned and rubbed at the back of his neck.

"He was shot, it looked like three times, right in the chest," he replied. She laughed and dropped the bag, clapping her hands together.

"He was shot!" she shouted.

"Jesus, keep your fucking voice down! Why is that cause to celebrate?" he hissed.

"Because I don't own a gun, Archer! I *couldn't* have shot him!" she explained.

She took a deep breath. She had honestly been worried. Had thought maybe he'd gotten inappropriate with her and in her drunken state, she'd hulked out and broken his neck or something. But gun shots, those were a whole different ball game.

"That's a good point," he agreed, nodding his head. She couldn't stop smiling as she picked her bag up off the ground.

"That takes a load off my mind. C'mon, let's go ask around about this dude," she sighed.

"Unless …"

She stopped in her tracks.

"Unless what?"

"Unless you shot him with *his* gun," Archer pointed out.

Hopes. Crushed. Her smile fell away and she frowned up at him.

"Thank you, Archer Calhoun. Thank you for that. You really know how to make a girl feel good about herself," she grumbled, then she turned and stormed off towards her job.

"Oh, c'mon, not this again," he groaned, chasing after her. "I'm just trying to think of everything."

"So you think I'm bad in bed, *and* a murderer," she stated, yanking open the door and striding inside. A bouncer behind a glass partition glanced up and when he saw it was her, he nodded and hit a buzzer. An inner door popped open, allowing them to enter the club properly.

"Hey, I never said either of those things," Archer told her.

"Oh, sorry. You implied them, my bad," she snapped as she wound her way through the tables towards the back of the room.

"I can't believe I've never been here before," he mumbled, and when she glanced over her shoulder, it was to find him staring at the stripper who was on stage.

"Because I said you weren't allowed, remember? Whoa, whoa, where do you think you're going?" she asked, coming to a stop when he almost followed her into the back room.

"I thought this was an investigation. I go where you go," he said, trying to step around her. She put a hand on his chest.

"Uh uh," she said, shaking her head vehemently. "I'm not aiding and abetting your perviness. Just wait here, try not to be a dip shit. I'll come find you when I'm changed."

She didn't give him the chance to argue or joke or be an idiot, she just turned and walked away.

A hallway led to a changing room, complete with mirrors rimmed in lights, and a long table covered in different make up products. Half naked women were everywhere, adjusting thongs, adding blush to nipples, gluing on pasties. Just a normal day at Bunny Love's strip joint—conveniently located between Hal's Steak Shack (now closed) and Boomer's Auto Car Wash.

Jo smiled at a few people, made small talk about feeling better and picking up an extra shift to make up for her missed days. Then she hurried back to her employee locker and quickly changed. Once she had everything in place, she hurriedly pulled her hair up into a decent looking bun and grabbed someone's red lipstick, smearing it over her lips. She glanced in the mirror and was happy to see she looked exactly like she did every other night she worked.

Most of the waitresses went all out on their looks—great hair and perfect makeup usually equaled bigger tips. But Jo hated her job, and hated the customers even more. She never wanted to give them more reasons to think they could touch her or perv over her, so she never put too much effort into her hair or makeup. That, combined with her bad attitude and the fact that Bunny Love's wasn't the most popular strip club, meant she made shit tips, but she didn't care. She just couldn't make herself do it, and especially not that night of all nights. So she called it good and grabbed an empty serving tray before heading onto the floor.

She came out on the other side of the stage, opposite of where she'd gone in, and looked around. She didn't see Archer anywhere, but it wasn't exactly easy. There were spotlights on the stage, but the rest of the club was almost entirely lit by red lights, and not a whole lot of them. Normally it didn't bother her, she'd gotten used to the low visibility. But that particular day, it creeped her out. Made her think of murderers and stalkers. Had her wondering how many men had watched her from the shadows.

"Hey!" she called out, spying another waitress nearby. Michelle, one of the girls who had gone out with her the night before. Jo and her were pretty good friends, had been to each others houses.

"Hey, I didn't know you were working today. How you feeling?" Michelle asked, clearing a table of empty glasses before turning to face her.

"Oh, good. Trying to make up for all that work I missed. So, last night was crazy, huh?" Jo jumped right into it.

"Yeah, it was!" Michelle laughed. "I had such a blast. I went home with this rich dude—he lived all the way out in Santa Monica and made me take an Uber back home at like four in the morning, but so worth it."

"Sounds awesome," Jo nodded her head. "You know, I met this guy there last night, it was so weird!"

"I saw you with him," Michelle laughed.

"You did?"

"Yeah. Your hot neighbor, right? When I went to leave, you were outside climbing him like a jungle gym," she told her. Jo gasped.

Kiss—he'd said she'd kissed him. There had been no mention of climbing.

"Well, you know how I am when I drink," Jo forced out a laugh.

"I don't blame you, girl. I've been telling you to fuck him for like the past year. Was it hot? He looks like he has a big dick," Michelle said.

"It's amazing, we should make a mold of it," Jo said through gritted teeth. "But you know, the night is kind of fuzzy. I met this other guy there, and he, uh, lost his wallet."

That lie worked for Archer, maybe it'll work for me.

"I hope it was full of fifties," Michelle laughed, then started edging back towards the bar. Jo followed after her.

"Thing is—we got to talking because he'd been here before," Jo babbled. She wasn't a very good liar, they didn't roll off her tongue like they did with Archer. "Here, to our club. He recognized us. I figured maybe one of you would recognize his name or something, so I can return the wallet."

"Oh, you know how I am with names, sweetie. Try Jaylah, or when Candell is done with her set, ask her," Michelle suggested, gesturing to the stripper that was now down to only a thong and a pair of very high heels.

"Okay. Thanks."

Jo sighed and after Michelle walked away, she went to turn around. Instead, she bumped into someone standing right behind her. Courtesy of the dead body in her trunk, her paranoia was at an all time high, so she let out a growl and immediately started slapping at the person.

"It's me!" Archer hissed, grabbing her wrists and holding them together.

"*Fuck*," she gasped. "You scared me!"

"I was sitting at a table over there," he said, letting her go. "I didn't even realize it was you till I heard your voice. So you think we should make a mold of my dick, huh?"

"Oh god, fuck off, I was just trying to stop her, otherwise she would've babbled on about penises all night," Jo growled. "Now can you actually be helpful and start asking around, as well?"

"Is this what you always wear?" he asked, ignoring her and frowning as he looked over her outfit. She glared and put her hands on her hips.

"No, I just thought it would be fun for today. *Yes.* Look around, all the girls are wearing this," she instructed, gesturing around the bar. He didn't look up, though. Just kept staring at her body.

"It's very ... shiny," he finally said.

"I'm sorry you don't like it, Archer, but it pays the bills. Now c'mon," she insisted, turning towards the bar. He grabbed her arm, halting her movement.

"I never said I didn't like it," he stated, and when she looked back at him, he was still staring at her body.

Her outfit was ridiculous, she knew that. The entire thing was made out of a distressed metallic gold lamé and was only two articles of clothing. Well, three, if she included the thigh high fishnet stalkings she wore. The other pieces were a short skirt that on her, with her long legs, showed the bottom swell of her ass cheeks. Normally, she wore a cute pair of black ruffly butt-covers underneath, but she'd been in a hurry and hadn't bothered with them that day. The top was a three-quarter sleeve V-neck number that tied in a knot between her breasts and stopped there. Everything from her ribs to her hips was exposed skin. A pair of boots typically completed the outfit, but she'd left them in the car and had grabbed a random pair of heels from the dressing room.

It was trashy and cheap, making her look like a two dollar hooker. But she also knew she had a great rack and a nice ass, so at least she was a sexy hooker. And judging by the way Archer was eyeballing all the aforementioned assets, he didn't seem to mind the trashy-cheap look.

"Well, then," she cleared her throat, and he finally looked away from her tits and into her eyes. "I'm glad you're enjoying the view. Pity the goods don't live up to the packaging."

"Huh?" he asked, and she pulled her arm free of his grasp.

"*Pretty good*," she reminded him, and he groaned, rolling his eyes.

"Jo, I didn't—"

"*Jodi!*"

A high pitched squeal interrupted them—her co-worker, Kim, the other girl who'd been out with her last night. She all but threw herself at Jo, giving her a big hug. Jo glared as Archer didn't even try to hide the fact that he ogling the two of them.

"Hey, Kimmy," Jo laughed, finally pushing the other girl away. "How you feeling? Wild night last night."

"O.M.G., wasn't it *the best!?* Lookin' good, Archer," Kim winked at him. He smiled big.

"Feelin' good, Kim."

"You two were so cute last night," Kim sighed, clutching her hands together. "The way you were all over each other! I swear, I almost melted."

"All over ..." Jo turned to stare at him. He cleared his throat and waved a hand in the air.

"So Kim, we have kind of a conundrum," he talked over her.

"A co-what?" Kim asked, scrunching her nose.

"A problem," Jo said, then she repeated the same lie she'd told to Michelle.

"Hmmm, what did he look like?" Kim asked. Jo swallowed thickly and tried to remember from her glances in the trunk that morning. He'd been laying face down.

"Like medium height," Archer filled in. "Brown hair. Older than us, I think, probably mid-thirties."

"Sounds like a lot of people," Kim pouted her lips out.

"But he said he came here a lot," Jo stressed. "And, uh, I think he said his name was ... Bernard?"

Kim gasped.

"Bernard!" she squealed. "Yeah, I know him! He was there? I wish I'd known, I love him."

"You know him, yes, thank you baby jesus," Jo gasped. "Do you maybe know—"

"He's so rich, he leaves the biggest tips," Kim kept talking. "You know, he's the one who told me about that night club."

Jo and Archer glanced at each other.

"He did?" she asked slowly. Kim nodded.

"Mmm hmmm. We were flirting one day, and I mentioned I was planning a ladies night. He said they had great drinks down there, said he could get us a free bottle. I can't believe he didn't say hi! He must have an eye for you, Jo," Kim laughed. Jo forced out a chuckle.

"Yeah, must have … so he comes here a lot?" she asked.

"Kinda. Like recently, I guess," Kim thought for a second. "I guess I noticed him a couple week ago. Started coming in every day, stays through the end of my shift. Sweet guy, tips big. Asks a lot of questions."

"Oh really? About what?" Archer kept his voice casual.

"The girls, what we like, what's allowed. Ya know, he's a Johnny type—wants to hook up with us chicks. I'm not surprised he likes you, Jo, he's into brunettes with long legs. Oh, table fourteen is calling, gotta run. Nice to see you, Archer!"

As Kim jogged off to help the customer, Jo and Archer stood side by side. It was a lot of information to take in. Mr. Bernard Krakow had recently started going to Bunny Love, within the last two weeks. He asked about all the girls, particularly leggy brunettes. *Jodi* was a leggy brunette. He'd been the one to suggest the nightclub they'd all gone to, and he'd most likely known who Jo was before he'd talked to her. It was all just … too much of a coincidence.

"Archer," she whispered, glancing around. "What if I didn't black out?"

"What do you mean? You were gone, you don't even remember

offering me a rim job."

"*I what!?*"

"You gotta work on your sense of humor," he chuckled.

"This is serious! I've never had a hangover like that, I've never … I mean, sure, okay, I've gotten black out drunk before—but I don't remember half the night. It's like a fog. Like I wasn't myself. I think he drugged me," she said. Archer raised his eyebrows.

"You got roofied?" he clarified what she was trying to say.

"I think I did," she nodded.

"He targeted you."

"I really think he did. Archer, I think he *knew me,*" she stressed. "I think he'd been watching me, and I think he wanted me at that nightclub."

"This is insane. We have to find out where he lives, find out what he wanted with—"

A man a couple tables away started shouting for her. Jo groaned and glanced around. A floor manager was in a corner, snapping his fingers at her and pointing to the customer. She nodded and hurried away from Archer, pulling an order pad out from her waistband.

After she'd taken the gentleman's order, she hurried off to the bar. She stood behind a gaggle of waitresses who were all flirting with the bartender, then finally she stepped up, slapping her ticket on the counter.

"Hey, Micah," she smiled big. He playfully glared for a second, then smiled.

"Hey, baby girl. You got something for me?" he asked, leaning towards her. She leaned over, as well.

"I've got an order, and a lot of questions" she said, slicking her tongue across her bottom lip. "Do you know a regular, Bernard? Bernard Krakow?"

"Hmmm, maybe," he flirted. "What's the info worth to you?"

"Oh, c'mon, I've got that money I owe you. Just tell me what you know about him, please?" she asked, pouting out her bottom lip.

"Why do you want to know?" he asked in a teasing voice. She resisted the urge to slap him.

"Because I have something of his, and I would like to give it back," she explained.

"Mmm," he moaned, and she shuddered when he reached out and traced a finger up and down her cleavage. "You've got something I'd like, too."

"Knock it off," she slapped his hand away. "If you don't know, then get me a bucket of Bud Light."

He paid no attention and his finger went back to between her breasts. Before she could shove his hand away again, though, someone crowded close to her side. She was shocked as Archer grabbed the bartender by the arm and used it to slam him face first into the bar top.

"She asked you a fucking question," Archer growled, leaning close to the other man. "So maybe instead of putting your hands where they don't fucking belong, you answer the goddamn question."

"You're gonna break my arm!" Micah the bartender squealed.

"If you're lucky, that's all I'll do. Now answer the fucking question."

"Uh, uh, yeah … Bernard dude. He, uh, comes in like every other day. Sits around and nurses a beer, hits on the girls. Has a hard on for Jo," Micah ground out.

"Why me?" she asked.

"I don't fucking know, you have nice tits?"

Archer lifted the bartender just enough to slam him back down.

"Mention her tits again—*I dare you.*"

"Alright, alright, damn! I don't know, he just likes you! Asked what hours you work, where you live!" Micah shouted. Jo glanced around. They were in luck; the bouncers and floor managers were busy with a rowdy bachelor party.

"And you fucking told him!?" Archer exclaimed.

"No! Of course not! That's against policy. He offered me a lot of money, but I swear, I've never told him shit."

"He didn't say anything else?"

"Just that he likes her … thinks she's special."

"What else about him?"

"Jesus, what do you want to know? He said he lives in some apartment off Ventura Boulevard. That's all I got, man!"

"Okay," Archer sighed, then he pressed down harder on the bartender's back. "Now apologize to Jo."

"What!?"

Another slam on the bar top and Micah improved his attitude.

"Shit, I'm sorry, Jo. Sorry for everything. Please, forgive me?" he begged.

"And the money she owes you—consider it paid back in full."

"What? It was fifty bucks! No, she has to—"

One more slam.

"She's had to deal with a piece of shit like you having the fucking audacity to look at her, touch her, *breathe near her*. I think that's worth more than fifty bucks. In fact, apologize for being a disgusting pig who shouldn't be allowed in the same room with her."

Jo didn't even know what to do, she was so shocked.. It was crazy—he had Micah's arm twisted up in some weird Kung Fu like grip, and Archer's face looked like he was ready to either have a stroke, or commit murder.

"I'm so sorry, Jodi," Micah said, and she was pretty sure he was crying. "I'm sorry. I'll respect the shit out of you from now on."

"Archer," she whispered, tugging at his shoulder. "Archer, let him go. People are looking!" He refused to move, though, obviously still considering murder. "Really, thank you. He deserved this, and it's awesome. But we have to go, or we're going to get kicked out."

He finally eased off, letting go of Micah's arm and standing upright. He didn't back away an inch, though, not even when it looked like the bartender might swing on him. Micah thought twice about it, though, and hurried away, disappearing into the stock room behind the bar.

"I'm still gonna kick his ass," Archer promised. Jo nodded, pulling on his arm and dragging him away.

"Awesome, and I will be happy to watch. But we have to get out of here!" she urged. The other bartender on shift was glaring at her, giving her the death stare. If Jo survived that weekend, it might only be to get fired.

She walked behind Archer, pushing on his back, guiding him around the outskirts of the room. She directed him down a hallway, then shoved him into an alcove. She stood in front of him, then peeked around the wall, watching what was going on at the bar.

"What the fuck was that about?" she hissed.

"What did you expect?" he whispered. "He had his fucking hands all over you."

"News flash, Archer—I work in a strip club. It comes with the territory," she said. A floor manager and a bouncer were at the bar, listening as Micah blubbered away.

"That shit happens to you all the time?"

"That 'shit' is nothing compared to the *real shit* I deal with—I'm probably gonna get fired," she informed him.

"*Good.*"

She whirled around.

"You know, it may be easy for you to go out and make a buck digging ditches, or whatever it is you do, but this is all I've got! What the fuck were you doing? Are you trying to fuck this all up?" she demanded.

"Are you kidding me right now?" he sounded shocked. "You think I'm going to just stand by while some dude mauls you and touches you like he—"

"I've worked here for years, and you've never had a problem with it before," she pointed out.

"Jesus, Jo, that was before I … I didn't know … you and I …" he stammered.

"Before what? Before you realized I really do work at a strip club? Before you knew that the men who come here treat us like pieces of meat? Before you and I had *pretty good* sex?" she snapped.

"Hey now, I didn't—"

"Just stop!" she held up her hand. "You're right, we shouldn't let 'stupid shit' get in the way of what we're doing. So I'm sorry you were drugged into having sex with me, and that my outfit offends you, and that you just now realized how men in strip clubs can act, but I—"

He grabbed her arms, gripping so tight she let out a startled squeal, but it was swallowed by his mouth. He yanked her close and kissed her hard, surprising every single thought out of her brain. Why was he kissing her? No one could see them, they were in a dark alcove surrounded by red light. They were about as invisible as two people could get.

"I know how men in strip clubs behave," he whispered when he pulled away. "And your outfit doesn't offend me—*it turns me on.*" He kissed her again, quickly. "And it wasn't the drugs back at the rave. I knew *exactly* what I was doing when I had the best sex ever with you."

She was stunned, and he took advantage of the opportunity. An arm coiled around her waist, pulling her flush with him, and before she could resist or ask a question or even think, he was kissing her again.

The first time they'd kissed, she'd been in a panic, worrying about a cop. The second time, she'd been high on ecstasy. This time … well, she was still panicking, and she was at work, and everything was fucked up, but it was different. She was completely aware of him in a way she'd never been before.

He was so tall. She'd always known that, but it was different being so close to him. Even in her heels, she had to tilt her head up to meet his lips. Was shocked at how strong his arms were around her, how tightly he held her. It made her light headed. She finally had to pull away, or she was going to pass out. She stared up at him, struggling to really see him in the shadows and dark lighting.

"Wait, wait, wait," she breathed. "I don't … what is going on here?"

"A really bad idea," he whispered, kissing along her jaw. "That we really want to happen."

"But you … you acted like it wasn't anything special, back at the rave."

"*I lied.*"

Her mind was blown and when he pulled her around, she went where he moved her. Allowed him to shove her against a wall. Groaned as his hands ran along the sides of her body.

"Why?" she moaned, lifting her leg to rub it alongside his hip.

"Because I'm no good for you," he said, squeezing her breasts. "You deserve someone better than me. That's why I could never do anything."

"Never? My god, Archer, how long have you been thinking this way?" she gasped. He leaned all his weight against her, pressing his hard on directly between her legs.

"I don't know," he whispered. "I've had at least a small crush on you since … remember prom?"

"I …" she couldn't even remember her own name. She clawed her fingers through his hair, pulling on the strands at the back of his head.

"You were sixteen, I was eighteen," he said, sucking at the sensitive spot behind her ear. "My senior prom. Anthony Skolnick invited you."

She'd all but forgotten him. A junior varsity basketball player and loose acquaintance of her brother and Archer, she had been delighted when a senior had invited her to prom. She'd grown tits over the summer and suddenly boys were noticing her. She would have much preferred to go with Archer, but he'd taken some slutty cheerleader as his date. They'd all gone together and had a good time, though her heart had broken a little when he'd left early with the slut.

I totally would've been slutty, if he'd ever asked.

"You've been wanting to do this ever since I was sixteen?" she double checked, then she nibbled on his earlobe.

"Pretty much. You have no idea how hard it is to be around you sometimes. Do you know how many guys I beat up in high school?"

"*No way.*"

"First Skolnick—talking in the locker room about screwing you after the dance, going to the—"

"I never slept with him! I was still a virgin!"

"*I knew it,*" he chuckled, and the sound rumbled in her chest. "And then Brian Murkel, talking shit about you."

"Oh, I totally slept with him," she laughed. Brian had been her first "real" boyfriend, but also a total dickhead.

"Shut up, Jo. All these fucking guys, so fucking bad for you. What the fuck?" he asked, circling his hips between her legs. She shuddered in his arms.

"I wanted you," she whispered, leaning close so her lips were brushing his. "I've wanted you since the first day I saw you. But you never noticed me. You're always with all these girls, and I was just … there. Just your pal. Why did you do that to me?"

"I told you," he sighed, pressing his forehead to hers. "You deserve so many things, Jo. Forget that shitty apartment, this awful job. You deserve someone who can take care of you, and make you laugh all the time, and someone who can make you feel amazing."

"Archer," she laughed, pressing a hand to the side of his face. "*You* already do all those things."

"You're killing me, Jojo. I can't …" his voice trailed off. There was no strength behind his words, though, and she didn't want to bother pushing it. She just wanted to be with him, always. In any way.

They kissed again, with heat and passion, tongues and teeth, clawing at each others clothing. There was an urgency in their movements, as if they didn't capture what was happening right that second, it would be gone forever. She could feel it, so she didn't stop him when he untied the knot of fabric between her breasts, causing her shirt to fall open. She was ready to strip completely naked for him, but a crashing noise and the sound of breaking glass stopped them.

"What was that?" she panted, looking down the hallway.

"I don't know. Shit, someone's coming," he hissed.

She dropped her leg and he shoved her into the corner of the alcove. While she attempted to put her shirt back to rights, he backed into her, blocking her from view. The space was dark, and the red light made it hard to see, but she still held her breath as a group of men walked past them. She recognized one of the guys as the owner of the club.

"Right this way, right this way," he was saying in an out of breath voice, leading them into his office. Everyone filed in, but there were too many bodies for the small room. Someone's shoulder prevented the door from closing.

"Shhh," she whispered, pressing her hands flat against Archer's back. "That's Buzz Tipton—he owns Bunny Love."

"Who are the other guys?" he whispered back.

"I have no clue. Buzz usually only comes to the club in the mornings—I've only met him once or twice. This is weird."

They both crept forward and leaned out of the alcove, straining to hear what was going on in the office. But there must have been a particularly acrobatic girl on stage, because the loud music and the cheering drowned out most of the sound. They finally crept across the hallway and stood against the wall, eavesdropping as best they could.

"I don't know," Buzz was saying in an insistent voice. "I don't know where your guy is!"

"He was supposed to check in at four o'clock."

"Well, it's almost four-thirty, maybe he just—"

"In the morning, Buzz. Been twelve hours, and nobody's seen him. Last anyone saw of him was last night, at our club, with one of your girls."

Jo gripped onto Archer's t-shirt, bunching it in her fists. They were talking about her in that office, and whoever owned the other voice, he didn't sound very happy. Or nice. She took a deep breath and leaned closer.

"I'm not their keeper. You think I got tabs on all these broads? Your boy was going through them faster than a junkie goes through smack. Talk to them," Buzz insisted.

"Nah, this girl was different. She was a waitress. He'd been sent here to find her," the other man explained.

Jo gasped so loud, the person in the doorway moved. Archer swore and immediately started back pedaling, shoving them backwards down the hall. Just as the office door swung open, they turned the corner, disappearing from view.

"Jesus, Jojo, are you trying to get us killed?" he hissed, grabbing her by the hips and propelling her through the club.

"Oh my god, oh my god, oh my god," she was chanting, moving on autopilot. He drove her back to the dressing room, and this time he ignored the "employees only" sign. He walked her straight back into the changing area, earning some yells and catcalls from the dancers who were wandering around.

"Jo," he said, whirling her around when they stopped at the far end of the room. "Snap out of it! We've got shit to figure out."

"Okay," she took several deep breaths. "You're right. Fuck, why was he sent here for me? Why me?"

"We're going to figure that out, just calm down," he said, keeping his voice soft. She realized he was running his hands up and down her sides, trying to soothe her.

"Alright, I'm trying," she told him, nodding her head.

He kept murmuring soothing words, kept petting her. She looked around the room, praying a bouncer hadn't seen them. Customers were strictly forbidden from entering the dressing room. She was thankful when she didn't see any large enforcer types lurching towards them. Most of the girls didn't seem to care about Archer's presence, and the ones that did were too interested in his good looks to kick him out. One particular girl was raking him over with her eyes, and a light bulb went off over Jo's head.

She abruptly pulled away from Archer, startling him. She didn't pay any attention, though, and walked across the room quickly. The eye-fucking stripper, Beeshonn, did a double take at her approach, then smiled.

"Hey, Joey-girl!" she preened. "You tryin' out for the stage?"

Jo was confused at first, then she looked down at herself. Her shirt was still hanging wide open, showing off her black lace bra and D-cups. She nodded her head.

"Uh, yeah. Totally. I mean, the money looks so good, and the guys you pull!" she laughed.

She wasn't making that part up—Beeshonn was known as the whore around the club, and which was saying a lot considering where she worked. If Bernard Krakow had really been sleeping with the girls at Bunny Love, then Beeshonn would've had a crack at him.

"Tell me about it, sweetie. But looks like you don't have a problem in that department," she said, looking back at Archer. "Who's your, uh, friend?"

"Him? Old friend of the family. He was asking about you—want his number?" Jo offered.

"I would love it. I like 'em big and tall," Beeshonn growled.

"Oh, he's big and tall all over. Tell you what, wanna trade numbers?"

"You want my number, too?"

"No," Jo stepped closer. "There's this guy, he's been hanging around the club. Real cutie, big spender. I was hoping you maybe knew his number, or knew where I could find him."

"Sure, who is it?" Beeshonn asked.

"Bernard," Jo said casually. "Comes in during the days a lot, so I keep missing my chance."

"Oh, Krakow! You sure? I mean, yeah, he's a big spender, but dude is kind of a freak. Does a lot of coke, gets ripped and wants to do crazy shit," Beeshonn warned her.

"Good thing I like crazy shit. Do you think he's busy tonight?"

They grabbed some paper off the counter and exchanged information. Beeshonn was even kind enough to scribble down Bernard's address—an apartment, right off Ventura. Just like the bartender had said. Jo recommended that Beeshonn wait to call Archer till the morning, when he would be at "peak" performance. Then she scampered back across the room.

"I'm super glad you're chill enough to have girl talk, Jojo," Archer growled. "But do you realize that at any second, a group of unhinged men could storm in here and carry you off for all sorts of rape and torture?"

"I know, I know, but I know her, and she's a total slut bag. I got Bernard's home address!" Jo whispered in excitement as she shoved the paper into his hand.

"You're shitting me," he gasped. She shook her head and bent over, sliding down her stockings as she kicked off her heels.

"Not shitting you. I feel like for the first time all day, we've made some real progress!" she told him, shoving her skirt over her hips. She let it pool at her feet while she slipped her top off her shoulders.

"Progress, yeah, uh …" his voice trailed off and she stood upright, wondering what was going on. She found him staring at her body and she looked down at herself. She was standing in front of him in only her underwear.

"What?" she asked, putting her hands on her hips. "You've seen it before."

"Um, last time, the walls were bleeding colors and I could hear my own heartbeat. This is a little different," he informed her. She laughed and pushed him away from her.

"Okay, lover boy, keep it in your pants. If we can solve this mystery, I will let you stare at my naked body all you want."

She got dressed in a hurry, almost falling over as she jumped into her jeans. She walked across the room while still pulling her shirt into place, and almost laughed again when Beeshonn winked at Archer.

"What was that about?" he asked, following Jo as she lead him out a back door into an alley.

"Oh, in order to get that guy's information, I had to give something in return. She thinks you're hot."

"She clearly has good taste. What did you give her?"

"Your number."

"Ah," he laughed. There was a brief pause, then he cleared his throat. "You gave her a fake number, right?"

Jo winced and turned around the corner, hurrying across the parking lot to her car. A slight chill was in the air, raising goosebumps along her shoulders. As she slid behind the wheel, she briefly wondered if maybe she had a sweater in the trunk, but then thought twice about looking.

"Shit, I didn't. I was in a hurry, I didn't even think about it, I just scribbled yours down," she replied when Archer got in the car.

"Dammit. Then I'm answering when she calls," he warned her as he took his phone out of his pocket. "And I can't be held responsible for the things I may agree to."

"And I can't be held responsible for the amount of times I might kick you in the balls," she sneered, shoving her key in the ignition. He smirked while his thumbs tapped against his screen. She wondered who he was texting. Wondered if Beeshonn had already sent him a message.

"I like this jealous side of you, Jojo. Pretty hot. Maybe later we can—"

His voice was cut off as the engine sputtered and coughed. They shared a concerned glance, then she tried again. It was even worse that time—like a smoker's cough, hacking through her engine. The dash lights flickered, then went out completely. When she tried the ignition a third time, nothing. Just the tell tale clicking noise.

"Fucking battery," she swore, smacking the wheel.

"I told you to put in a new one last month."

"Thanks Archer. Maybe we should start keeping a list of all the things you've told me to do that I didn't do that are now coming back to bite me in the ass."

There was a long pause.

"That would be a really long list."

"We're fucked," she sighed, climbing back out of the car. "We can't exactly go back in there and ask for a jump. There's a gas station maybe a mile down the street, but I doubt we could get anyone to come back and jump us."

"It's not the end of the world—at least we know it's somewhere it won't get towed," Archer pointed out, getting out of his seat and shutting the door behind him.

"True. But it could get stolen," she replied. He shook his head and held up his phone.

"It'll be fine. I'll get an Uber and we can ..."

His voice died off and Jo raised her eyebrows. Then he groaned, shook his phone, and she watched as he pressed his thumb hard against the power button. It didn't take a genius to figure out what that meant.

"Fuck. Your phone didn't just die, did it?" she groaned. His lips were pressed together in a hard line, but he managed to nod.

"Yeah. *Fuck*."

"How are we going to get there, now?" she asked. "Both our phones are dead, and there's no cabs around here this time of day."

"We have to walk, we don't have any other option. Let's go home and get my bike, then we can go buy cables, or fuck it, a new battery," he suggested.

"Seriously? Walk that far? How?"

"You have feet, Jojo. They were originally invented for walking, you know."

"Sometimes ... it's like my hatred for you overflows my body," she breathed, letting her eyes fall shut.

"When you talk like that, I know it's your way of saying you love me. Now c'mon, let's move out!"

And with that, Archer wrapped his arm around her shoulders and dragged her out of the parking lot.

4:40 P.M.

DAY ONE

They walked in silence for a while and Archer couldn't help but stare down at her. She looked so different, back in her jeans and tank top. Jo had an amazing body and it was evident no matter what she wore, but in that sparkly gold work uniform? He couldn't get it out of his head.

He'd seen her in all sorts of sexy get ups, of course. Halloween was his favorite time of year—she'd been a naughty nurse last year. But something about that gold outfit was really sticking in his brain.

*Probably because it was the first time you not only got to see her being sexy, but you got to touch her, taste her, and fully experience her sexiness. Well, **almost** fully …*

"So," Jo finally started speaking again, startling him. "Senior prom, huh?"

"What about it?"

"You wanted to take me?"

"Yeah. But you know, now I'm kind of glad I didn't."

"Why? Because if you had, we might not be such good friends now?" she guessed, smiling up at him. He snorted.

"Because you just told me you were still a virgin back then—you never would've put out."

"Such a dick," she growled, punching him in the shoulder.

They went back to silence, but only for about two minutes. He smirked when she couldn't take it anymore and opened her mouth. Jo was a habitual last-word-haver.

"And who says I wouldn't have put out?"

His smirk fell away and he jerked his head to look down at her again.

"Seriously?"

"You should've asked," she replied, shrugging her shoulders. "Who knows how the night would have gone?"

"Oh, c'mon. You were a good girl, Jo. Nothing would've happened," he said. She laughed.

"A good girl, huh? You know, just because I never had sex with my prom date doesn't mean I didn't do anything else with him."

"Huh. Like what kinds of things?"

"You should've asked me, then you'd already know."

Now it was Archer's turn to punch her in the shoulder. He barely biffed her and she laughed at him.

"Alright, Miss Sexy Sex Time," he teased her. She rolled her eyes. "So since we have quite the walk ahead of us, maybe we should use this time to plan our next move."

"Okay," she agreed, nodding her head.

"I think we should go back to your apartment and write everything down. It's easier to go through it all when it's on paper," he suggested. She thought for a moment, tapping her nails against her bottom lip.

"You know, maybe it's time to call the police," she sighed. He nearly started choking.

"No," he practically shouted, then he winced at how loud it had come out.

"Why not?" she asked, glancing up at him.

"Because ..." he racked his brain for a suitable excuse. "We look worse now than we looked this morning. How are we going to explain driving around all day with the body before calling the police?"

"How would they know? Unless one of us told them," she pointed out.

"Do you even watch CSI? They'll know, Jo. They always know."

More silence. He prayed she bought it. Finally, she sighed and nodded her head.

"Okay. So still no cops. We'll write everything down."

"Yeah. You can make us some food while I do all the writing, and then we can go grab some jumper cables and get your car started. After that, we should go search Krakow's apartment," he suggested. She shuddered.

"So creepy."

"What?"

"We'll be walking through a dead guy's apartment. It's ... weird."

"No weirder than driving around with his dead body in your trunk."

"Please don't make this worse than it already is," she groaned. He laughed, then on an impulse, he hooked his arm around her waist and pulled her close.

"And then after searching the place," he continued with the plan-making. "We can go back home. We can stay at your apartment."

"We can?"

"Yeah. Strictly for security purposes."

"Ah. I see."

"Safety in numbers, and whatnot."

"Very cautious of you."

"Probably best if we sleep in the same bed, too."

"For security purposes?"

"Well, duh. Wouldn't want one of us to get caught unaware."

"Don't you just think of everything?" she laughed, leaning against him.

"Sometimes."

It was ridiculous. They'd been on the run all day, and Archer knew it was going to get a lot worse before it got better. *If* it got better. Still, he couldn't help feeling happy. Finally touching her, being close to her. Feeling her nestled into his side. She was so small next to him. Delicate. All dainty and soft. *Feminine.* He loved that about her. Could stare at her all day.

This is wrong, and you know it.

The unbidden and unwelcomed thought burst into his brain. He cleared his throat and used the sound as an excuse to pull away from her. He coughed into his fist, then shoved both hands into his pockets.

"You okay?" she asked, staring up at him.

"Yeah. Just cold. Let's pick up the pace," he said, increasing his stride. She struggled to keep up.

"Geez," she laughed. "Why don't we just jog there?"

"Certainly would be faster."

No matter what happened, no matter how beautiful Jo was, or how amazing he felt around her, he had to remember—she wasn't his. If everything went well, this weekend together would be all they had, it couldn't go any farther. She deserved better than him, and he had to keep that in the forefront of his mind.

Because if he didn't, then one weekend would never be enough and they'd both be screwed.

And not in the good way.

5:01 P.M.

DAY ONE

They walked in a silence for a while. Without cell phones, they couldn't call any friends or order an Uber. They trudged along, hoping they could flag someone down—it was eight miles to their apartment building.

Finally, Archer was able to score a ride by sticking his thumb out. The driver was kind enough to let Jo use his charger, so she plugged her phone in and after it had reached fifty percent battery power, she turned it on. When the screen finally lit up, she was surprised to see seven missed calls.

"Who is it?" Archer asked, leaning between the seats.

"It's Beeshonn, I think," Jo mumbled, pressing a button to call the number back. She glanced at Archer, then lifted the phone to her ear. After four rings, the line connected.

"Jo! I've been calling you and calling you!" Beeshonn spoke in a stage whisper. There was loud music in the background, but it was quickly fading, as if she was walking away from it.

"Yeah, my phone was dead. What's up?" she asked.

"Right after you left, Buzz came into the back. He was acting all weird, going through your locker and shit. He was all red, sweating everywhere. I thought he was having a heart attack!"

"Why was he going through my locker?" Jo asked, though she wasn't exactly surprised.

"That's what I wanted to know—so I followed him to his office, was sweet talking him, giving him a massage, and I notice he's got your file on his desk!"

"Wait ... what? What file?"

"Ya know, like your application and payroll stuff. It's spread all over the place, even a head shot of you. So I asks him what's going on, and he says nothing, so I sit in his lap and breathe in his ear like he likes, and he says you're in trouble with some bad people. Some guys had come lookin' for you, so he'd given them your address!" Beeshonn told her. Jo gasped and spun in her seat, staring at Archer.

"My address!? You're sure?"

"Yeah, sweetie, down to your apartment number. I don't know what you did, but I thought you deserved a heads up."

"*Fuck,*" Jo hissed.

"I'm so sorry, honey. I hope you figure stuff out. I just didn't want you walkin' into an apartment full of debt collectors or something," Beeshonn explained.

"No, yeah. Thank you. Seriously, I can't thank you enough. You're amazing. I am so sorry for all the times I called you names," Jo gushed out. Archer whacked her in the arm.

"You called me names?" Beeshonn asked.

"What? No, I would never," Jo spoke quickly. "I love you, Bee. Serious. If I'm alive on Monday, I'm going to goddamn marry you. Thank you, thank you, thank you. From the bottom of my heart."

She didn't wait for a response, just hit the end call button.

"They know where you live," Archer spoke immediately.

"Yeah. Yeah, I think so. Holy shit, they're probably at my apartment!"

"We don't know that, Jo. We don't know anything. Let's just go stake out the place. I have my keys, we can easily grab my bike," he told her.

They didn't have much of a choice, anyway. Their ride was going to a street just a couple blocks down from them. He gave them a bunch of weird looks, and after letting them out down the street from their building, he wished them good luck.

Jo was scared out of her mind as they walked down the street, so she just followed Archer's every move. Walked hunched over, almost in a crouch. When he veered off into some bushes, she stayed right behind him. They finally came up to the hedge that lined their parking lot and got down on their hands and knees, crawling up and peeking through the branches.

"I see a car," Archer whispered. She saw it, too. It was idling in front of the building, and a very large man was standing by the driver's side door.

"Who is that?" she asked.

"No clue. Look, at your window."

"Oh no," she gasped, looking at the building. Her apartment lights were on and large figures were moving behind the blinds.

"Shit, Mandy isn't there, is she?" he asked, asking about her roommate.

"No. No, she went to San Diego for the weekend, she's visiting her parents."

"May want to call her and tell her to stay the week."

They huddled in the hedge forever, staring up at her window. Every now and then, someone would bump the blinds, cause them to rattle and shake. Though they never lifted, Jo knew what was going on. The men from the club, the ones who had been giving Buzz the shakedown about her and Bernard Krakow, were now in her apartment. Tossing it. Though for what, she had no clue.

What the fuck does any of this have to do with me!?

"I feel like I'm going to be sick," she moaned. Archer glanced down at her, then rubbed a hand up and down her back.

"Let's get out of here," he offered.

"Where? Where are we gonna go?" she demanded.

"I don't know, a motel," he suggested.

"We already spent like eighty bucks on gas—the rest of that money has to last us," she replied.

"Do you have a better idea?" he asked. She opened her mouth to respond, but then the sound of something breaking in her apartment echoed across the parking lot.

"No," she replied meekly. "My home, Archer. It was an awful apartment and I didn't have much, but that's my home."

"It's just stuff," he whispered, hugging her close to his side. "We have each other. That's more important. Look, I'm gonna go get my bike. Wait here, don't make a sound, and I'll drive around, then you run out and hop on. We'll go somewhere … somewhere no one will think to look for you, and then we'll figure out our next move."

She couldn't think of a better plan, so she simply nodded her head.

"Okay. But be careful," she insisted, gripping onto his arm when he went to pull away.

"Baby, my middle name is careful."

"One time you got distracted by a Baywatch rerun and tripped on my rug and chipped a tooth."

"Shut up, Jo."

It was their nature to tease and bicker and banter, but in reality, she was terrified. These were serious bad guys, shit was going down. Archer could get hurt, or worse. Just the thought of it made her heart crack and splinter. What would she do without him in her life? When he went to stand up again, she jerked on his arm, almost causing him to fall back. Before he could snap at her, she leaned in and kissed him quickly.

"I'm serious," she whispered with her lips still touching his. "I don't want anything to happen to you."

He smiled against her, and when she looked up, she could see that a street lamp was catching his eyes. The hazel appeared dark brown, with a quicksilver rim around his iris. His eyes moved to her lips, his full lashes drooping with the motion.

"Me, too. Be back in a second."

He kissed her once more, then he was gone, scurrying along the back of the hedge. She watched until he got to the other end, then he disappeared around the corner. Jo held her breath and looked back through the branches, watching as he made his way behind a row of cars.

He made it all the way to the end of the row no problem, then ducked between vehicles to move closer to the building. Their luck ran out after that—his bike was parked in a spot without any other cars around it. She finally let out the breath she'd been holding and started panting.

"Careful, Archer. Careful, careful, careful," she whispered.

Everything in the apartment complex had been quiet up till then, but suddenly there was some sort of commotion in the entry way to the building. The big man standing guard next to the idling car turned around, and Archer made his move. She bit down on her bottom lip as he dashed across the pavement to his bike, then almost passed out when he swung a leg over his seat. She let her eyes fall shut and sent up a thank you to heaven.

He made it, we're safe. We're good.

"Over there!"

Jo's eyes popped open and she almost screamed. Several men were standing on the stairs and one of them was pointing at Archer. Everyone held still for a moment, suspended in time.

Then everything happened at once. The men started running down the steps. Jo almost threw up. Archer kick started his bike, then spun it around in a tight circle. She was pretty confident he could get away before any of the men could reach him, and definitely before they could get in their car to chase after him. But then one of the men whipped out a gun and every ounce of self-preservation she had flew out of her body. Without one single thought for her own safety, she leapt to her feet.

"*ARCHER!*" she screamed as loud as she could.

Every single person in the parking lot turned towards her. Including Archer, who almost lost control of his bike. He managed to stay upright, though, and zipped out of the parking lot, flying over a curb.

Jo expected a barrage of bullets to come flying her way, so she dropped back behind the hedge and began crawling towards the street as fast as she could. Gun shots rang out and she started screaming again.

None of the bullets were coming her way, though. They didn't seem to know where she was, so they kept shooting in Archer's direction. As he came around the outside of the lot, a dumpster wound up between him and their pursuers, and she shrieked as bullets ricocheted of the heavy metal.

"*More your ass, Jo!*" he shouted at her.

She glanced once over her shoulder and saw that there were two men with guns, and both were reloading. With her heart threatening to beat right out of her chest, she jumped to her feet and went into a dead sprint.

Archer slowed down just enough for her to leap onto the back of his bike. She'd barely settled in before he gunned the engine, almost throwing her off. She screamed and wrapped her arms around his waist, holding on for dear life as they raced down the street at suicidal speeds.

"*Remember everything I taught you!*" he yelled back at her. She had her cheek pressed to his back and she nodded. She'd been on Archer's bike a couple times, and he'd explained to her how she needed to just do whatever he did; keep her weight back when he braked, and hold on tight when he accelerated.

Hold on tight—not a problem today.

They drove forever. She kept her eyes closed the entire time, just trying to remember how to breathe correctly and feeling his body. She was shaking and she was hyperventilating and she was *absolutely fucking terrified.*

When she finally lifted her head, it was to find that they'd stopped in some park. She didn't remember it happening. She was completely out of it, her mind back in her torn up apartment. She had a death grip around his waist and he had to work to get free from her.

"Are you okay?" he asked, squirming to get off the bike without dislodging her.

"Fine. I'm fine," she whispered, staring straight ahead. He turned to look at her and moaned.

"Jojo, don't cry," he begged, cupping her face in his hands.

"I'm not."

"Jo."

"What?"

He wiped his thumbs under her eyes and she could feel the moisture. She *was* crying. More like sobbing. She gasped and choked on air as she stared at him.

"We're gonna die," she croaked out.

"No, no, no," he whispered, pulling her off the bike. "I won't let that happen."

"They had guns. They shot at you. I thought they were going to kill you, and then you'd be another body in a trunk," she sobbed.

"They didn't kill me. That won't happen," he insisted, rubbing his hands up and down her arms.

"How do you know that? I don't want to die, Archer. I don't want you to die," she cried.

"No one is going to die, Jo."

"Someone has already died!" she yelled.

"Please don't cry," he whispered, pulling her into a hug. "It kills me when you cry. I can't stand it. Tell me how to make this right. Tell me what to do, and I'll do it. I'd do anything for you, Jo. Anything. Just please, *don't cry.*"

But she couldn't stop. She gasped for air and soaked the front of his shirt and just cried. Cried and cried and cried.

6:08 P.M.

DAY ONE

Jo sighed and wrapped her arms around her legs, resting her chin on her knees. She stared straight ahead, squinting her eyes as a strong breeze washed over her.

They were on the famous Mulholland Drive, at the Universal City Overlook. It was a good twenty or so minutes from home, but it was probably her favorite spot in the whole world. And Archer had known that, so he'd taken her there. Without asking, even. Had just driven straight to it without a word, parked, then walked way from his bike, leaving her alone with her thoughts.

She liked that spot, liked looking out at all the twinkly lights. When she'd been growing up, that had been her dream. For Archer Calhoun to fall in love with her, and then they would run away to the big city together. She'd get some fabulous, yet easy, job working for a production company. He'd be all sexy and successful in a minor sports league. They'd make enough money to be comfortable, but not enough to turn them into douchebags. They'd vacation in Mexico, and post annoying selfies from Malibu.

But she'd never made it. In fact, by moving to Van Nuys, she'd gotten farther away from her dream. The closest she ever came was the occasional club night, and only ever at some of the least reputable clubs. The last couple years, she'd completely forgotten about her dream. Archer had never shown any real interest in her, and she made nowhere near enough money to move downtown. L.A. was a lost cause.

It should have depressed her, looking at something she could never have, but it didn't. It was beautiful, and she'd always appreciated beautiful things. Looking at the cityscape while sitting next to Archer actually reminded her that maybe, just maybe, some dreams weren't so far away. Maybe she just had to look at them from a different angle.

Compromise. Life is about compromises.

"I can't go home," she whispered, her eyes locking onto a large apartment building. She wondered what the people inside were doing, if they had any problems half as serious as hers.

"No, home would be a bad idea right now," he agreed.

"Okay," she shook her head, clearing out the bad thoughts. "So let's go over what we know—the body in my trunk is Bernard Krakow. He's been watching me for like two weeks."

"He orchestrated you going to that club last night, he wanted you there," Archer added.

"Yeah. They said he'd been 'sent' to watch me—so someone else told him to come after me," she continued.

"Yes. And now they know where you live."

"I can't go home, and I can't go to the club, and you can't go home, and …" she let her voice trail off.

"And …" he tried to contribute and failed.

"Fuck, Archer. We still haven't learned anything!" she snapped, slamming her fist into the ground. "Other than a name. Bernard Krakow—which means nothing to me. So we're no better off than we were this morning."

"That's not true," he argued, wrapping an arm around her

shoulders and forcing her to lean into his side. "We know your boss is willing to sell you out at the slightest hint of trouble. We know bad guys are chasing you. We know Krakow's been stalking you, and best of all—we know where he lives."

"*Used* to live," she chuckled, then was immediately embarrassed at her dark humor. "Oh god, I'm sorry. Jesus, I'm going to hell."

"No, you're right. They've probably figured out by now he's most likely dead, so they know he won't be going back to his apartment. *He* certainly won't be going back to his apartment, soooo …."

The puzzle pieces lined up and she gasped.

"So there's an empty apartment sitting on Ventura Boulevard that no one will be checking out," she finished.

"*Exactly.*"

"Maybe," she started to get excited and she moved to kneel next to him. "Maybe he has like a laptop, or a computer, or whatever … notes, I don't know. Maybe we can find out what the fuck this has to do with me!"

"Yeah, maybe. We should get going. We'll get there and we can hole up—take showers, order food. We've been moving all day, we can take a break. Make a plan," he suggested.

"Yes, please, that would be *amazing*."

They got back onto his bike and as he revved the engine, she took one last look at her happy spot. At the Los Angeles skyline. She may have been nothing more than strip mall trash, but she still felt like she belonged down there.

Some day. Some day, it'll happen.

At the best of times, Archer drove like a prison inmate late for a conjugal visit, that's why she rarely ever rode with him. On that night, he was even more maniacal than usual, though admittedly, it was for a good reason. Jo squeezed her eyes shut tight, prayed to every god she could think of, and held on for dear life.

Google directed them to a small nondescript apartment building on a hill. After they'd stashed the bike down the street, Jo started to get nervous again. What if the bad guys were waiting? What if his building had a doorman? Or a secure door? How would they get inside?

Archer solved the problem by pulling out a ring of keys when they got to the unmanned door. She stared in awe as he tested several keys before finding one that let them into the building.

"How did you do that?" she whispered, following him inside.

"When I got his wallet this morning," he replied in hushed tones as they hurried into an elevator. "I found the keys in his jacket pocket. Thought they might come in handy, so I took them."

Mr. Bernard Krakow lived at the very top of the building, his apartment taking up the entire floor. It certainly wasn't the nicest, ritziest place in the Los Angeles area, but it still couldn't have been cheap. The penthouse in any building meant top dollar, and when Archer let them into the apartment and Jo saw the view, she knew why Bernard had chosen to live there.

"Wow," she breathed, walking up to floor-to-ceiling windows and pressing against them. There was a pretty good view of the neighborhoods sitting below them.

"I'm fucking starving," Archer groaned, shutting the door and bolt locking it. "I'll look around the place—you go find something to munch on."

A wide galley style kitchen sat off the living room and Jo was slow as she walked through it. Everything was very nice and very clean, but looked like it had come straight out of the 1980s. When she glanced back into the living room, she saw a white leather sofa and a gold standing lamp, all courtesy of the decade that brought the world Cyndi Lauper and parachute pants. Apparently, Mr. Krakow spent all his money on rent, but not on redecorating. In fact, if she had to guess, she'd say he must have moved in fairly recently. There were no personal touches about the apartment, and the furniture looked beyond old.

She sighed and started pulling open cupboards, but she was

surprised to find almost nothing. A couple cans of cream-of-chicken soup, some dry pasta, and an expired box of pop tarts were the best his kitchen had to offer. The fridge had a case of beer and moldy cheese in it. There were dirty dishes in the dishwasher, but no indication of *how* they'd gotten dirty. Bernard Krakow didn't seem to have any groceries.

There was a door in the back wall that she'd assumed was a broom closet, but when she opened it, she found a pantry. The light from above the stove showed her a couple bags of off brand cereal, but it was too dark to see anything else. She stepped inside and patted the walls for a light switch, but found nothing. Another step and something hit her in the face. She swung her hands wildly in front of her and smacked what felt like a string, batting it away from her head.

Probably a pull cord for a light—this is the apartment time forgot, after all.

She stuck her arms out straight and waved them around, hoping to connect with the cord again. Instead, her hands connected with something else, knocking it off a shelf. A pouch of sorts hit her on top of her head and virtually exploded. Suddenly, she was surrounded in a cloud of dust. She yelped and coughed and gagged on something dry in her mouth. She back pedaled out of the pantry, rammed into the door jam, ricocheted into the fridge, then stumbled into the living room.

"What? What!?" Archer yelled, and she could hear him running from another room.

"Oh my god!" she screamed, looking down at her hands. They were covered in a white powder. The same white powder that was now covering her face and coating the inside of her mouth.

"Jesus," Archer exclaimed, coming to a stop in front of her. "What happened to you?"

"Oh my god, is this coke?" she yelled, holding up her hands. "This is coke! Oh my god, I've never done this drug! I inhaled,

Archer! *I INHALED!*"

"Just calm do-"

"This looks like a lot!" she started to panic. "Is this a lot? Did I just OD? Oh my god, am I ODing right now!? Call an ambulance, for fuck's sake, I'm an OD!"

"First of all, you're not ODing!" he shouted, reaching out and grabbing her hands. "Second of all, calm the fuck down and let me look at you!"

"How would you know?" she demanded, watching as he dragged a finger through the substance on her palm. "Have you ever ODed? It's happening. Holy shit, I can feel my heart in my nose. I'm having a heart attack. Archer, I think I'm having a heart attack!"

"Shut up," he growled. As she watched, he stuck a white-tipped finger into his mouth.

"What are you doing?" she was shocked. He sucked on his finger for a bit, then he started laughing. Guffawing, really. Loud and hard.

"Jojo," he gasped for air, pressing a hand to his stomach.

"I'm glad my possible overdose and eventual death are so hilarious!" she snapped.

"*Baking soda,*" he managed to choke out. "You're covered in baking soda."

She blinked a couple times, then stuck her own finger in her mouth. She'd never tasted cocaine before, but she was pretty confident it didn't taste floury and bitter. Plus, in the movies, dudes were always rubbing coke on their gums and getting a rush. She didn't feel anything.

"Oh jesus," she groaned, dropping her hands. Archer kept laughing.

"'*I just ODed!*'" he mocked her. "'*I'm an OD!*'"

"Shut up."

They went back into the kitchen and she bee-lined for the sink, holding her face and hands under the faucet. When she'd cleaned the last of the baking ingredient out from under her fingernails, she turned the water off and moved back towards the pantry. Archer was standing in it with the light on, his head tilted up as he looked over all the shelves.

"Why does Bernard Krakow have a shit ton of baking soda?" he wondered out loud as she walked up next to him.

"He's a baking enthusiast?" she guessed, though it didn't seem likely. Literally every shelf in the pantry was lined with bags of baking soda.

"Sometimes," Archer spoke slowly. "People use baking soda to cut cocaine."

"They do?"

"Yeah. I mean, it's total garbage coke. Makes more product at a shitty quality which you can sell at the same price as the good stuff."

"You can?"

"Sure you can—doesn't make it a good idea, though. Sell to the wrong person, and you'll wake up with a shotgun in your face. Still, it looks to me like that's what our buddy Bernard was doing."

"You think so?"

"Yeah, I found a huge package of cocaine in the bedroom. He's been fucking over his boss by cutting the pure stuff with baking soda, selling it, and keeping the difference," Archer guessed.

"How do you know so much about this?" Jo asked, glancing up at him. He chuckled.

"A combination of shitty friends and the A&E show 'Intervention'. C'mon, you take a shower and I'll order pizza," he offered, then he pushed her back out into the kitchen.

"No olives," she insisted. "I think today of all days, I get to call the pizza shots."

"You're a pizza Nazi," he replied, but when she went to argue, he held up a hand. "But you have had a shitty day, so fine, no olives."

Jo stood under the shower for a long time. Too long, the water started to turn cold before she got out. She felt kind of bad because it meant Archer wouldn't be getting any hot water, but once she'd stepped under the spray, she hadn't been able to move. She'd sat down on the floor and wrapped her arms around herself, her knees up to her chest, and had just let the shower beat down on her.

She couldn't wrap her brain around it. Twelve hours ago, she'd been sleeping off a hangover, oblivious to the entire world. Twenty-four hours ago, she'd been getting ready for an evening out with friends, pre-gaming in her kitchen. The same things she did every weekend, for pretty much the past four or five years.

In fact, *nothing* had changed in the past four or five years of her life. She worked all week so she could spend all her tips on the weekend. She went out with random guys all while pining over Archer, who—it turned out—had been pining over her for years, too.

I'm such an idiot.

That's what Jo felt like—stupid and young. Clueless and oblivious. She'd never been a big "goals" person, she hadn't been one of those kids in drama class or junior achievers or anything like that, but she'd had some pretty basic dreams. Get a solid job, meet a nice man. Get married some day, have some kids, all that jazz.

Is that asking so much?

Sure, she'd never done much in her life, but she hadn't done bad, either. How had she ended up in such a mess? What had she done to deserve any of this? She'd gone over and over it in her mind. Had she flirted too much with a customer? Had she invited the wrong person to a party?

No. The answer was no, none of those things. She was somewhat notorious at work for being a frigid bitch—hence why her tips weren't very good. And she didn't let strangers into her home, not even when Archer showed up at her parties with all his random construction buddies in tow. She made them party at his place.

So why the fuck had some drug dealing piece of shit been stalking her, on behalf of his evil bosses? And how had he ended up dead in her trunk?

"Think," she growled to herself as she stomped into Bernard

Krakow's walk-in closet. "Think, Jojo!"

She put on her underwear, then searched through his clothes. Mr. Krakow hadn't been a very large man, it seemed. She couldn't remember what he looked like standing up, but according to the inseam on his pants, he was a little shorter than her. She finally pulled on a large sweatshirt. It settled over the tops of her thighs as she padded out of the room.

Archer was taking his shower, so she wandered into the kitchen and found a large pizza. She put a couple slices on a plate, grabbed a beer out of the fridge, then stood in front of the windows for a while. She ate while she contemplated, balancing the beer on the back of a Barcalounger.

Maybe she was going about it the wrong way. She'd been trying to figure out what her role was in the whole thing, but she hadn't gotten anywhere. She'd had the thought before—she needed to start looking at it from a different angle. Who was Bernard Krakow, and more importantly, who did he work for? She knew she hadn't done anything wrong or illegal, so what the fuck had Krakow been up to?

After she finished her pizza, Jo went back into the bedroom. The shower was still going and she stared at the door for a second. Archer was inside, scrubbing and cleaning and wet and ... naked.

Stop it. There's slightly more important things going on right now.

She found a laptop that was dead, so she plugged it in so they could investigate it later. Inside the closet, she stood back and once again looked over Krakow's clothes. He favored a practical look. Lots of dress shirts and pants, with pullovers and plain dress shoes. Muted colors—navy, forest green, brown. So much brown.

There is not one thing about this man that stands out in any way.

All his shoes were arranged by light to dark colors, and while shuffling around them, she stubbed her toe on something hard. When she knelt down, she found a small safe. She frowned as she picked it up. What was the point of a safe if someone could just pick it up and walk off with it? She poked and prodded at the combination lock while she carried it back into the bedroom.

"Wha'd you find?"

She looked up to find Archer standing at the foot of the bed. He was wearing a pair of briefs and was in the act of pulling on a t-shirt. She cleared her throat and walked around him so she could crawl onto the mattress.

"I don't know," she finally replied, sitting with her back against the headboard and the safe between her legs. "I can't get it open."

"Weird," he mumbled, and she felt him stretch out next to her.

"What's weird?"

"He has a safe."

"So? He's a drug dealer, he's paranoid. Makes sense to me," she replied, glancing at him. He was staring at the fireproof metal box.

"Yeah, and I get all that, but if drugs and money aren't valuable enough to go in his safe, then it makes me really wonder what was worth enough to put in there," Archer asked, then he pointed across her lap. She followed his finger and saw a large brown package on the nightstand. Several bands of duct tape went around the middle, but a small tear had been made in a corner and a pinch of white powder had fallen onto the table top.

Jo glared. A safe without anything valuable in it. A man who was as bland as dry toast. A dead body in her shitty car.

"Fuck this," she growled, flipping the safe over. It tumbled to the floor with a loud thump. "I am *so tired* of not knowing what the hell is going on."

"C'mon, Jojo," Archer teased. "How is this different from any other time in your life?"

She snapped out her leg and kicked him in the side.

"Eat a dick, Archer."

Before she could pull her leg back, though, he grabbed her ankle and held it in place. Then both his hands were on her feet, giving her a light massage.

They didn't say anything for a while. Archer leaned over her foot, digging his thumbs into her sore muscles. She bent towards him, her heavy brown hair falling over her shoulder. Eventually, he sighed and moved his hands, massaging her calves.

"You never wear your hair down," he stated abruptly. She looked over at him.

"Excuse me?"

"Your hair," he repeated himself, glancing up at her. "You always have it up in a ponytail. Even when you go out, it's like up in a knot or whatever. I didn't realize it was so long."

Jo grabbed a hank of hair, holding it up in front of her face. It was still damp, just barely starting to dry. It would be awkwardly wavy and frizzy in the morning.

"I know. I always think I should cut it, but then I just can't bear to," she explained.

"I like it. I mean, I like it long. Looks good on you."

"Why, Archer Calhoun, was that a compliment?"

"Shut up, I compliment you all the time."

"You say things like 'nice tits' or 'great ass'—sometimes it's nice just to hear something … nice," she told him. He snorted, but he was smiling as his hands worked their way up and over her knee.

"Right after we graduated, when your brother knew he'd be moving away and I'd still be living down the street, he made me promise I wouldn't mess around with you," he told her. She was a little surprised. No one had ever told her. Andy had never paid much attention to her, so it was kind of hard to fathom him being concerned about who was or wasn't "messing" with her.

"Why would he say that? I mean, you guys were friends," she pointed out.

"Yeah, exactly—he knew how I was with chicks. Plus, you're his baby sister. He's a dick most of the time, but the way he talks about you, he thinks you're like a princess. No one was good enough for you, but especially not me."

"Okay, I can't even process this," she laughed. "Andy thought no one was good enough for me?"

"Yup."

"And why especially not you? I mean, you were his best friend. He had to have thought of all people, you'd be good enough."

"Because we were such good friends, he … I'm kind of a dick, too, Jojo. I make fucked up choices and do the wrong thing most of the time, and I'm just an idiot. Like us, for example. We've known each other forever, I've wanted to put the move on you for years, so what happens? I practically eat your face off at a rave."

She burst out laughing, pulling her leg away from him as she bent over again. She pressed her hands to her face, trying to stifle her giggles.

"Practically," she agreed when she got her laughter under control. "But I wasn't exactly complaining. I've wanted you for a lot longer, and I never had the balls, either."

"It's not just about that," he sighed, reaching out and stroking his finger over her toes.

"Then what's it about?" she asked.

"I agree with him. I think you can do better than me," he said plainly. She lost her smile.

"Maybe I don't want better than you," she countered.

"Hell of an argument, Jo."

"I feel like I'm getting dumped," she said. "And we aren't even dating."

"You're not," he assured her. "I don't know what we're doing, or what's gonna happen in the morning, and I just wanted to tell you …"

He was still touching her foot, but he was staring absently across the room. Jo took the opportunity to study his face. He had almost two days worth of stubble, giving him a sexy, rugged look. He always kept his hair pretty short on the sides, but he'd let it get long on top, so the ends almost brushed his eyebrows. It gave him a sort of boyish look, the way the locks curled at the very tips. Paired with the naughty grin he was always flashing, he was almost impossible to resist.

From the neck up, his most defining feature was probably his eyes. She loved them because at first glance, they just looked light brown. But they were hazel, and upon closer inspection, they were always shifting and changing, depending on the light or his mood. That moment, they were an almondy color, with just a hint of green. His thick lashes made them pop out of his face—it really wasn't fair, she spent a fortune on mascara to get the same effect.

Jo could stare at him for hours, and felt like she had at different points in her life. At his amazing body and long legs. Those thick arms and broad shoulders. He was built like how she felt a man should be built, tall and strong and broad. A little dirty and a lot naughty. *Perfection.*

More than ever, though, now she was noticing the other parts of him. How thoughtful he was—stealing the newspaper from the shut-in down the hall so she could read the funnies every day. Bringing her lunch before she had to go to her evening shift. Fixing her internet whenever the router gave her attitude, and letting her come over *whenever* she wanted, day or night.

Like helping her. He'd just automatically trusted that she hadn't killed the guy in her trunk. And when she'd pushed him about it, he'd said he would bury the body for her. How could she have been such an idiot? Was there anyone she treated half as nicely? Was there anyone she would bury a body for?

Archer Calhoun, if you asked me to, I would dig a grave for you.

She leaned forward and kissed him, catching him off guard. He was motionless for a couple seconds, then his hand was on the back of her head, his fingers curling in her damp strands of hair.

"It's okay, Archer," she whispered. "I like you, too."

"That's not what I was going to say," he whispered back, all while smoothing his free hand up her bare leg.

"Then what? What is it?" she asked, scooting closer to him and putting her hands on either side of his face.

"I don't know how to say this …" he sighed. Jo felt like her heart was going to pound right out of her chest.

Holy shit, this is really happening. Be brave. Say it first.

"It's really okay," she managed to say in a shaky voice. "I feel it, too. I think I've felt it for a while. I think … I think I'm in—"

Her sentence was cut off as he quickly kissed her again. It was different from the first kiss, much more aggressive. Breath taking. She gasped as his hand shot up her thigh, squeezing where it reached her crotch.

"You know," he said as he started pulling at her sweater with his other hand. "You really do have nice tits."

"I know, Archer. And a great ass," she laughed, ducking her head and lifting her arms so the material could slide free of her body.

"How are those not nice things to say?" he asked, stretching out alongside her.

"They're great. Super. But you know what's even better?"

"What?"

"If you don't talk at all right now."

As she ran her hands under his t-shirt, Jo wondered if she would ever get used to having such free reign to touch him. Not that she'd never touched his bare skin before—he had little to no shame when he was at home, he was always walking around bare chested or in his boxers. But it was different now. Actually running her hands over his skin and feeling it jump and react to her touch. It filled her with a sense of power.

"How did we go for so long without doing this?" she whispered, moving her hand up his chest and through the neck hole in his shirt, smoothing her way to his jaw. She tapped her nails against his bottom lip.

"Sheer will power," he chuckled, then he nipped at her fingertips. She laughed and pulled her hands free of his clothing. "And a lot of cold showers."

"This isn't right," she moaned as he rolled them so she was laying on top of him. "We're in someone else's bed, it's been such a fucked up day. There's so much to do, and we're doing *this*."

"Jojo, if you can think of anything else you'd rather be doing right now, please. Inform me."

She wasn't given the chance, though. Before she could open her mouth to make some smart ass comment, he sat upright. She squealed and held onto his shoulders, almost toppling over backwards.

"I would get so mad at you."

He was whispering, his voice close to her ear. Then he bit down on her earlobe and she gasped, digging her nails into his shoulder blades.

"Me? Why?"

"I knew what you were doing."

"What was I doing?"

"When you slept with that guy after Thanksgiving," he hissed, and he paid her back by dragging his own nails down the length of her back. "And the one guy from our softball team."

"I …" she couldn't properly respond as his nails went back up to her shoulders.

"So competitive," he chuckled as he moved his teeth to her neck. "You wanted to show me how grown up you were. Wanted to make me *jealous*."

"It's funny," she was panting as he bit hard enough to leave a mark. "I never thought you noticed."

"Oh, I noticed. And I'm not laughing."

"No. Not laughing at all. You fucked anything with tits. Fair is fair, Archer."

"It was different," he sighed into her skin. "Completely different."

"How?"

"You were doing it to get back at me. I was doing it to *stay away* from you."

"But why—"

She gasped when he squeezed her breast, rolling her nipple between his fingers.

121

"They really are perfect. You have no idea how many times I've fantasized about this," he told her, lowering his lips to her flesh.

"That makes two of us," she panted, scratching her fingernails through his hair.

He was moving too slowly, almost methodically. It was driving her insane. While his tongue lapped at her areola, she started squirming around on his lap. Desperate for more speed, more friction, more everything.

"So pretty," he breathed, moving to her other breast. She tugged at his hair.

"Archer," she growled.

"What?"

"Let's make up for lost time."

He laughed, but got her message loud and clear. She helped him pull off his pants and after she'd chucked them across the room, she watched as he took off his t-shirt. While he was still struggling to get the material over his head, and she reached out and stroked the tattoo on his side, the large tree.

"What does this mean?" she asked, lightly tickling his ribs. His skin jumped and flinched, making him chuckle as he pulled away from her.

"Something special," was all he said as he gently pushed her onto her back and went about removing her underwear.

"I know everything about you, but I can't know about a tree tattoo?"

"You don't know everything."

"I know a lot."

"You do," he whispered, kissing his way up her stomach. His stubble scratched against her skin, making her moan and hiss.

"So why can't I—whoa, *fuuuuuuck*," she groaned, her eyes rolling back in her head and her back arching off the mattress. Two fingers. Without a word or a warning, he'd thrust two fingers inside her.

"Goddamn, Jojo," he breathed, and she felt his lips against her neck. "I will never get tired of seeing you like this."

"Never tired. Nope."

"Writhing. Moaning. Wet. Needy."

"Dying. I'm pretty sure I'm also dying."

He laughed out loud, causing her to laugh, then her hand found its way to his dick and they were both groaning again. His forehead dropped to her breast bone as she began stroking him.

"Yeah," he panted. "Dying sounds accurate."

"How could you keep this from me for so long? So unfair," she groaned, rolling her thumb over his sensitive tip.

"Grossly unfair," he agreed, sucking air through his teeth. "I'm going to make up for it, right now."

She moaned when he pulled his fingers away, then shrieked when he yanked her upright. He pulled her back into the position they'd been in before—both sitting upright, her on his lap with her legs around him. His erection stood up between them, drawing all her attention.

"You're so fucking beautiful," she whispered, and he laughed again.

"Look at me."

She lifted her head to stare at him, and didn't break eye contact as he wrapped an arm around her hips. Kept staring as he lifted her, and still managed to hold his gaze as he lowered her back onto his shaft. She struggled to catch her breath and even moaned as he slowly filled her, past the point of comfortable even, but she still didn't look away.

"If this ... is a contest ..." she was so full with him, she felt dizzy. "I think I won."

"Then I guess you'd better claim your prize."

God, she loved being so close to him. She was a tall, somewhat gangly girl, but she felt small and delicate in his arms. They were also good enough friends that she didn't feel awkward or self-conscious, either. And thankfully, their ecstasy-induced bang session had done away with those pesky first-time-jitters.

Good. Because I could really use a stress reliever right now.

They moved in sync, one of Archer's hand on her hips, keeping her in time with his thrusts. She reached her arm out behind her, leaning back to grab the headboard so she could use it as leverage to push harder against him. He slid his free hand up her back, his fingers sliding around on her sweat slicked skin, then he scratched his way back down to her ass.

"Holy fuck, Jo," he grunted through clenched teeth. "You're so … fuck, this is better than any dream. Any fantasy."

"So much better," she agreed, then she bit down on her bottom lip.

He was so deep inside her, so large, it was creating a paradox of mind blowing pleasure and an insane level of uncomfortable. Her nerve endings didn't know what to focus on, it was driving her body crazy. She felt like she was going to explode at any moment.

"I'm gonna fix everything, and then we are going to be doing this *constantly*," he groaned, his head dropping back.

"All the time," she agreed.

"You need to quit your job," he urged.

"Okay."

"You're going to move in with me."

"Alright."

"I take care of you. You fuck my brains out."

"Deal."

"*Fuck*," he swore when all her muscles contracted. "And we are definitely going to—"

"Archer," she interrupted him with a whine. Her whole body was trembling and she couldn't keep up with his thrusts anymore. "I can't … I'm going to … you're going to make me …"

She almost started choking when he abruptly stopped moving, leaving her impaled on him. Then he kissed her hard, his tongue taking over her mouth at the same time as he gently pushed her away from him. He wouldn't let her complain, just kept moving his tongue against hers as he urged them both onto their knees.

"Don't worry," he whispered when he finally pulled away.

"*Please,*" she begged, her trembling turning into shaking. "Please, please, please, Archer."

"I'm going to make you come so hard," he promised, and she moaned at his words. "But first I'm going to do something I've dreamed about for years."

She was in no position to argue. She couldn't even make coherent sentences. So when he started pushing her and moving her in a circle, she had no choice but to go along. Didn't say a word as he put both her hands against the headboard. Sighed when he swept his hands down her back, then moaned when he pulled her hips back towards him. Then a long, shuddering groan escaped her mouth when she felt him moving behind her, forcing his hard length into her from behind.

"Better," she whispered, letting her head drop forward as he held still for a moment, his fingers digging into her hips so hard she was sure she'd have whole hand prints on her skin.

"The best," he corrected her, and she chuckled.

He was gentle, at first. Really, he'd always been gentle with her, in all their interactions. So it didn't surprise her. But then he started picking up speed, his hips slamming against her ass. She cried out with each thrust, curling her fingers around the top of the headboard so hard, her knuckles turned white. When he slapped her on the ass, she gasped.

"Jesus, fuck, where has this guy been this whole time!?" she shouted, then she moaned when he gripped her hair and yanked back, forcing her to look straight up.

"Hiding—I didn't think you could handle him," he growled, leaning over her back.

"I don't think I can, either," she agreed, then she groaned again when she felt him biting into her shoulder.

"Jojo," he grunted, letting go of her hair and letting his hand wander down her back.

"Yes. Yes, god, yes, anything, whatever you want, please," she babbled, her whole body starting to shake again as his hand continued on a path over her hip and around to her front, slipping and sliding between her legs.

"I want you to come for me, and I want to know it's not because of drugs, or some fucking party, or some stupid fantasy. I want it to be only for me," he told her, breathing hard. She nodded her head.

"Only you. It's only for you. Only ever you. So close, Archer. So close."

"*So close,*" he whispered.

He pinched his fingers together and she burst apart at the seams. Screamed and pounded her hand against the wall. A second, larger wave of pleasure rolled over her and she was reduced to groans and grunts, collapsing her front half onto the pillows. She sobbed and yanked at the blankets around her, unable to handle all the sensations running through her body. Every nerve ending was firing because of her tsunami sized climax, and she couldn't catch her breath. Archer's dick was pounding her inside out. He hadn't slowed down at all for her, had fucked her straight through her orgasm.

"Goddamn, that was spectacular," he grunted from behind her.

"So ... good," she managed to pant, then groaned when he slapped her on the butt again.

"Such a perfect ass," he whispered, petting his hand over a cheek before slapping it again.

"Perfect," she agreed, still not quite sure what planet she was on, let alone what he was saying.

"Fuck, Jo, you're too much ... I can't ... *fuck, I'm gonna come.*"

Her ass was stinging, her hips were throbbing, and she was pretty sure her pussy was broken. It certainly wouldn't be any good for any other men, ever again. So when he slammed home one last time, then hitched his hips in tight, moaning and twitching against her, only one response came to her mind.

"*Thank you.*"

5:22 A.M.

DAY TWO

Archer slid sideways out of bed, then glanced back over his shoulder. Jo was on her side, still breathing heavily, obviously asleep. He hadn't disturbed her.

Good.

She was facing away from him, and a sheet was wrapped tightly around her waist and legs. He knew if he walked around the bed, he'd be treated to the magnificent sight that was her breasts. Then he remembered waking up next to her at the rave, when she'd been sleeping on her stomach, only his t-shirt covering her ass. She clearly had no problems with sleeping in the nude.

God bless her.

He shook his head and forced himself to look away. Sleeping with Jo was a bad idea. So frickin' stupid. And had he been imagining things, or had she been about to say she loved him!? She totally had. He'd stopped her because … he couldn't handle hearing those words. Not now, or at least, not yet. Not until he could say them back with a clear conscience.

And to do that, he had to get to work.

Archer grabbed the charging laptop and moved into the bathroom, gently shutting the door behind him. He quickly got dressed, then he sat on the toilet and opened the computer on his lap. It made a loud noise as it booted up, the Windows logo flashing across the screen. He grimaced and glanced at the bathroom door, praying Jo hadn't woken up. When he didn't hear anything from the bedroom, he got to work, fumbling around through different programs and files.

Why were you following Jo, Krakow? And why were you doing your boss dirty and selling bad coke?

Bernard Krakow had some notes that made it obvious he wasn't the only one in on his baking-soda-coke scam. He had a partner. Someone he e-mailed fairly regularly, going over deals and shipments. All strictly business—ounces, payments, measurements. His partner never gave away his name, just signed his messages with the letter *R*.

When the emails didn't lead anywhere, Archer moved on to dig through Krakow's personal files. The computer seemed to be pretty much empty, at first. Then Archer hit pay dirt—a whole shit ton of photos. He'd found them buried in a junk file, in a folder marked "taxes", because of course, who would go rooting through someone else's taxes? Boring.

Luckily, Archer *was* that kind of person, so he'd opened the folder and found a cornucopia of pictures. At first, he'd thought they were just Krakow's porn stash. A little strange, a grown man who lived alone hiding his own porn on his own laptop.

But after about the fifth picture, Archer started to notice something. The pics were all of a very specific nature. Women who all looked like they'd been banged up, tied to chairs, their clothes ripped in various places. BDSM was all the rage anymore, but this seemed different. A porn star would moan or smile in pleasure for the camera. None of these women looked happy. They all looked terrified.

Beyond that, though, there was the setting. Archer's breath

caught in his throat as his eyes wandered over the backgrounds of the photos. Then he stood up and cautiously opened the door so he could peek into the bedroom.

Jo was still sleeping on the plain queen sized bed. There were nightstands on either side of the mattress, and a dresser against the wall by the door. On the opposite side of the room, there was enough space between the nightstand and wall for a cushioned chair. It had wooden armrests and looked very unassuming.

Archer looked at the laptop screen. Then looked at the chair. Back at the screen. So much rage started rushing through his body, he thought he was going to snap the computer in half. He backed into the bathroom and sat down again, taking deep breaths as he did so.

Those women had been tied up in Bernard Krakow's bedroom, to the exact same chair Archer had just been looking at. Krakow had roughed them up, then he'd forced them to get their picture taken. Archer clicked through more of the photos, but they just got worse. Some of the women had their tops ripped off, and some were completely nude. Some looked fine, others were sobbing. *All* of them looked scared.

And beneath each photo was a caption. "July job—Tonya. Released." "April job—Marie. Released." "October job—Sammy. Divested." "June job—Roxanne. Released." "March job—Hannah. Divested."

Released clearly meant those particular women had been let go. But divested? What the fuck was that supposed to mean? As he scrolled through the photos, he saw "divested" more often than he saw "released". He had a general idea of what "divested" meant, but he decided to look it up. Just in case he was wrong.

Divest. Verb. Rid oneself of something that one no longer wants or requires, such as a business interest or investment.

He was not wrong. Some of the women in the photos had been allowed to go home, but most of them had been killed. *Divested.* Presumably by Bernard Krakow. But why? Was he a drug dealer *and* a serial killer?

No. Maybe a little crazy, and clearly lacking in sympathy, but not a psychopath. Every picture had the word "job" under it—keeping those women had been a job. Archer felt safe in assuming that meant there was a boss somewhere down the line, ordering Krakow to do these things. To … maybe … follow these women. Learn their habits and patterns, so when the time came to kidnap them, it would be easy. Maybe he'd even met them first. Had gotten them to lower their guards by, say, buying them drinks and dancing with them.

Jesus fucking christ, Jo. So close. I was so fucking close to losing you.

Archer growled and slammed the laptop shut. He didn't want to see those images anymore. Wanted to burn them from his brain. He paced around the small bathroom, trying to calm down before he had to get back in bed.

So Bernard Krakow had been following and stalking Jo, most likely in hopes of capturing her and torturing her and possibly killing her. Now the real question was—who had asked him to do it? Who had "hired" him for this particular job? And *why?* Why Jo? She had no real connection to the drug world, no reason to be kidnapped and tortured, no reason to be anybody's "job" or anything like that.

No real connection …

Archer tiptoed across the carpet and climbed into bed. He laid on his side and stared at Jo for a while. Then she mumbled in her sleep and rolled onto her back. She yawned, then kept moving, pulling the blanket up to her chin as she turned to face him. He held still until he was sure she was still asleep.

"Jojo," he whispered, reaching out and brushing a lock of hair away from her face. She always looked young—whenever they went out, she got carded. She *was* young, though; and fragile. He'd tried for so many years to be her protector. Her defender. Her best friend. A guy she could always trust. A guy who might some day be worthy of her.

130

Some day.

"I'm so, so sorry, Jo," he finally sighed. She mumbled again, then snuggled closer to him. He turned onto his back and she rested her head on his shoulder. Her warm body was flush against his side, silky soft and smooth to the touch.

But he barely noticed. He stayed awake for another two hours, trying to get the mental image of her tied to Krakow's chair out of his head.

7:58 A.M.

DAY TWO

Jo yawned and stretched. Instead of cracking her knuckles against the bare wall behind her bed, she bonked into something soft. She opened her eyes and looked up at a padded headboard. She blinked a couple times, then looked around Bernard Krakow's bedroom, remembering where she was and what was going on.

Archer was sleeping next to her, stretched out on his stomach on top of the sheets. He must have gotten up at some point in the night, because she remembered them falling asleep naked, yet he was almost fully dressed, wearing his t-shirt and pants. He was facing away from her, but he had his left arm stretched out behind him, as if he was reaching for her in his sleep.

She smiled at the thought, then slipped out of bed. Her clothing was scattered about the room—Archer seemed to like to rip stuff off her and then just fling it every which way. She tip toed around and slipped on her panties and bra, then wiggled back into Krakow's sweater that she'd grabbed out of his closet. Then she headed into the bathroom and almost screamed when she looked at her reflection. After all their acrobatics the night before, and then sleeping on it all crazy, her hair looked beyond wild. Lank and frizzy around her face, and a big rat's nest on the back.

She leaned over the tub and stuck her head under the shower, getting her hair damp enough to calm it down. While she was trying to work her fingers through the tangle, she thought she heard something over the water. She frowned, holding still and trying to listen.

"Jo!"

She hadn't even realized Archer was in the bathroom, yet there he was, grabbing her from behind, his arms wrapping tightly around her. She shrieked as he pulled her off her feet, then they were both falling backwards, hitting the ground a second later. Her back was pressed to Archer's chest and she clutched at his wrists.

"What the fuck are doing!?" she demanded. One of his arms moved and suddenly his hand was clamped over her mouth.

"They're here," he hissed.

"*Hmoo's hmere?*" she mumbled through his palm.

As if to answer her, a pounding sound reverberated through the apartment. Jo went completely still.

"*Police! Open up!*"

She was a little surprised to feel relief flooding through her veins. They probably should've gone to the police from the get go— now that they were at the door, she could just unload everything onto them. The body could become their problem, it couldn't be too hard to prove she hadn't done anything. She'd spend a night in jail, maybe two. No big deal.

Awfully convenient timing. Why are the police here?

"Don't say a word!" Archer breathed as he removed his hand and started shifting around underneath her.

"Why not? What's going on?" she whispered, rolling off him and watching as he crawled out the door. He moved awkwardly, and she realized it was because he was clutching his cell phone in one hand. They'd found some chargers the night before and had juiced up their devices. His screen was lit up with missed messages.

"Those aren't the police," he finally answered her, and she followed behind him on her hands and knees. They left the bedroom and headed across the living room. A large sofa sat with its back to the windows and Archer came to a stop behind it. Jo sat next to him, resting against the piece of furniture and shoving her hair out of her face.

"How do you know that?" she asked.

"Call it a hunch. Wait here, and don't move," he urged, then he stood up and started moving across the living room.

"Police! Open the door, now!"

She looked over the back of the couch, watching as he crept across the apartment. He lurked around the door and peeked through the peep hole. After a second, he ducked down, as if the people on the other side could see him. Then he hurried back to her. She stood up when he got close.

"That's not the fucking police," he said in a low voice. "Two guys in plain clothes."

"Maybe they're detectives?"

"Please don't talk right now. Let's find a way out of here."

"But maybe they could be—"

"Seriously, are we arguing about this right now? Just do what I say! C'mon, the guest room is over the parking garage, maybe we can find a way to climb down to its roof," he suggested, turning and looking back towards the bedrooms. She leaned around him, following his gaze. The pounding at the door was becoming violent, making the wood shake in its hinges.

"Alright, fine. Whatever, let's get out of here."

Before either of them could make a move, though, gun shots ripped through the room. Whoever was on the other side of the door had decided they were done with knocking.

Most officers would just break down a door, not shoot through it. Archer was right.

The window-wall behind them exploded, glass going everywhere.

Jo screamed as a gust of wind rushed through the apartment. She ducked down and Archer stepped in front of her, presumably to protect her from the flying bullets, but then he accidentally bumped into her. With all of her weight behind her, she was immediately thrown off balance. She windmilled her arms for a second, then proceeded to topple over backwards.

And this is how I die—falling out a window. Fuck my life.

Jo screamed as she went through the window, reaching out her arms to grab onto something, anything. At the same time, Archer lunged for her, grabbing her by the wrist. She screamed again as she slammed into the side of the building.

"I've got you! Hold on, I've got you!" he yelled through gritted teeth.

"Don't let me go, Archer! Don't drop me!" she cried. She watched as he glanced over his shoulder.

"Do you trust me?" he asked as bullets flew over his head.

"What!? No! Now pull me up, please!" she begged. He looked back down at her.

"Trust me, Jo!"

He used both his arms to swing her away from the wall. Before she could ask him what he was doing, though, he released his grip. Four stories above the ground, and he just let her go.

God, what a dick.

Jo screamed all the way down. She was mid-breath, ready to start screaming again, when she made contact with the ground. Only, it wasn't solid. She smacked into a body of water and was so shocked, she sucked in a lungful of liquid as she went under.

Falling forty feet into a pool wasn't a picnic. She'd hit the water hard on her thigh, it already stung. She hacked and coughed as she tried to orient herself and push off the bottom. When her head finally broke the surface, she gagged and spit out chlorinated water, then looked up just in time to see Archer land about three feet to her left.

"*I CAN'T BELIEVE YOU LET ME GO!*" she screamed, hitting

him when he resurfaced.

"Stop it! I knew there was a pool, you're fine!" he shouted, managing to dodge her blows and get behind her. His arms wrapped around her middle and he began dragging her towards the side.

"I've been chased, I've been shot at it, I've been thrown out of a building, and I nearly drowned. What's next!?" she moaned, going limp in his arms.

"Oh, stop it. C'mon, upsy daisy."

The concrete lip of the pool scratched against her bare stomach as Archer shoved her up over the side. She scrambled to her feet, trying to untwist the oversized sweater from around her chest. She watched while Archer hauled himself out of the water, then they both looked up.

"Holy shit," she breathed, suddenly glad she hadn't been looking down during her fall.

"Right? We gotta go before they start shooting down here," he urged, gently pushing against her back and guiding her to the front of the building.

"I'm not wearing any pants or shoes!" she squealed, running on tip toes over grass that ran alongside the sidewalk. Archer was at least mostly dressed, looking almost normal. Unfortunately, he hadn't had time to grab his shoes, either.

"Wanna go back up there and get them?" he offered, breaking into a jog and moving past her into some bushes.

"Not really. Shit, I forgot we have to take the bike!" she moaned, raking her hands through her wet hair as he rolled his motorcycle out from its hiding spot and into the road.

"Our only option. C'mon! They're coming out of the building!" he hissed as he jumped onto the bike. She chewed on her bottom lip while he kick started it, then looked over her shoulder. Two guys were hustling up the street towards an SUV. Then she looked back at Archer. He was leaning towards her, his arm outstretched, offering her his hand.

Beats walking down Ventura Boulevard in your bare feet with your ass hanging out.

She took his hand and climbed on, then clung to him as they raced off down the street.

10:10 A.M.

DAY TWO

Jo sat on top of a picnic bench with her feet resting on the seat below her. She would've much rather been sitting inside, but McDonald's apparently had a strict no-pants-no-service policy. *Nazis.*

Of course, she was also barefoot, and her hair was absolutely crazy. After Archer's insane drive through every single back road he could find, the wind had completely blown up her hair. It was easily sticking up eight inches all around her skull, giving her an interesting looking halo. People walking in and out of the fast food restaurant stared at her like she was rabid.

"Okay, I got you two sausage egg McMuffins, a hashbrown, and coffee—black," Archer popped up next to her and specified before she could ask about the drink. She took the warm cup first, holding it between her cold hands and blowing into it.

"Thanks," she grumbled, taking a sip. He sat down next to her and she listened as he dug around in the bag of food he'd brought out.

"C'mon, Jojo. You can't still be mad at me. I knew the pool was right under you," he insisted. "It was like … thirty, forty feet, tops. I wouldn't have dropped you if I'd thought there'd been any chance you could get hurt."

She sighed.

"I guess I can cross cliff diving off my bucket list."

"There's the spirit!"

They sat in silence for a while, munching on their sandwiches and sipping at coffee. She felt like she was missing something, though. Something important. They hadn't learned much at Krakow's, she'd never gotten a chance to go through the guy's computer, but still. There was an important clue somewhere back there, and she just wasn't seeing it.

I can't think straight while my ass is freezing off.

"C'mon," she said, sliding off the table and gently lowering her feet to the ground. "Let's get out of here."

"Huh?" he grunted, looking up at her, his mouth full of hashbrowns.

"Let's go to Walmart. I need pants and we need jumper cables," she told him.

"That's it? Don't you want to talk about getting shot at? Or eat your food? Or bitch about … everything?" he asked, sounding skeptical.

"Shut up, Archer, I'm trying to be nice for a change. I can't run around all day without pants on. If you go slow, I can eat the other sandwich while you drive."

"Whoa now, both hands around my waist at all times—I haven't risked my life all weekend just to have you fall off the back of my bike," he said, climbing off the table as well and handing her the bag of food.

"Well, at least keep it under fifty."

"I make no promises."

Luckily, someone in Jo's condition didn't get many double looks at Walmart. She bee-lined for the clothing section and grabbed the first pair of shorts she saw that weren't absolutely hideous. Then she grabbed a t-shirt from a clearance rack, and on a whim, a nice light-weight athletic jacket.

After spending about fifteen minutes in a changing room, try-ing to get her hair back under control, she went and found a pair of sneakers. She hopped up to a check out line, all the tags in her hands, while slipping into a pair of socks. Archer appeared behind her, also looking more like a human being. He'd changed into fresh clothing, and had not only grabbed a pair of jumper cables, but also an entirely new battery. He was also holding a basket full of random tools and car accessories and a backpack.

"That's going to take a lot of our cash," she pointed out, trying to remember how much money they had left.

"I want to get that car started," he explained simply. "We can use my card for this stuff."

"You have enough to cover this?" Jo asked in a skeptical voice as she took in all the junk they were buying. Archer didn't look at her, just started loading things onto the conveyor belt.

"Yeah, I should be fine."

Before they got back on the bike, Jo yanked her thick brown hair all up into a tight bun. She wasn't dealing with that mess again, if she could avoid it. Archer handed her the backpack full of the car stuff, then they were racing off towards the strip club.

She wasn't sure whether to laugh or cry when they pulled into the parking lot and she saw her shitty car still sitting there. She'd half-way expected it to have disappeared, or for it all to have been some sort of horrible nightmare.

But it had all been real. The car was still there—as was the body, as a quick glance in the trunk confirmed. They tried once to get the engine to start, then Archer got to work, laying out everything he would need to change out the battery. Jo sat behind the wheel for a while, but she couldn't hear anything he was saying, so she eventually moved to sit on the roof of the car.

"So let's go over everything," she suggested, trying to match up the puzzle pieces in her mind. She still felt like she wasn't grasping something she'd learned back at Krakow's apartment. While she thought, she scanned the roads around them. She wasn't sure what she was looking for, just knew that she wanted to be able to run before any more bullets started flying.

"Huh?" Archer grunted from under the hood.

"Dead dude in the trunk. Bernard Krakow. Been following me for … what, like two weeks?"

"Sounds about right."

"We don't know why."

"Sure."

"He's a drug dealer," she added. "And has friends who are looking for him."

"Yup."

"Friends he is most definitely fucking over with that baking soda trick you told me about."

"Okay."

"But …" she let her voice trail off as her brain raced.

"Sounds good."

"I stopped talking," she laughed. He glanced around the hood.

"I haven't been paying attention. C'mon, let's test this sucker out."

She hopped to the ground and got back behind the wheel. With a hope and prayer, she cranked the ignition, then nearly cried when the engine roared to life. Archer clapped, then gathered up all the tools and tossed them into the backseat.

"Finally, something goes right. Will my bike be okay here?" he asked as he slid into the passenger seat. She frowned, trying to remember what they'd been talking about before they'd restarted the car.

"Yeah, it should be fine," she mumbled, tapping her nails against her bottom lip. He finally glanced at her.

"What's up?" he asked.

"Thinking. Baking soda … Krakow … friends …" she prattled off, trying to recapture her train of thought.

"Friends who know your boss well enough for him to give up your information," Archer added. Jo snapped her fingers as every single thought slid into its proper place, possibly for the first time since their whole ordeal had began.

"Hey! Yeah, his friends! Those guys shooting at us, at his apartment? I saw them, before I got on your bike. Two of them looked like the dudes from our place, the ones who shot at you last night," Jo told him.

"So? They shot at us last night, they shot at us this morning," he said. She shook her head and put the car in reverse before peeling out of her spot.

"That's the thing—how could they have possibly known we were at Krakow's place? I had thought at first they were there looking for their friend. But why the whole 'police, open up' act? Why start shooting? Is that how they say hi?" she asked, pulling into traffic. Archer nodded.

"Yeah … yeah, I hadn't thought of it that way. Why start shooting at their buddy's apartment? Maybe they knew about his baking soda trick," he suggested.

"Maybe … but still, why the whole act? Why not just break down his door and pistol whip him?"

"Pistol whip?"

"Whatever drug dealers do," she said. "I don't know. Shooting through the door seems a little overkill. Seems a little like they didn't think Krakow was there, at all. Seems like they somehow *knew* we were there."

"Yeah, it does seem that way," he said. "You didn't tell anyone? Didn't text anyone?"

"No, no one. Who am I going to text? My stripper friends? My

142

mom? The only person I'd text this kind of crazy shit to is you," she laughed.

She had expected him to laugh, too, but when she looked over, Archer wasn't even smiling. He looked confused, and even a little angry. His brow was furrowed and he had his hand on the back of his neck, rubbing back and forth.

Nervous gesture.

"Yeah …" was all he said, his voice low.

"What are you thinking?" she asked, glancing between him and the road.

"I'm thinking that it looks like you're heading home," he replied, pointing ahead of them. Jo frowned.

"Force of habit, I guess. I always go straight home after work. Do you … could they still be there?" Jo asked. He shrugged.

"I don't know. I doubt it—they were looking for us, and obviously we weren't there. Do a slow drive by first," he suggested.

They did just that, cruising past their building's parking lot at a slow speed. Jo sunk so low in her seat, she could barely see over the dash. Archer laughed at her and pointed out that a car moving without a driver was more suspicious than just acting normal, but she held her position till they were clear of the complex.

There were no strange cars out front, and no henchmen looming in the doorway, so they decided to risk it and circled back. Jo parked away from the building's entrance, close to the sidewalk, in case they had to make a quick get away. Then Archer made her wait in the car while he checked out the front door. It felt like a lifetime had passed before he leaned out and waved that it was all clear. She got out of the car and jogged over.

"What if they're in the apartment?" she whispered, clutching Archer's t-shirt as they moved through the entryway and up the stairs.

"We'll go slowly," he assured her, stopping at the door to the second floor. "Stay behind me at all times—if it looks like someone is in there, we'll go right past and head to my apartment, okay?"

"Okay."

Archer opened the door and peeked his head out. Jo held her breath, then let it out when they moved into the hallway.

They tip toed along, Archer hugging the wall, and her practically hugging his back. Everything was quiet, and when she glanced around him, she saw that her door was closed. That didn't mean much, though, because the bad guys could be sitting in her living room. Commenting on her thrift store furniture, watching her illegal cable.

Fuckers.

Before they could reach her apartment, though, another door opened. Jo nearly had a heart attack, but before she could collapse, Archer all but slammed her back against the wall. He pressed his back to her front, completely hiding her from view.

"Your little girly has done it now! That party last night was ridiculous! I called the police, I did, but the rat bastards never showed up. Typical! I'll be calling the building manager, do you hear me? Your girly will get evicted this time!"

Mrs. Copernicus, the old woman Jo had yelled at just yesterday morning. Had it really only been twenty-four hours?

Time flies when you're having fun.

"We've been gone all night, Mrs. C," Archer said in a careful voice. "What party?"

"Nice try, Archer!" she snarled, brandishing her cane. "All that noise, thumping around, breaking things! On and on, until almost three in the morning. My cats were terrorized. Stupid cops, good for nothings. Wasted my breath calling them."

"Wait," Jo finally spoke up, and she stood on her toes to look over Archer's shoulder. "You called an actual police station, and they never sent anyone?"

"Not anyone! Called three times. They claimed they sent a car around, but no one ever came. This town is disgusting. But don't you worry, the manager will hear about you!" Mrs. Copernicus assured Jo.

"I promise, Jo was with me all night," Archer insisted. For whatever reason, the old woman had always taken a shine to him and tended to believe anything he said. He was the only one who could calm her down when she got into one of her temper tantrums.

"Then who was making all that racket? No protecting her this time. I'm onto you!"

And with that, Mrs. Copernicus stepped back and slammed her door shut.

Apparently there's no calming her down this time.

"Three in the morning," Jo said. "They must have come back after the shoot out and kept looking around."

"Yeah. Sounds like they're not here anymore."

Archer started moving again, walking faster down the hall than before—Jo jogged to catch up to him in front of her door. They both stood still for a second, taking in the broken lock and dangling knob, then he pushed the door open.

Jo had been expected the apartment to be a mess, but it still came as a shock. Cushions ripped up, shelves knocked over, her tv broken, the fridge standing open. They shuffled through the mess and moved into the kitchen, taking in the spoiled food and broken dishes.

"Don't move," Archer suddenly said, and he jogged out of the room. Jo turned in a circle, feeling overwhelmed as her eyes combed over the mess. By the time she came back around to face the door, he was walking back into her apartment.

"What's out there?" she asked, slightly out of breath.

How long will this take to clean? I hate cleaning.

"Checking out my place. They hit it, too. Looks just as bad," he told her, standing next to her.

"What were they looking for? What could they possibly expect to have found in here? I'm a waitress, for christ's sake," she groaned.

"I'm sorry, Jo. For now, though, let's … just collect some stuff, okay? Anything that's important, you know? Some clothes, any money you may have stashed away, whatever," he suggested.

"Okay. Yeah, the closet. I keep all my important paper stuff there," she sighed, going back into the living room and heading to the large closet near the front door.

Of course, it had been ripped open and all the contents were spilled across the floor in front of it. Jo dropped to her knees and started sifting through everything, tossing aside scarves and shoes so she could pick through the papers that were underneath them. Clearly, the bad guys weren't interested in identity theft because she found all of her important documents right away, like her social security card and her birth certificate.

She was still digging around when she heard a creaking noise in the hallway. The one thousand year old elevator that she was too scared to take—apparently, someone wasn't afraid of it. It was groaning its way up the building. She glanced over her shoulder, finding Archer standing stock still in the kitchen.

"Get away from the door," he ordered, and she immediately stood up and backed into the kitchen with him.

"Maybe it's just—" she started to whisper, but was cut off by the sound of the elevator doors dinging open on their floor.

"Move. Right now, move," Archer hissed, shoving her down the hallway. She tripped over her feet and stumbled through the door at the opposite end. Her bedroom hadn't been left untouched, but she was glad to see it didn't look quite as bad as the rest of her apartment.

"Please just be a neighbor," she prayed, moving so she was behind Archer, who was against the wall next to her door. *"Please, please, please."*

"No such luck," Archer sighed as the sound of heavy footsteps entered her living room. More shocking, though, was the gun he produced from behind his back.

"Where the fuck did you get that?" she asked, her voice barely above a breath.

"I grabbed it when I went over to my apartment—they forgot to look in the toilet tank," he explained.

"You just love hiding shit in toilet tanks, don't you? Why the fuck do you have a gun, Archer?" she demanded.

"Just be glad I have one, I—"

"*We know you're back there!*"

Jo was so startled, she almost choked on a breath of air. She coughed into her jacket collar and tried to listen to whoever was yelling from her kitchen.

"If you know that," Archer shouted, "then you should also know we're armed and dangerous."

"Awww, that's cute. He's armed and dangerous, you hear that?"

"I heard. *Adorable.*"

Jo screamed and hit the floor as bullets started flying. Before that weekend, she'd only been around guns a couple times in her whole life. Now it felt like she'd been running through a hail of bullets for the last twenty-four hours.

And though she'd thought the bad guys' gun shots were loud, coming from the end of the hallway, they were nothing compared to Archer firing his hand gun out her door. She gritted her teeth and clamped her hands over her ears, watching as he peeked around the door jam while he fired the weapon. The booming went on through ten shots, then just quiet clicking, over and over.

"Please tell me you hit them," she groaned, daring to get up into a crouch.

"Clipped one in the leg, but nothing that would scare them off," Archer said, crawling over to her closet.

"Shit. You have more bullets, right?"

"Nope. That was it. Do you have anything in here that would work as a weapon?"

"You only had ten bullets?" she asked.

"The gun only holds ten. C'mon, weapons, think. Anything," he snapped, digging through the mess of clothing on the floor.

"Well, I keep my semi-automatics in my underwear drawer, and my—"

"Jojo. Not helping."

"What do you think I have in here!?" she snapped, glancing back at the door. Their assailants were still taunting them from the kitchen, thankfully. "I have around sixty pairs of cheap underwear, a ton of shoes, some Bacardi from your birthday, and a shitty Beanie Babies collection. Not exactly an ammunitions depot!"

"I don't know! Anything we can fashion into—wait, Bacardi? What kind?" he asked, turning on his haunches to face her.

"Are you serious?"

"Yes. Where is it?"

"Oh, for fuck's sake …"

Jo angrily crawled over to her night stand and yanked open the bottom drawer. A bottle full of amber liquid rolled around and she picked it up. She held it out to him, the label facing up.

"I never thought you being an alcoholic would save my life. I could kiss you," he sighed, taking the bottle from her and quickly unscrewing the cap.

"Alcoholic!?"

"No worse than me, don't worry. Now for the panties," he said, turning away from her and going to her dresser. He pulled open the second drawer and started rifling through her underwear.

"What do you need my underwear for?" she asked, then realized something else. "And how did you know which drawer they were in?"

"You think I've never snooped around your bedroom? I'm a guy, Jo," he snorted, pulling out a plain white cotton pair. A couple gun shots were fired and they both ducked again.

"That's awful, and an invasion of privacy," she informed him. "And … what the hell are you doing?"

She watched as he sprinkled some of the rum over her panties, then he bunched up the material and forced it into the neck of the bottle. It made a makeshift cork and he turned the bottle upside down, further soaking the cotton inside the glass.

"Collect anything you love, right now," he told her, glancing around. Her laptop was on top of her dresser and he grabbed it, practically throwing it at her. She managed to catch it and put it on her bed, along with the documents she'd collected in her living room. She picked a ratty backpack up off the floor and started shoving things into it. The papers and computer, some pictures from her night stand, any clothing that was laying anywhere near her.

"Holy shit," she gasped for air, trying not to hyperventilate as she filled the pack to almost overflowing. "Oh my god, that's what I think it is, isn't it?"

"It is," he nodded, moving so he was against the wall right next to her door. "Anything above eighty proof burns really well. We're lucky you like your drinks strong—nothing like good ol' 151 to get the job done."

"Mandy is going to be so pissed," Jo groaned.

"Do you have renter's insurance?"

"What do you think?"

"We don't have a choice, Jo. They're gonna start coming down the hall as soon as they catch onto the fact that I'm not firing back. Got a light?" he asked, shaking the bottle at her.

Jo clutched the backpack to her chest and stared at him. Archer Calhoun was holding a Molotov cocktail in her bedroom, and he was ready to toss it at some drug dealing henchmen in her kitchen. What had happened to the world?

"Yeah," she sighed, going to her dresser and rooting around in the top drawer. It was mostly full of junk, and after a second of searching, she found her lucky Zippo. It had an American flag on one side, and the Anarchist symbol on the other. She held it out to him and he wrapped his hand around hers, squeezing tight for a second.

"I'm sorry, Jo. I really am," he told her, staring very directly into her eyes. She managed a watery smile, just barely holding back tears.

"It's not your fault. I hated this place, anyway. Light it up."

Archer did as told, holding the flame to the cotton. When it caught fire, he handed the Zippo back to her and then peeked out the doorway. Jo shoved the lighter into her pocket, then she hunched over and plugged her ears. She didn't really want to hear if he hit his mark.

He may have had shit aim with his gun, but he didn't miss with the bottle. He dashed across the open door, throwing the incendiary device as he moved. It exploded somewhere down the hall and despite her makeshift ear muffs, she could still hear the bad guys screaming.

"Shit," Archer hissed, now on the other side of the door from her and looking through the crack on that side. She let her hands fall away from her ears.

"What?" she asked.

"I was hoping it would hit in the kitchen, on the tile. Maybe buy us some time. Landed at the end of the hall, the walls are already on fire," he told her. There was more screaming and the sound of stomping. Someone falling to the ground. She hoped they'd been taught to stop, drop, and roll.

"Shit. What are we going to do? I don't want to burn to death, Archer!" she whimpered.

"That's not going to happen," he assured her, and he rushed over to her window. It was open and he leaned outside as she hurried up behind him.

"Two stories isn't so bad," she said. "We could survive a two story jump, right?"

"Maybe," he said. "But I have a better idea—there's a dumpster halfway under Mandy's window. Move, go to her room."

He didn't wait for her to follow instructions, just started shoving her down the hallway. She hissed as a wall of heat slapped her across the face. Flames were licking their way down her walls, racing towards the bedrooms. She squealed and hurried into her roommate's room, going straight for the window. She struggled to open it, then shrugged into her backpack while she looked outside.

"What is it with today and jumping out windows?" she asked, swinging a leg over the window sill and straddling it for a moment.

"You always wanted to bungee jump, remember? Think of it like that," Archer suggested, rubbing her shoulders comfortingly as she moved her other leg so she was sitting on the ledge.

"This is not bungee jumping, Archer. It looks a lot farther than two stories. What if I miss the—"

She screamed when he shoved her from behind. She barely had time to throw her hands in front of her head before she landed face-first in a pile of trash. There was shouting from above her and she scrambled backwards, banging her head painfully on the partially closed lid. She scooted under, and a second later Archer landed in the same spot she'd just vacated.

"I'm beginning to think drug dealers aren't the only ones who want me dead!" she hissed, kicking at him while she struggled to push the lid open.

"The door was on fire, I didn't have time to baby talk you through it. You okay?" he asked, sitting upright and shoving the lid up.

"Peachy keen. Let's get the fuck out of here."

They both fell out of the dumpster, picking trash and food off their clothing as they hurried across the car park. By the time they got to Jo's car, the building's fire alarm was going off and residents were starting to stream into the parking lot. She frowned as she turned on the vehicle.

"Everyone is gonna be okay, Jo," Archer assured her. "The sprinklers in your kitchen had already gone off, the fire won't go beyond your apartment."

"But what if it does?" she asked, watching in her rear view mirror as Mrs. Copernicus hobbled her way out of the building, carrying four of her cats. Her grandson followed close behind, holding the rest of the scratch-happy kitties.

"It won't. The doors are all steel, the hallways and apartments all have sprinklers. The building was made to be fireproof. Look at the window we just jumped out of, do you see any flames? It's probably almost out, already. No one will get hurt. It'll be okay," he promised, rubbing her shoulder.

She knew it didn't really matter if she was upset or not—they had to keep moving. So she nodded her head and pulled out onto the street. She turned a corner and felt a little relief when a fire engine went screaming past them.

"It's just like Krakow's apartment. How the fuck did they know we were home?" she asked after they'd gone a couple blocks. "We'd barely been there … what, ten minutes? Fifteen minutes? They couldn't have followed us. Could they have?"

"I don't think so …" Archer mumbled, but when she glanced at him, he was glaring out the windshield.

"We should just go to the police," she finally said what she'd been thinking since morning. "This is too much for us. We just set a building on fire!"

"No," he shook his head. "No police. It's too late for that now. Did you hear Mrs. C? She called and no one came—they're probably dirty cops, paid off to let these guys do what they want."

"This isn't a movie, Archer! A James Bond villain isn't lurking somewhere, orchestrating all this," she insisted.

"No, this is real life, Jo. Which means whoever is behind this probably makes a James Bond villain look like a pussy. Don't be naive, I don't have the energy for it today."

"Fuck off. What do we do then? Go on the lam? Should I drive to the border?" she asked in a snide voice.

"No. We …"

She waited for a second, expecting him to finish the sentence. He didn't.

"We … what? What do we do? Where do we go?" she demanded. He let out a long, pained sigh.

"We go to my dad's house," he breathed.

"Great idea! Yeah, we should just lead the bad guys to our childhood neighborhood! Maybe introduce them to our moms!" she laughed angrily. He didn't smile. Just sunk lower in his seat and looked away from her.

"No. Not that house."

"Then what house?"

"My *real* dad's house."

12:06 P.M.

DAY TWO

Jo had known Archer Calhoun since he was fifteen. She'd been to his family home, had met his mother and step-father. She'd also met his grandmother, his two aunts, his one uncle, and six of his cousins.

She knew that as a young child he'd struggled with a minor case of dyslexia. She knew about the night terrors he'd dealt with until the age of eleven. She even new about how his step-dad used to slap him around, before Archer got bigger than the guy. She knew his favorite color, the way he liked his steak cooked, and all about his secret obsession with pop music.

So how *IN THE FUCK* did she not know about his real father!?

As far as Jo had known, Archer didn't even know who is real father was—that's what he'd always told her. All their lives. His mother and father had split up before he'd been born, and he'd always been told his dad didn't care about him, didn't want him, didn't love him.

"How could you not tell me something this huge?" Jo asked again, staring at him from across the car. He shrugged and glanced to his left before making a turn.

"It's … complicated. I'll explain everything when we get there," he replied.

It was pretty much the only answer he'd give her. They'd stopped at a gas station to grab some water, and when she'd come back outside, he'd insisted on driving. Once in the car, he'd immediately gotten on the freeway and headed south. After about half an hour, though, he'd hooked west, passing Santa Monica and heading onto Highway 1— the scenic coastal highway. For a while there was nothing but ocean on their left, and national park on their right. It took over twenty minutes before she'd realized where they were heading.

Malibu. Archer's real dad lives in Malibu!?

"You're kinda freaking me out. Where are we going?" she asked as they cruised through the posh community.

"I told you, I'll—"

"Archer."

He finally glanced at her.

"Jodi."

"I have been thrown out two windows today," she said in a slow voice. "Been shot at. Been chased. Been threatened. And it's barely noon. Please, *please*, just tell me what's going on."

"Okay. Okay, we're basically here," he sighed, and she sat up straight, glancing around. They were on Malibu Canyon Road and he turned onto a smaller, more residential road. They wound their way past intimidating gates, which were all locked in front of large properties. In the distance, she could see palatial homes.

"Your real dad lives here?" she said, her voice full of awe as they rolled to a stop at a dead end. The only way to continue forward would be through a scary iron gate that had spikes at the top of it.

"Yeah."

He climbed out of the car and she hurried to get out of her side. She hesitated at her door, though, unsure of whether to grab her backpack or not. At home, she never left anything in her vehicle that might tempt someone to break in. But she highly doubted there were car thieves creeping around in the bushes, so she shut her door and moved to stand with him at the front of the vehicle.

"This …" she tried to collect her thoughts. "Archer, this is not a normal home. What does your dad do for a living?"

"That's the thing. Jo, I …" his voice trailed off, and somewhere in the distance she heard a buzzing noise. She peered through the gate, watching as something behind the hedges moved.

"Yeah?" she asked. He gently grabbed her by the shoulders and forced her to face him.

"Before everything goes to shit," he started talking fast. "I want you to know something."

"Why? What's happening?" she asked, getting nervous again. He glanced at the gate.

"Everything I did, was because of you. *Everything*. Even if it seems fucked up—and it will—it was because of you. Because I wanted to be close to you but I knew I wasn't good enough for you, and I wanted to be better, but I just couldn't, and I had to keep you safe. From me, from them, from everybody. Jo, I've always—"

She was a little blown away by his rambling speech, and she held her breath, waiting for those words she'd been dying to hear. Words she felt like she kind of wanted to say, herself. His fingers were digging into her skin and he was staring at her so hard, she couldn't look anywhere else but into his gaze. His eyes were back to a mossy green and she felt herself getting lost in them. She swayed towards him, soaking in every sentence.

Before he could finish what he was saying, though, there was another buzzing sound. Much louder. She winced and turned her head, watching as the gate slowly creaked open. A vehicle drove towards them—it looked like a war-ready golf cart, decked out with big wheels and a roll bar and camouflage paint. It came to a stop maybe five feet away and the driver jumped out, a bounce in his step as he headed towards them. He wore a black suit with a crisp white shirt, the top couple buttons undone. An artfully messy red pocket square stood out against the dark material of his jacket, and when he finally reached them, he smiled a toothy grin that looked oddly familiar to Jo.

"Archer," the man said, not bothering to remove his shiny sunglasses.

"Mal," Archer nodded his head.

"Going to introduce me?" the guy called Mal asked, turning his smile to Jo.

"No."

"Awww, you're no fun!"

"It's been a shitty weekend."

"Really? That's too bad, Archie."

"It is. I need to speak to him."

"He saw you on the cameras, he sent me down to get you."

"We can drive up on our own."

"Seriously, little bro, you have to lighten up," Mal laughed.

"Little brother?" Jo asked.

Mal smirked and removed his glasses, and she gasped. He was tall, but smaller in size than Archer, not quite as broad. Leaner. He had much darker hair and much fairer skin. They really didn't look alike at all—except for their identical hazel eyes.

Wow, it's just like looking into Archer's eyes.

"By five years," Mal informed her. "And you must be the famous Jo. I've heard *so much* about you."

"I wish I could say the same," she replied, glancing at Archer. He was busy glaring at his brother.

"Let's go," he said, grabbing her arm and leading her to the tricked out golf cart.

Mal rambled on and on. He was pretentious and snide. Spoiled-rich-kid poured off him in waves. He seemed to love to hear himself talk, and was trying his hardest to embarrass Archer.

"On and on," he was chuckling as they cruised up a long drive-way. "Jo this, and Jo that. Jo, Jo, Jo!"

"Shut up," Archer grumbled. Jo managed a small smile, staring at the backs of their heads.

"That's kind of sweet," she said, poking him in the shoulder.

"Oh yeah, the girls *love it*," Mal sighed. She stopped smiling.

"Girls?"

"Shut up, Mal," Archer growled.

"I have a question," Jo ventured, and she noticed as he stiffened up. "What do you do, Mal?"

"What do you mean, Jo?" he asked, chuckling.

"Like for a living. I assume you don't just live with your dad," she laughed. She had no reason to dislike him, really, but it was clear he liked taking the piss out of Archer, and that got her hackles up. Only she was allowed to do that—no one else.

"A funny one! I love it. No, I don't 'just live' with Daddy. I can't believe Archie here hasn't told you, considering he's so—"

"We're here!" Archer shouted, jumping out of the cart before it came to a stop. Before Jo could even open her mouth, he was pulling her out behind him.

"He's in the games room," Mal said, then peeled off without so much as a goodbye.

"That was *bizarre*," she snorted, trying to keep her feet under her as Archer dragged her up some marble steps. "He's your brother?"

"*Half* brother," Archer corrected her. "Same dad, different moms."

"So he's not Mal Calhoun?"

"No, he's Malcolm Rodriguez. Calhoun is my step-dad's name. Mal was raised by my real father."

"Malcolm, Mal," she repeated his name softly, but she wasn't really paying attention. Archer was rushing her through an amazing home. A stained glass dome over the main entrance, a split staircase curving up the sides of the walls, gold inlaid everywhere. Such opulence.

And women. So many women, just wandering around. Bikinis

everywhere. Jo knew she was good looking and had a good body—to work at her job, a person had to look a certain way—but the women surrounding her actually made her feel a little self conscious.

On top of that, they all seemed to know Archer. They called out greetings, leaned in to kiss his cheek. A few even tried to hug him. He shrugged away from them all, explaining that he was in a hurry, that he was only there to speak to Santana.

"Who's Santana?" Jo asked, struggling to keep up as they practically ran up a flight of stairs.

"My dad. Santana Rodriguez."

He stopped her outside a huge pair of double doors. Laughter and giggling could be heard from the other side of them, and the sound of pool balls clacking and clinking together.

"Your dad's name is Santana?" she laughed.

"It's a nickname. Jo, I just … remember what I said outside, okay?" he asked, and he was staring at her again. She stopped laughing and nodded her head.

"Okay, Archer. I promise."

"Remember, and *trust me*," he added. She frowned.

"Okay, but you're making me nervous."

"You're about to get a lot more nervous."

He didn't give her a chance to respond, he just turned and opened both doors.

The way he'd been talking, she hadn't been sure what to expect, but the scene in the room looked pretty normal. Three more bikini clad women stood around a pool table which sat in front of a curved wall. Big windows behind it let in lots of sunlight, negating the need for any lamps or overhead lighting. Against one wall were shelves full of basketballs and tennis balls and volley balls and soccer balls—basically just a lot of balls. The opposite wall was bare, and painted on the hard wood floor in front of it was a shuffleboard.

An impressive space, for sure, but not enough to distract her from the only other man in the room. He was wearing a cream colored linen suit, no tie, and when he came out from around the table, she was surprised to see he also wore no shoes. His thick, long brown hair was brushing his collar, and a trim beard obscured the bottom half of his face.

Still, there was no mistaking who he was; Malcolm Rodriguez may have looked nothing like his younger brother, but Santana Rodriguez looked *exactly* like his younger son. It was uncanny. He was an older version of Archer. The tan skin, the generous smile, the broad shoulders. When he got close enough, she could see he also had the same gorgeous hazel eyes.

"My boy!" his dad laughed loudly. He even had the same laugh as Archer. "I was wondering where you've been all weekend."

"It's been a rough one," Archer sighed, then she felt his hand pressing against her lower back. "Dad, this is Jodi Morgan. Jo, this is my ... dad."

Jo automatically stuck out her hand, but Mr. Rodriguez ignored it and pulled her into a great big bear hug, picking her up off her feet. She grunted as the air was forced from her lungs, and she managed to turn her head to shoot a worried glance at Archer. He couldn't see her, though, because he grumbling and staring at his feet.

"Finally!" his dad laughed again as he set her back down. "I've been bugging this kid to introduce us for a while now."

"Uh ..." Jo responded articulately.

"I know, I know, sounds a little weird. Archer here has mentioned you a time or two. Has shared some of your wilder adventures. Gotta say, I was annoyed at first, thinking some little flirt was stealing my son away right after I found him, but eventually I could tell it was the real deal," he told her. She raised her eyebrows.

"Real deal?"

"Oh, he may not have said it yet, but Archer here is head over—"

"*Dad*," Archer practically shouted. Everyone in the room turned to stare at him. "Sorry, it's just ... shit has been *really* crazy this weekend, and I have a lot to fill you in on. *In private*."

"Geez, why didn't you say so? C'mon, my office. Jodi, feel free to stay here, or you can—"

"She goes where I go, I'm not leaving her alone in this house."

Jo wasn't sure why, but she got the impression Santana Rodriguez wasn't someone who was often interrupted, and now Archer had done it twice. The two stood still, staring at each other. Archer had maybe an inch or two on his dad, but Mr. Rodriguez had a steely confidence that only comes with age and extreme wealth. He narrowed his eyes at his son.

"It's okay," Jo said quickly. "I can wait here, Mr. Rodriguez."

There was silence for a second longer, then his dad grinned again. His arm wrapped around her shoulders, hugging her to his side, and he started walking out of the room.

"Please. My father was Mr. Rodriguez. Everyone calls me Santana, the boys call me Dad, and my name is Carlos. Take your pick," he offered as he guided them out of the room and down a hall.

"Ah, I get it," she laughed nervously. "Santana. Carlos. Carlos Santana."

"I love a good guitar player," Santana sighed.

They walked into his office, which was filled with lots of leather and wooden furniture. Heavy drapes were covering the windows, making everything dark and masculine. Large, expensive looking leather chairs were pulled up to a huge rosewood desk and Santana deposited her in one of those chairs. Archer sat next to her and immediately leaned forward, resting his elbows on his knees.

"We have a real problem," he sighed.

"Seems like it," his dad agreed, sitting behind the desk and opening a drawer. He rooted around in it for a second before pulling out a large cigar.

"Like I said, it's been a shit weekend. I left here Friday and did that job for you over in Marina Del Rey," Archer started.

"Yeah, seemed like it went well."

"Perfect, no problems. Then I went home and changed and …"

Jo was confused. He'd been in Malibu and Marina Del Rey on Friday? He'd told her he'd worked all day Friday, which should have meant he'd been at his construction site in Reseda—that's where she'd assumed he'd been when she'd tried to get a hold of him all night Friday. Had he been on a different site in Malibu? She wasn't sure why, but she was pretty positive the answer was *no*.

"Are you a contractor?" she suddenly blurted out, interrupting Archer. Both men turned to look at her, and she could tell Archer was upset with her question, but she didn't look away from his father.

"What?" Santana asked, blowing a stream of smoke over his shoulder.

"He said he did a job for you—he works construction. Are you like a contractor, does he work at job sites for you?" she asked. Nothing had been said, so she couldn't be sure why she felt sick, but her stomach was definitely cramping up. Nerves were setting her entire body on edge, and not in a good way.

I bet Archer's never even been on a construction site ...

"Construction?" his dad asked, chuckling as he glanced at his son. "Is that what you said?"

Archer groaned and turned towards her.

"Please, please, please don't freak out," he urged. "Let me just get this over with, and then you can freak out all you want. But right now, please just—"

"What do you?" she spoke through him, still staring at his dad. The older man sighed and leaned forward, setting his cigar in an ornate crystal ashtray.

"I know this isn't what you wanted, Son," he said. "But best just to get it over with."

Archer ignored his dad and reached across the space between the chairs, gripping onto her hand.

"Please, Jojo," he whispered.

"I'm an entrepreneur, I guess you could say. I have a lot of real estate, some shares in some production companies, a trucking business," Santana explained. Jo blinked and glanced at Archer.

"That seems pretty normal."

"I'm also one of the most successful cocaine dealers in the greater Los Angeles basin."

Jo sucked in air so hard, she started choking. Archer jumped to his feet and began pounding on her back, but she shooed him away. When she finally caught her breath, she stared at Mr. Rodriguez.

"I'm sorry," she breathed. "I've had a weird weekend, I'm half deaf from listening to gun shots. What did you say?"

"I import cocaine," he said, resting his arms on his desk and lacing his fingers together. "Vast quantities of it, from Colombia and Mexico. And then I turn around and distribute it to gangs and lower level drug rings. Some premium clients, we deal with ourselves. I set up the deals, and Archer and Malcolm facilitate the trade offs."

Jo stared at him for a moment, then turned to stare at Archer. He was holding her hand so tightly, she was starting to lose the feeling in her fingers.

Ten years around each other, and I don't even know this person.

"You're a drug dealer," she stated in a loud clear voice. He winced.

"Jesus, don't say it like that, it's not like I'm lurking around high schools, selling to kids," he argued.

"Oh, I'm sorry. You're a *rich* drug dealer," she corrected herself.

"Jojo, stop."

"Don't call me that," she hissed, yanking her hand away.

"I'm sorry you had to find out this way, I hadn't realize Archer was keeping it a secret from you. I told him from the get go leading two lives was virtually impossible. He was right about one thing, though; it sounds like we don't have time for you to 'freak out' right now. You will have plenty of time later to rake him over the coals. Right now, sounds like you've both got a problem you need help with," Santana said.

"The problem is a dead *drug dealer* in my trunk!" Jo yelled. Santana's eyebrows shot up, his eyes bouncing between her and his son.

"Someone we know?" he asked in a casual voice.

"Bernard Krakow," Archer sighed.

"Hmmm. One of Danny's guys," Santana grumbled. Jo held up her hands.

"You *know* him!?" she shouted.

"I never met him," Archer spoke fast. "A guy named Daniel Nguyen runs a drug ring out in West Covina, mainly dealing meth and coke. But recently he's been edging into our territory. Krakow started running drugs for him around Hollywood, that's when we first heard his name. He only popped up in Van Nuys a month or two ago."

"You knew him," she breathed, at a total loss. The moment was surreal. She briefly wondered if she'd never actually come down from the ecstasy she'd had yesterday.

"So now he's in your girlfriend's trunk. How did he get there?" Archer's dad asked.

"I'm not his girlfriend," she snapped.

"Jo, shut up," Archer groaned. "And we ... we don't know. Jo and I were at a club downtown Friday night, the dude drugged her drink and tried to take her outside. Next morning, he's sleeping off a couple bullets in her trunk. We've been on a wild goose chase ever since. Found out he's been stalking her, lurking around her work, was the one pulling the strings to get her to the club he met her at."

"Did you know any of this was going on? That he was following her?" Santana asked.

"No. You told me to leave him alone, so I left him alone. Seems like he didn't want to return the favor."

"She mentioned gun shots. How big of a mess am I going to have to deal with?" Santana sighed.

"That's the thing," Archer's voice got animated as he scooted to the edge of his seat. "Wherever we go, these assholes keep popping up! Big heavy dudes. We're at her work—they come in asking about her. We go to our apartment building—they're there tossing the place, even shot at us when we tried to get away. So we go to Krakow's apartment. I figured I could search the place and figure out what's going on—they turn the place into Swiss cheese the next morning. We had to jump out a four story fucking window into a pool."

"You *dropped me* out a window," Jo corrected him, clenching her teeth together so hard she halfway expected one to crack.

"Jojo here pointed out that they keep magically showing up everywhere we went, which I was like yeah, that's pretty fucking weird. So I take us back to our building and while I'm checking to make sure they're not hanging out downstairs, I made a call," he said.

This was news to Jo. She'd sat in the car while Archer had made sure the entrance to their building had been clear. She'd assumed he'd just checked the stairwell and the elevator, she hadn't realized he'd been making phone calls.

"Obviously not to me," Santana noted. "I'm a little upset to hear you've been getting shot at for two days straight and you didn't think to tell me. You know better, Archer. I could've helped."

"I didn't know we'd end up getting shot at. And …" his voice trailed off as he looked back at Jo. "I thought I could postpone this moment for a little longer."

"Can't postpone the inevitable," his dad pointed out.

"Besides, I didn't think I'd need your help because I thought I already *had* help. Someone I'd been messaging all weekend. So when we got back to our building, I called my little *helper* and told him where I was and what we were doing. Maybe fifteen, twenty minutes later, guess who shows up?"

"Nguyen's thugs?" Santana guessed.

"Yeah. Wound up pinned down in her bedroom. I had to set the fucking apartment on fire."

"I thought I saw something on the news about a building fire in Van Nuys."

"That would be us."

"That would be when he threw me out a window for the *second time* in two hours," Jo added, glaring at Archer.

"Well then," Santana sighed, leaning back in his chair. "We knew we had a double-cross. Sounds like you found him. Do I want to know?"

"I don't think you'll even believe me," Archer replied.

"Wait, wait, wait," Jo tried to catch up. "You're a big time drug dealer, and Archer is a little mini-drug dealer."

"Mini-drug dealer!" Santana laughed. "Archer took to it like a duck to water, he's my second in command. He'll inherit everything one day, if I can ever get him to leave Van Nuys."

"He's a second in command drug dealer," Jo continued talking. "Whatever. And you guys have someone working for you who's been double crossing you for this other big time drug dealer, Danny who-ever. Danny, who probably sent Krakow after me, all because Archer is a drug dealer, too. And yet, some how, bringing me here seemed like a *good idea!?*"

She had turned in her seat while she'd been speaking, and when she finished, she was staring straight at Archer. He stared right back, but he was rubbing at the back of his neck. She knew him well enough to know what that gesture meant.

I don't know him at all.

"It was a good idea, because it means we can plug up the leak we seem to have, and then we can deal with your little problem, as well. Who's the leak?" Santana asked.

"Mal," Archer said simply.

"What does Malcolm know?" Santana looked confused.

"No, Mal *is* the leak," Archer sighed. "I told you he'd been weird lately. Not showing up to jobs, shady late night meetings. He's the only person I've been talking to all weekend. Every time I texted him what was happening or what we were doing, fifteen minutes later we would be surrounded. It *has* to be him. Literally no one else knew where we were."

There was a long silence. As upset as she was, even Jo knew better than to interrupt it. Father stared at son, clearly not wanting to believe what he'd just heard. Jo didn't know Mal at all, but the accusation didn't surprise her. Santana may have been some kind of drug lord, but he also seemed genuinely nice. Malcolm Rodriguez, on the other hand, had "bad guy" written all over him.

"How can you be so sure?" Archer's father finally asked. "Your little girlfriend here could have been texting any—"

"Check my phone, I've used it once to make exactly one phone call all weekend, and it was to a stripper named Beeshonn. I doubt she's in on your little drug war," Jo snapped at him.

"And I haven't spoken to one single other soul besides Mal," Archer said again.

Santana let out a long sigh and stared up at his ceiling. It probably wasn't easy, hearing that his first born was not only a traitor, but had also pretty much tried to get his brother killed. Living a life of crime clearly wasn't as glamorous as movies made it out to be.

This is why I don't get involved with drug dealers or pushers or addicts or bad people in general, ARCHER. YOU FUCKING DRUG DEALING BAD PERSON!

"I didn't want to believe it. I've had my suspicions, even before you brought up yours. Ever since I brought you into the fold, he's had issues. He's always been jealous. Apparently it finally got the better of him," Santana sighed. "So he's working for Nguyen. They've been specifically poaching our long term clients, now we know how and why. And now Mal's using Krakow and Nguyen to come after you. Probably because he thinks if he gets rid of you, he'll inherit everything."

"And Krakow and Nguyen were into some fucked up shit. I found all this stuff on Krakow's computer. Jo wasn't the first girl he'd followed around. He's been doing this kind of thing for a while, kidnapping chicks and keeping them. Torturing them, killing them."

"*What!?*" Jo all but screamed. This was all news to her, she hadn't even known Archer had gotten on the laptop.

"It's a pretty regular thing. Kidnap a rivals girlfriend or wife or sister, and you can get him to do just about anything you want," Santana nodded his head while he spoke.

"You sound like you speak from personal experience," Jo snapped and both men glared at her.

"Be quiet," Archer hissed. "So yeah, Mal was gonna have Krakow take Jo, probably to get me to leave Malibu and the drug scene."

"And if he couldn't accomplish that, then he'd have a sweet job with Nguyen and home over in West Covina," Santana added.

"Not for long," Archer snorted. "I found all these emails between Krakow and someone going by R. *R* for Rodriguez. *Malcolm* Rodriguez. They had a scam going, they were cutting Nguyen's coke with a shit ton of baking soda and selling it at full price."

"Sounds like he was trying to screw everyone over."

"Especially me. I mean, I knew he didn't like me, but I didn't realize he wanted me gone."

"And what about me? I'd never even met him," Jo pointed out. Archer frowned.

"Because he knew how much you mean to *me*. It's like my dad said—if Krakow had gotten you, I would've done anything they asked me to do."

"Oh my god," she groaned, bending in half. "I'm being chased by some drug gang because I made the epic mistake of having a crush on my brother's best friend from high school."

"It's a little more than a crush at this point, Jojo."

She sat upright and started punching him. While he struggled to grab hold of her wrists, his dad groaned and stood up.

"You deal with this," he said, gesturing to Jo. "I'll go have a *discussion* with Malcolm. We need to nip this in the bud right fucking now."

Jo and Archer both held still and watched as the intimidating man walked out of the room. Santana didn't say another word, just slammed the door shut behind him. Jo almost felt bad for Malcolm.

*Santana seems like a man I never, ever, **ever** want to have a "discussion" with.*

12:35 P.M.

DAY TWO

As soon as she couldn't hear Santana's footsteps in the hallway anymore, Jo started hitting Archer again, slapping him hard across the side of his head.

"What the shit, Jo? Stop it!" he yelled, grabbing at her arms again. She yanked free and leapt out of her seat.

"Don't touch me! You don't get to fucking touch me! Drug dealer!?" she shouted, backing away from him as he stood up.

"I know, I know! I lied to you. I lied so much to you," he groaned, following her as she tried to move around the large desk.

"No shit! Jesus, who are you, Archer?" she demanded, shoving a leather and wood office chair at him before scrambling to the other side of the room.

"I'm still the same guy," he insisted. "You've known me forever. I like carrot cake, and I drink too much, and I'm completely stupid for my sexy neighbor."

"Too bad she doesn't feel the same way."

"I think she feels *exactly* the same way."

"Stop it!" she shrieked. "Stop being cute! *Who the fuck are you!?*

How could you not tell me any of this?"

"Because I know you, Jo. You're a good person. Way too good for someone like me. That's why I never asked you out, why I never tried anything with you," he explained, following her as she kept moving around the room,.

"But I'm not so good that you couldn't just leave me the fuck alone? Years, Archer! We've lived down the hall from each other *for years*, I see you almost every day. How could you not mention any of this? How have you been hiding all this?" she asked, getting trapped between a ficus tree and a bookshelf as he walked towards her.

"Construction seemed like a good cover," he told her. "Something that would keep me busy, sometimes has weird hours, would take me far away from home."

"I can't believe this. Everything has been a lie," she moaned, closing her eyes and thinking back over the years. Two years ago, for his birthday, she'd gone all out and bought him a really expensive, nice tool belt.

I wonder if he uses it to carry coke around Beverly Hills.

"I had to, Jo. I don't know what happened, but … okay, look. When I was twenty, I was working at my step-dad's garage, remember? And I basically hated life. Your brother was in college and hardly ever had time for me. All our friends had gone off to school. Home was shit, and you were way out in Van Nuys, and we weren't really that close back then. I felt like I was gonna be doing that forever, working some shit job I didn't even like, and going home to my mom and a step-dad I couldn't fucking stand.

"Then one day I'm working on this Chevy, and it's right before closing, and this guy walks in. Asks if I can work on his Aston Martin, which c'mon—who in that area has an Aston Martin, and even if they did, why would they come to some shit hole garage for it? So I climb out from under the Chevy and this guy … he looks really familiar. We're talking about cars and I'm telling him we're not the right garage for his Aston, and I can't shake this feeling that I must know this guy."

"What a touching story of a father-son reunion. Did he ask you to sell coke right then, or later?" Jo snapped in a snide voice, finally opening her eyes again. He didn't look mad, though. He looked … hurt.

"Later. It was amazing, Jo. Here I am, struggling to make a dime, and you know what my home life was like. And in walks my real dad, like a rich as fuck fairy godmother, offering to change everything. I never asked how he made his money, I was just excited to be around him. Then I found out I have a half-brother, and that just made everything even more awesome. I went and stayed with them for Easter, for like two weeks. It was incredible. A mansion near the beach, half naked women everywhere, more money than I'd ever seen in my life."

"Is this supposed to endear me to you?"

"And then one night, my brother decided to take me for a little drive. Said he had to deliver a package downtown. I was so stupid, I really thought that's all we were doing—at fucking one o'clock in the morning. We go to this club, these big bouncers lead us into the back, and I shit you not, something like three Grammy winners from that year were hanging out in a VIP room. I was so star struck, I didn't even realize Malcolm was spreading out a shit ton of coke on a table until people started cutting it up," he said. Jo stared at him for a second.

"So while we've been slumming it out in Van Nuys," she spoke in a careful voice. "You've been going back and forth between there and Malibu, selling drugs to celebrities?"

"Yeah. Look, Jo, just think about it. Suddenly, there's this man in front of me, offering me attention and hugs and love and respect, and hey, all I have to do is sell some drugs to rich people? Rich people who, by the way, are already doing drugs anyway. I couldn't sign up fast enough. The deal was I would start out in the 'burbs, out there in Burbank and those neighborhoods, learn the ropes and prove my worth. Then after the summer, I'd be moved out to Malibu, to work directly underneath him."

"But after that summer, you moved to Van Nuys," she was confused.

"Because I came out to visit you that summer, and … shit, Jo, you were just the best time. I'd always had a small crush on you, and then with your brother out of the picture, it was just the two of us. I thought I'd end the summer with a bang, partying it up with you. Maybe get laid."

She hit him in the chest.

"Dick bag."

"Hey, I'm a guy, you have an amazing rack. But the more we hung out, the more fun we had, the more I didn't want to leave. I wanted … I wanted to be with you. A little crush turned into a big fucking deal. But like I said, you're a good girl. Strip clubs and body shots and crazy parties aside, you really are, Jo. You're probably the best person I know. Every time I thought about telling you what I was doing, about my dad and his 'business', I got scared that you'd stop being my friend. It was already hard enough not being closer to you. I couldn't handle losing you all together."

Suddenly, Jo's schoolgirl crush on Archer seemed small in comparison to whatever he must have felt for her. She was a little blown away. He'd hidden so much from her. It was kind of sweet, but also a little alarming.

"So basically, you've been selling coke since you were twenty," she said. He nodded.

"Yeah. Pretty much."

"But you're always broke."

"Umm …"

"Okay, so you pretend to be broke so no one will figure out you're selling coke."

"Pretty much."

"*And* you've had a serious thing for me since you were twenty."

"Pretty much."

"But you couldn't tell me because you thought I wouldn't be understanding of the fact that you're a drug dealer."

"At first, yeah. Then the longer I did it, the more I realized how dangerous it can be—there's rival gangs, dirty cops, and a lot of people don't want to pay. It can get ugly. I had a coked out sitcom star put a gun to my head once. I didn't want you to be anywhere near any of that," he told her.

"A gun to your head? What did you do?" she asked.

"He got distracted and I beat the shit out of him with his own gun."

Her heart started to race. This was all so foreign to her. Archer was the goofy, sweet guy from down the hall. From her youth. He went with her whenever she visited her grandmother, always made the old woman laugh and blush. It was hard to imagine him pedaling coke and carrying guns and beating people. For the first time ever, Jo was afraid of Archer, and it broke her heart a little.

It also made her sharper. Made her think about things more clearly.

"Archer," she breathed, licking her lips and glancing around the room. "There's something I still don't understand."

"I'm sure there's lots. I know I lied to you, Jojo, but only so I could be with you. I never lied about how I felt, and I never lied about—"

"How did Bernard Krakow end up in my trunk?" she blurted out.

Archer went completely still, and Jo's heart sank.

No no no. I can forgive a lot of things, but I don't know if I can forgive this ...

"He was following you, Jo. He was going to hurt you."

"That's not an answer."

"He got shot and he—"

"*Stop lying to me!*" she suddenly screamed, covering her face with her hands.

"Calm down," he said in a soft voice, and she felt his hands on her wrists. She hadn't realized it, but she was starting to hyperventilate.

"How the fuck did he end up in my trunk, Archer?" she demanded as he pulled her hands away from her face.

"Malcolm has always hated me, he—"

She tried to yank free from his grasp.

"Malcolm hired Krakow to follow me," she growled, stumbling around and bumping into the shelf as she tried to break his hold. "You said that. So what the fuck does Malcolm have to do with Krakow getting shot? Are you trying to say Mal killed him? Why would he shoot the guy he'd hired to kidnap *your* girlfriend?"

There was a long silence. She rammed into the shelf again, sending a couple books flying to the ground. Then she stepped the other way, knocking over the ficus. The whole time, Archer stared down at her.

"I can't stand the thought of you being scared of me," he whispered, reading her mind. Her fear must have been written all over her face.

"Well, it's a little too late for that! *How the fuck did a dead body get in my car, Archer!?*" she yelled.

"He was going to hurt you," he sighed. "I can't ... the thought of someone hurting you, Jo. Remember when that guy on New Year's shoved you?"

She did—some drunk idiot had almost knocked her down. Archer, who had been even drunker, had turned and shoved the dude hard enough to send him to the ground. The whole place had erupted after that, and they'd barely escaped without getting arrested.

"Yes."

"Well, this was like that, only actually dangerous, and I was mostly sober. I followed him as he practically carried you outside, then I made up some story to get the bouncer inside. Then I confronted Krakow. He dropped you and tried to pull a gun. I don't know how to explain it. I just instantly saw red. You were laying on the ground, not moving, and I'm thinking this guy is gonna shoot you. I tackled him, he hit me, I hit him back. Then we rolled around, fighting for the gun. I got it and he lunged and … I shot him. Jesus, Jo, I shot him. Three fucking times, right in the chest."

She was going to be sick. She was going to vomit all over Santana Rodriguez's expensive Persian carpet and antique wood floors. She wasn't sure what part of Archer's story was more upsetting—the fact that she'd almost been date raped and kidnapped, or that he'd almost been shot, *or* that he'd actually shot somebody.

"How …" she ran out of air and had to clear her throat. "How did nobody see you?"

"It was after one in the morning at a shitty club in a shitty neighborhood, and we were between a huge truck and your car. I shot him and he went down. Happens all the time."

"Not to me, it doesn't."

"It does to coke dealers."

"Oh my god," she breathed, and went back to yanking at his grasp. "How many people have you killed!?"

"Christ, Jo, no one! I'm not some murderer!" he shouted at her.

"Except you are, Archer! You murdered some guy, then you hid him in my trunk, then you let me believe you didn't know anything about it! *For two days!* You even let me believe there was a chance I might have killed him! *What the fuck is wrong with you!?*"

She surprised him by changing tactics and shoving him in the chest. He stumbled backwards, and she used the distraction to break free. She ran for the door, but he caught her before she could make it and lifted her off the ground.

"You knew who he was!" she yelled. "You knew who he was and you knew how he died—how was this weekend supposed to go, Archer!?"

"I thought we either wouldn't figure anything out and I would convince you to dump your car, or I could distract you while I did some of my own investigating. I knew it couldn't have been random, that specific guy sniffing around you—he had to have known me, had to have been sent by someone. I knew running around and asking about him, I'd figure it all out. Hopefully before you would."

"It never occurred to you that all your secrets would come out?"

"Honestly … I don't know, maybe I was kind of hoping they would? I don't like lying to you."

"You could've fooled me."

"I may have done it for years, but I never once enjoyed it."

"Archer Calhoun, a drug dealer with a goddamn heart of gold."

"Thank you, Jo. Your confidence has always been, and continues to be, truly inspiring."

His grip had loosened a little, so Jo swung her leg back as hard as she could. Her foot made painful contact with his shin and he grunted, dropping her. She took one step forward, but then felt his hand gripping the back of her jacket. He yanked hard and she swung around in a circle, ramming into the desk with a grunt. She hesitated only a second before scrambling over the piece of furniture. She'd hit it so hard, she'd knocked a couple drawers open, and one clipped her left foot, causing her to fall to the floor.

"Are you gonna shoot me, too!?" she shouted while glaring at the drawer. Then she saw what was inside it.

"What? Don't be stupid, Jo, I—"

She grabbed a pistol out of the drawer and leapt to her feet, pointing it straight out in front of her.

"Stop. Talking," she was gasping for air.

"Ooookay," Archer spoke slowly as he raised his hands so they were up by his head.

"I am going to leave now," she informed him, moving so she was kneeling on the desk. She'd assumed that as the gun got closer to him, he'd back up, but he didn't budge an inch. He just shook his head and stood his ground.

"It's too dangerous, I can't let you—"

"This thing is loaded, Archer, and I know how to use a gun," she warned him. One of his eyebrows quirked up.

"You're just full of surprises, Jojo."

"Not as much as you."

"Look," he sighed. "I know this has been a long weekend, and you just learned a lot of really fucked up shit. But I think if you'd just calm down, we could talk—"

She cocked the hammer.

"Did you seriously just tell me to calm down?" she snapped. "An angry woman with a loaded gun pointed at your chest, and your re-action is to say 'calm down'? You are the stupidest man I have ever met."

"You know, you're not the first person to say that to me."

"Keep dicking around, and I'll be the last."

"You can't shoot me, Jojo."

"Don't call me that!" she yelled. "What the fuck is wrong with you? You're a fucking sociopath! You lied to me! This whole time! Who the fuck are you?"

"Stop saying that," he yelled back. "I'm the same guy! I lived down the street from you, we practically grew up together."

"That guy never would have lied to me. That guy is long gone. Now you're just some piece of shit drug dealer!"

"I didn't lie about everything, I promise. I had to … I just couldn't tell you certain things. Believe me, I wanted to. All the time. So many times," he told her.

"Oh, really? What stopped you? Wait, let me guess, you got dis-tracted while buying impulse cocaine," she said snidely.

"Impulse may have been an exaggeration," he chuckled.

"You think? So what's the plan here, Archer? Am I going to wind up in my trunk by the end of the day?" she demanded. He actually laughed out loud.

"Do you really think I could ever hurt you? I just discovered you can put your ankles behind your head—I was thinking about propos-ing to you."

"My answer would be no, just to warn you."

"Aw, c'mon, Jojo, you love me."

That hit too close to him. She clenched her teeth together

"Just shut up! Shut the fuck up. I'm going to call the police, and then you can be a smart ass with them. See how well they like it," she threatened, knee walking closer to the edge of the desk, ready to jump down and run past him.

"Fine. Go call the cops, because frankly, you're starting to scare me," he told her.

"Good!" she shouted, jerking the gun at him, trying to get him to move. "You should be scared!"

"I'm scared you'll hurt *yourself*," he clarified.

"Oh, fuck you, Archer. Fuck you and your stupid smiles and your big lies and every single moment we ever spent together. I hope you—"

Her tirade was cut off as she let out a shout. Faster than her eyes could follow, he lunged forward and grabbed her behind her knees. Next thing she knew, her legs were yanked out from under her and she was falling backwards off the desk. The gun went flying out of her hand, hitting the floor with a thunk.

Jo didn't lose a beat. She scrambled around, digging her elbows into the rug as she moved. Archer was already on top of the desk, leaping towards her. She screamed, rolled onto her front, then jumped to her feet.

Gun. Get the gun. You don't want to end up in a trunk, Jojo!

"*STOP!*"

He roared so loud, so close behind her, it actually worked. Jo shrieked and came to a stop, wrapping her arms around her head and ducking down. She wasn't even sure what she was doing, she just knew she was terrified and didn't want to get hurt. She held still as he grabbed her arm and yanked her around so she was facing him.

"Please," she whimpered, and she realized she'd started crying. "Please, I won't tell the police. I won't say anything."

"Jo," he groaned, pulling her out of her crouch and wrapping his arms around her. "I'm not going to hurt you. I could *never* hurt you. I lied to you so you *wouldn't* get hurt."

"Too late," she whispered, her face pressed against his chest.

"This is killing me," he whispered back.

Bad choice of words.

"Then let me go," she urged. "You have my car, you have the body. You know who your double cross is. I'm in more danger here than I ever was at home. Than I ever was before you moved down the hall."

"Don't say that," he groaned.

There was a long silence. Jo wasn't sure what to do—she was in some drug lord's mansion in Malibu, and apparently her best friend-slash-the guy she was probably in love with was also a drug dealer. Oh, and he'd also murdered someone and put the body in her trunk. No big deal.

She let out a growl and rammed her knee into his crotch, as hard as she could. He let go of her and made a choking noise as he dropped to the ground.

Jo didn't waste a second. She turned and bolted from the room. It was too much, how was she supposed to deal with all this? She just needed a moment. She'd spent all weekend with Archer, thinking all the wrong thoughts, believing all the wrong truths. She just needed a goddamn moment to herself.

The house was absolutely huge. She couldn't remember how they'd gotten to Santana's office, but she knew she didn't have time to stop and think about it. She spent half a second looking around, then she ran down the hall. Went down the first set of stairs she came across, kept going for about three flights, then came out in a huge kitchen. She immediately ran towards a set out of glass doors and found herself outside, right at the edge of a large pool.

Figuring that running would only draw more attention, Jo managed to slow it down to a fast walk as she hurried across a cement deck. Once she got around the corner of the house, she went back to running, streaking along the side of the house and heading for the front.

She was on the lawn and almost halfway to the gate when her cellphone went off. She let out a yelp, startled as it vibrated, then she pulled it out of her back pocket and looked at the screen. Archer. She ended the call, then frowned as she looked at her screen. A lot of missed calls from both her parents, her roommate, a couple from her brother, and even one from Archer's mother. There were also several unknown numbers that she had to assume were from her building's management, the police, and possibly the FBI at this point. Her frown turned into a glare and when Archer called her again, she answered.

"Just leave me alone, okay? I just need to be alone for a minute," she snapped, stomping across the grass towards a guard station.

"Where are you?" he demanded. She rolled her eyes.

"I'm still in your drug compound, don't worry."

"It's not a drug ... Jo, please. If you want to hate me, fine, we can work on that later. But for now, we need to stick together, okay?"

"Not okay! I wouldn't be in this situation if it wasn't for you! Sticking with you has done nothing but ruin my entire fucking life!" she hissed, skirting around some huge potted plants that towered over her.

"Don't say that, Jojo. You're mad right now, but you know you love me."

Not the words she wanted to here right then.

"Get fucked, *Archie*."

"Don't ever call me that. Look, I'll leave you alone, I promise. Just come back to the house. We don't have to be together, but I just have to know where you are. I have to know you're okay," he stressed. She grumbled and walked around the small building. It was stationed maybe fifty feet from main gate, and she figured someone could get said gate open for her.

"Well, I'm okay, and I'm at the front of the driveway," she sighed, peeking through the windows. She frowned when she saw the station was empty. What was the point of a guard station if there weren't any guards? Maybe they only worked at night. But how was she supposed to get the gate open?

"Don't leave!" Archer practically yelled. "Krakow's dead, but if Malcolm is really in on this, we're both still in trouble. It's safest inside the house."

Fear trickled down Jo's spine as she slowly moved through the open doorway. She swallowed thickly as she looked around. There were several monitors, all displaying the footage from multiple cameras around the property. Except for one—its screen was just full of static and snow. Everything looked fairly normal, she supposed, except for an over turned chair, a broken window on the far side of the small room, and a liquid that had been splashed across the monitors.

"Archer," she breathed, taking a couple steps forward.

"What?"

"I think you were right," she whispered, leaning down close to the screens. It had looked brown from the doorway, but upon closer inspection, the liquid was definitely red. *Blood* red.

"Right? What's happening? Why are you whispering?"

Jo dropped into a crouch, ducking beneath the windows. She inched back towards the door and pressed herself up against the wall next to it. She glanced outside, not even sure what she was looking for—maybe a windowless van? Gun men in fancy suits?

You've seen too many movies.

"Something's happened," she said, gripping the door frame as she looked around it. She didn't want someone to sneak into the room behind her and catch her unaware.

"I'm coming," Archer's voice sounded slightly breathless, and even through the phone she could hear the sound of his feet pounding down a set of stairs. "What happened?"

"I came to the guard station," she kept whispering, her eyes never leaving the driveway. "I thought they could open the gate for me, but no one is here. One of the cameras isn't working, and there's blood in here."

"Goddammit, Jo, this is why we should've stuck together!"

"I'm sorry I got scared of being in a room with a murderer!" she hissed through clenched teeth.

"I'm not a murderer!"

"Oh, well then, what do you call a person who's killed another person?"

"Shut up. Are you hiding?"

"I'm in the station," she breathed, daring to lean out the door a little to look the other way down the drive. "I'm hiding under the windows, looking out the door."

"Okay, just stay there. I'm coming to get you."

"Fuck," she groaned. "Now I'm stuck here. I've gone from my shitty apartment, to a drug dealer's penthouse, to a drug lord's mansion, and I'm probably gonna fucking die here."

"Stop being dramatic. And this time, when I save you, don't kick me."

"I make no promises. Hurry up."

"Can you see any one?"

"No, no one. It's totally—"

Jo screamed as her head was yanked back. Her hair was still up in its bun and someone had their hand wrapped around it, using it as a knob to control her head. She was dragged away from the open doorway, then jerked up into a standing position. She gripped her phone in one hand and swung her other arm wildly, hoping to hit her assailant. She was twisted around and she saw that behind her had been another door, partially hidden behind a file cabinet.

"What's happening!? Jo, talk to me! What's going on!?"

Archer's voice was tinny and far away as he shouted through the phone line. She screamed again as she was pulled towards the secret door, and at first all she could think was that she was dead. That she was being dragged away to her death. Then Archer's voice got louder over the phone and a memory flashed through her mind. One of her favorite movies, some ridiculous, over the top, incredibly violent film that featured Liam Neeson kicking ass all over Paris.

Do something. If you're being taken, then make sure Archer can find you!

"He's got me! Someone's got me!" she yelled, hooking her leg inside the door frame before she could be pulled clear of it. With her free hand, she reached back and started clawing at the fingers in her hair. She twisted around and though it meant she lost her hold on the doorway, it also meant she was able to see who was grabbing her.

"Who!? Hold on!" Archer shouted over the phone, and she thought maybe she could also hear him in the distance.

Put up a fight. Hold out. Just long enough for Archer to get here and turn this asshole inside out.

"It's Mal!" she shouted, then she screamed as Malcolm Rodriguez backhanded her. She fell to the side, ramming into the side of the guard station and dropping her phone. Mal grabbed her by the hair again and she started yelling. "It's Malcolm! He killed the guards! He's trying to take me!"

"*MALCOLM!*"

Archer was definitely outside, and as Mal's arm wrapped around Jo's neck, he turned just in time for her to see Archer running around the side of the main house.

"You know," Mal sounded out of breath. Jo struggled at first to get free, and then in panic as he cut off her air supply. "I really didn't think I would enjoy kidnapping a defenseless girl. But seeing the look on Archer's face, it's actually totally worth it."

Her vision was going black around the edges. She was pulling at his wrists with one hand, and with her other arm, she was reaching out. As if she could grab hold of Archer while he was still a couple hundred feet away. She kept telling herself it would only take a minute for him to reach her. Just a minute, and he would save the day. Sixty seconds, and he would make up for all the other bad shit he'd done.

But it turned out she didn't have sixty seconds. She barely had ten seconds before everything went completely black and she fell unconscious.

12:51 P.M.

DAY TWO

"Just a minute. Hang on, Jojo! Just one more minute!" Archer was practically screaming as he ran.

That's the thing with minutes, though. They're always longer than you think. Shorter than you realize.

He watched as Malcolm dragged Jo's limp body into a car. Shouted as Mal got behind the wheel. Archer was able to grab onto the spoiler of the car when the tires started squealing. He tried to hang on, but the vehicle whipped in a tight circle, throwing him onto the lawn. Then rocks and dirt were spit into his face as the car raced out of the driveway.

"*FUCK!*" he yelled, pounding his fist into the grass. "No! No, no, no, no!"

"What happened!?"

He looked up to see his father jogging across the lawn. Several men trailed behind him, all carrying semi-automatic weapons.

*How is this my life? What the fuck am I doing here? **What the fuck have I done?***

"Mal took her," Archer panted as he climbed to his feet. "He killed the guard on duty, he choked her out, and he fucking took her."

"I knew I should've kept that boy in counseling," his dad sighed.

Archer glared and suddenly had an acute idea of how Jo must have felt a lot of the time. One liners and constant quips were only funny when he was doing them at someone else's expense. It wasn't so much fun when it was at *his* expense.

"Should've drowned him at birth," Archer growled.

"Calm down," his father urged. "We'll get her back. He must have some kind of plan, or he just would've killed her out here. We need to think right now—it's the best thing we can do for her. I'm gonna make some calls."

While Santana did that, Archer walked over and picked Jo's cell phone up off the ground. The wallpaper was a picture from a party, just a couple weeks ago. A group selfie. Archer and Jo were nestled in the middle of the group, him with his arm around her, holding her close. He smiled as he remembered the moment—he'd grabbed her butt, which accounted for the surprised, open-mouthed look on her face.

Then he frowned. That was the same night he'd hidden the coke in her toilet tank. A deal earlier in the night had gone bad and he'd gone straight to her party afterwards, intending to take the coke back to his father in the morning. But then some chick had spilled red wine all over his pants and Jo had offered to wash them in her sink, before the stain could set. She'd been very insistent and he hadn't wanted her to find the drugs. So he'd taken off the pants in her bathroom, hid the coke in her toilet, then walked around the party with a towel wrapped around his waist.

I am the worst fucking person on the planet, and now she's going to die because of me. I never even got to say—

"I have our friends at the precinct looking for his license plates," his father's voice interrupted his thoughts. "He's disabled the GPS in the car so we can't track him that way, and his phone is off, so that won't work, either. Does Jodi have her—"

Archer waved her phone, cutting off the question before it could be asked.

"No. Fuck. *Fuck*. Where would Mal go? Does he have an apartment in the city?" he asked, running his hand through his hair.

"Not that I know of, but it seems like he's full of surprises. He'd go somewhere private. Somewhere no one else would be—he can't exactly haul an unconscious girl all around Los Angeles without someone noticing."

"Krakow's apartment," Archer whispered.

"What?"

"The dead guy in the trunk," Archer snapped, glancing down the driveway and seeing Jo's car parked outside the open gates. "His apartment—Malcolm knew him, knows where it is, knows it's empty."

"You can't be sure—what are you doing!?" his dad demanded as Archer started running down the drive.

"Going there!"

"You don't even know if that's where he is! Just wait, he'll call at some point. Be rational!"

"I'm leaving. Krakow's apartment is on Ventura, I'll message you address," Archer said.

"This is stupid!" his father yelled.

"Probably! But I can't just sit here. When I send that address, you better send every gun you have after me!" Archer yelled back before sliding behind the steering wheel.

"Please! Just wait a couple minutes, so we can ready a car and we can all go—"

The growl of an engine cut him off and Archer peeled out of the spot. He raced down the winding road, pushing the vehicle to its max speed.

Jo's car was old. A real piece of shit, with two-tone doors and an engine that was barely clinging to life. He was always joking with her that he was going to buy her a car someday, though secretly he'd been serious. Someday, he was gonna buy her the car of her dreams. A vintage Chevelle SS.

Someday, Jo. Someday, I'll buy you the frickin' moon—just hold on. I'm coming for you. **Hold on.**

2:15 P.M.

DAY TWO

Jo came to with a snort, her head jerking upright so fast she rammed it into something behind her. She groaned and tried to lift her hand to rub at the spot, but found she couldn't move. She blinked her eyes open and looked around.

She was in a large open space. Industrial, with metal walls and concrete floors. She lifted her head to take in high ceilings and patches of rust. A warehouse, if she had to guess. An unused warehouse.

Next she looked down at herself. She had ropes wrapped around her chest, hips, and ankles, tying her to some sort of metal support beam. They were tight enough that she couldn't free herself right that moment, but there seemed to be some wiggle room. She was pretty sure if she moved around enough, she could get an arm loose.

"She awakes!"

A voice boomed and echoed across the large space, startling her at first. She craned her neck around to see Malcolm Rodriguez walking towards her. He took off his suit jacket as he moved and dropped it on an empty chair. She could see he was wearing a gun harness, the kind that strapped across his shoulders and back, the guns resting just under his arms. Pearl handles winked and gleamed in the sun-light streaming through a hole in the roof.

I have to admit, he looks pretty bad ass.

"Where are we?" she asked, her voice a little slurry. It felt like her tongue was numb.

Somewhere safe," he assured her, unbuttoning his cuffs as he talked. "Sorry about being so rough earlier."

"Um … that's okay," she spoke slowly. He was talking to her like they were having brunch somewhere and he was giving her a weather report. Very calm and natural.

"I don't have anything against you, personally, I want you to know."

"Thank you?"

"You see, it's always been just my father and I," Mal explained, moving out of her view behind the beam. There was a scrapping noise and he dragged a second chair around so he could sit in front of her. "My mother died when I was young. Then suddenly, magical-ly, five years ago I find out I have a little brother. Awesome, right?"

"I don't know, I don't get along with my brother too well," she replied. He threw back his head and laughed, startling her again.

This guy is a few sandwiches short of a picnic, isn't he?

"Then maybe you'll understand. I wanted to like Archer, I really did. Took him under my wing, showed him the ropes of the family business. I didn't know he was going to steal it all from me."

"Steal?" Jo asked. He leaned forward, resting his elbows on his knees.

"Yeah. This fucking guy. This … *nobody*, this nothing, this … this … this piece of North Hollywood trash just strolled into my life and—"

"Burbank isn't really North Hollywood," Jo interrupted.

He was out the chair before she could blink and she shrieked as he slammed his palm against the beam above her head. He was so close to her, she could feel his breath on the side of her face.

"Do I look like I give a fuck?" he growled. She squeezed her eyes shut and turned her head away. "Some fucking stupid guy just walked in and stole my father, stole my position, stole my inheritance. I was supposed to be next in line, I was supposed to be my father's right hand man. So what if I skimmed a little off the top? Who cares if I was using every now and then? It was my birth right, I'd earned it. I was first born, for shit's sake!"

Jo stayed silent, and after a moment, she felt him move away. When she finally opened her eyes, he was sitting back in his chair. She took a deep breath and thought quickly.

"Yeah, um, I guess I could see how that would be awful. Someone you don't even know suddenly getting all the attention," she spoke fast, just trying to say whatever she thought he'd like to hear. He nodded and raked his fingers through his hair.

"And it was like he couldn't just wait to point out my fuck ups, you know? Fucking Archer. Just me and my dad, taking on the world."

"Okay," she whispered, then she cleared her throat. "Okay, I know how you feel. You know everything about me, right?"

"I had Bernard Krakow following you for about two weeks, so between that and Archer's big fucking mouth, yeah, I know pretty much everything."

"Then you know I have an older brother—that's how I met Archer, they were best friends. Everyone loves my brother Andy. He got good grades, he got records in every sport he ever participated in, he got a scholarship to college. So I know how you feel, I really do. It's like … being invisible. It's the worst," she sympathized with him. He stared at the ground while she spoke, and she took the opportunity to shimmy her shoulders up and down, trying to work her arms loose.

"The worst," he whispered.

"But I still don't really understand. What do I have to do with any of this? I never even knew Archer was dealing drugs, let alone that you or your father even existed," she told him. He sighed and lifted his head. She held still.

"Archer is my dad's favorite thing in the whole world," he grumbled, staring off into the distance. "I couldn't touch him directly—it would kill my dad, and then my dad would kill me. I had to get rid of Archer, but couldn't figure out how. I thought about hiring a hitman, but I couldn't be positive it wouldn't get back to me. So I realized I had to find a way to make him leave on his own."

"Blackmail," she whispered. He nodded.

"My father offered to buy Archer his own home in Malibu, but he turned it down so he could stay close to you. That makes you a big fucking deal. I knew if I took you, he'd do whatever I wanted. He doesn't care about money or drugs or women or any of that bullshit. Just you," he told her.

I suppose I should be flattered.

"So that was your whole plan? Have Bernard Krakow kidnap me, hold me hostage or whatever, until Archer did whatever you asked?" she clarified.

"Pretty much."

"And then what?"

Silence. She swallowed thickly and felt sweat break out around her hairline. He was still doing his thousand yard stare, so she decided to risk it and she started working on her bindings again.

"Like I said, nothing personal, Jojo," he chuckled as he used her nickname.

"Of course not. What's a little thing like killing an innocent woman?" she laughed, almost wrenching an arm free. He abruptly looked over at her and she turned into a statue.

"I couldn't have you getting the law involved. It would've gotten back to my dad," he explained. She nodded.

"Sure, sure."

"I don't know how it all got so fucked up," he grumbled.

"How what got fucked up?"

"The plan. Danny Nguyen's been desperate for years to get inside my dad's operation, so it was easy enough to get in with them.

I fed them information, and in return, I was basically given Bernard Krakow as my personal assistant. He was supposed to be showing me the way they did business, but I could see it was a shit show. So easy to take advantage of and manipulate. We came up with a plan to fuck over his boss, Nguyen. By the end, the shit we were selling for him was more baking soda than cocaine. And then I had him—Krakow had to do whatever I wanted. I told him if he didn't, I'd rat him out to his boss. I'd be fine, I could always run home to Daddy. I thought it was the perfect plan. Get rid of Archer, and make a shit ton of money on the side. *Perfection.* What the fuck happened?" he growled.

"Um, sounds like maybe you needed more time to plan things out?" she offered.

"Suddenly I'm getting text messages from Archer, saying he fucked up and there's a dead body and it's Krakow. What the fuck was I supposed to do? I knew it would all lead back to me, so I called in Nguyen's thugs to take care of it. Kill you guys, and then it would just look like Bernard was the traitor, not me. It's all fucked now, though. Can't go home because Archer tattle taled to Dad, and by now, Dad will have told Nguyen everything, so I can't go back there, either. All because of you guys. You two are like cockroaches, you know? Fucking impossible to catch and kill."

"We do our best."

"You know," he started laughing as he slowly stood up. "I can see why he likes you, but I honestly can't see why anyone likes him."

"Sometimes, I think the same thing."

"But at least I can do one thing right before I leave the country," Malcolm sighed, pulling his phone out of his pocket.

"Uh … what's that?" she asked nervously.

"I have you, which means I can make Archer regret ever coming into my life."

While he'd been talking, he'd started pushing at things on the screen of his phone. Jo took the opportunity to finally yank her right arm free of its restraints, but held it close to her side. As he lifted the phone to his ear and stared at her, she hoped he didn't notice the slackness in the ropes.

"Yeah," he said as someone picked up on the other end of the line. "She's fine, Archie … no … no … keep talking that way, and it'll happen a lot sooner … you won't find us, I'm miles from Malibu now … of course you can, hold on."

The phone was pressed to the side of her face. Her heart hammered in her chest—he was on her right side, and she was scared he would see that her hand was no longer inside the ropes.

"Hello," she said in a shaky voice.

"Are you okay?" Archer asked immediately. She chewed on her bottom lip.

"Depends on your definition of okay. I'm tied to a beam and your brother is very, very, *very* upset. But other than that, yeah, I'm okay," she answered, all the while staring at Malcolm. He smiled back at her. It was unnerving, staring into eyes so similar to Archer's in a face that was so different.

In a body that's so frickin' crazy.

"Where are you?" Archer continued.

"Um, I don't think Malcolm would appreciate me describing our current location," she replied, and Mal nodded quickly.

"Fuck," Archer swore.

"I know how you feel."

"Anything. Give me something, Jo. Help me find you," he urged, but she was barely listening. Malcolm had taken one of his guns out of its holster and was spinning it around in his free hand.

"Archer," she sniffled, then she took a deep breath.

"Don't cry," he said. "Please, don't cry. Everything is going to be fine. We're going to find you, and I'm going to make him eat—"

"I'm sorry I kicked you," she said in a low voice as one tear fell down her cheek.

"It's okay. You can kick me as many times as you want. Help me, Jo! I can't do this without your help. Are you in Malibu? Van Nuys?

I'm out here, just help me find you!"

"And I'm sorry I got so mad at you. I wish … I wish I'd told you so many things, before this weekend. I shouldn't have been such a pussy," she started sniffling again as the tears kept falling.

"Stop talking like this!" he yelled. "You can tell me all the things you want as soon as I get you free. You're a smart girl, Jo, think! Think, goddammit! Tell me where you are!"

"What is wrong with me?" she moaned, blinking through the tears and looking straight up, trying to calm down. "I've been in love with you for so long, and I never said anything. Why didn't I say anything?"

"Jodi Morgan," he spoke in a serious voice. "I am going to forget you said that to me, and I'm not going to say it back, because this *will not* be the first time we say those words to each other. I am going to find you, and I am going to save you, and then I won't ever stop saying those words."

She laughed for a moment, choked on a sob, then laughed again. Her eyes wandered over the high ceiling while she listened to him speak. While she remembered all their moments together. His stupid jokes and her silly games and how at least two times, she'd gotten to experience true magic with him.

Granted, once had been in a dead drug dealer's apartment, and the other had been on a nasty mattress in some …

She gasped so hard she started choking again. As she coughed and hacked, she stared up at the ceiling again. In one corner, the roofing was completely gone. Crumbled in, exposing metal beams and rafters, which seemed to be homes for several different birds that were flying around.

"What's going on!? What's happening!? Is he choking you!?" Archer was yelling, but she ignored him and glanced around the room.

She hadn't recognized the space. She'd been nervous the first time she'd seen it, and mad and hungover the second time. Plus, what with a psychotic drug dealer threatening her life and all, she hadn't been paying much attention to her surroundings.

"I'm fine," she croaked out, glancing at Malcolm to see if he'd noticed her reaction. He was still looking down at his gun. "I'm fine. My throat is just dry, I ... I could really go for some orange juice right now."

"I will get you all the orange juice you want," Archer promised. "You just need to—"

"OJ," she stressed. "A great big glass, it sounds great. Remember the last time we drank orange juice?"

"Why the fuck would I remember ..." he started snapping, but his voice trailed off as he caught on.

"Your impulse purchase," she spoke quickly. "Where'd you find a good place to, uh ... pawn it?"

Please please please, don't be your usual stupid self. Please catch what I'm throwing out there.

"Malcolm," Archer hissed. "He's the one who told me about the rave."

"What the fuck are you talking about?" Mal demanded, suddenly catching onto the strange nature of her conversation. She took another deep breath.

"He's crazy, Archer," she started speaking fast. "He's going to kill me, he's got guns. He wants to hurt me, and he wants to hurt you. He wants to punish you for—"

Wow, getting slapped never felt good, did it? Mal's palm crashed across her face so hard, she was pretty sure she'd have a permanent hand print on her cheek. When she finally lifted her head again, Malcolm had walked away and he was yelling into the phone. She practically started jumping up and down, trying to work her left arm free.

"You hear that?" he shouted. "I'm gonna put a bullet in your fucking girlfriend! And there's nothing you can do to stop me!"

Then he shouted and threw the phone across the room. It hit

the concrete floor hard, and Jo watched as different pieces cracked and flew off.

"I'm sorry!" she gasped as he rushed back to her. "I'm sorry, I was scared! I'm sorry!"

"What the fuck is wrong with all of you!?" he bellowed, and suddenly both his hands were in her hair, shaking her head back and forth.

"*Stop it!*" she screamed.

As he jerked her around, slamming the back of her skull into the beam a couple times, her left arm finally fell free from the ropes. She raked her nails down his face, and in the split second he stopped shaking her, she jammed her thumb into his eye as hard as she could.

He bellowed in pain and stumbled away from her, falling to his knees. She didn't miss a beat, she instantly began shoving and pulling at the ropes around her shoulders, sliding out from under them. Then she bent over and yanked at the ones around her ankles, literally falling out of them. She was sobbing and crying and she was pretty sure she had a concussion, but she was free.

"You bitch! You stupid goddamn bitch!" Malcolm was screaming.

She was scrambling around on her hands and knees, just trying to crawl away from him, when he pointed his gun straight out and started pulling the trigger. He had one hand over his right eye though, which clearly seemed to effect his aim. Bullets flew around the room, but none of them came even remotely close to her. She was able to get to a door in the far wall and she crawled through it.

Once she was on the other side, she jumped to her feet and started running. She didn't remember the lay out at all, so she took a chance and ran through one doorways. It led to an abandoned office. While she stood there, breathing hard and looking around, she heard a door bang open.

"*Jooooodiiiiii,*" Malcolm's voice sang out, followed by two rapid fire gun shots. She dropped back to her hands and knees. "There's no where to go! No one knows where you are, and no one is coming for you!"

Don't listen to him. Just get somewhere and hide. Archer knows where you are, and just pray that his dad really does love him more than Malcolm and is willing to turn that psycho into pig food.

There was a door in the wall to her right, so she crawled over to it and slowly pushed it open. It led to some sort of work room, with lots of long tables. She cursed under her breath, then crawled between them to another wall with a door in it.

"Jojo! C'mon, maybe we can be friends!" Malcolm's voice was disturbingly close. In front of the office she'd just left, if she wasn't mistaken. "I could treat you better than Archer ever did! I would never lie to you, and I would certainly never hide a dead body in your car!"

Almost tempting.

She moved through the door and found herself in what looked like a large storage closet. There were no other doors, and she almost yelled at herself for running into a dead end. If Malcolm came into the work room, she was as good as dead. But then she looked around, trying to see what was lining all the shelves.

It looked like paint cans, but she couldn't read the labels from the doorway. She crept all the way inside and slowly closed the door behind her, then she risked standing up and walking to the shelves. Some of them were paint, but mixed among them were also cans of paint thinner, primer, and turpentine.

All which are extremely flammable.

Jo had no clue what the warehouse had been home to before it had been abandoned, but clearly it had involved painting in some way. On another shelf, she found drop clothes and stacks of newspapers. She almost felt like it was Christmas.

After getting one can of turpentine open, she splashed it all over the floor, careful not to get any on herself and to keep it away from the door. She put a pile of newspapers and a drop cloth in a corner, then covered them in primer. Not enough to completely soak them through, but definitely enough to act as fire starter.

Shit, to start a fire you need actual fire. How am I going to—

The door to the work room burst open, causing her to step back so she was against the wall. She had another can of opened turpentine in her hand and she held her breath, trying not to breathe in any of the fumes.

"Seriously, Jo," Malcolm was yelling. "Please don't make me search every room. I will be very unhappy if I have to do that."

She gasped as she remembered something. With her free hand, she felt all around her pockets. Her lucky Zippo! Archer had lit his Molotov cocktail with it, then he had *handed it to her*. She pulled it out of her fifth pocket and almost started crying again.

*You can do this. **You will do this.** Just stay calm.*

The door knob next to her rattled and she took a deep breath, trying to slow her heart rate. Malcolm was still babbling away. She had guessed right when she'd first met him—he really loved to hear himself talk. So much so, he wasn't paying attention to much else as he pulled open the storage room's door.

NOW!

Keeping as much of her body behind the door frame as possible, Jo leaned over and chucked the turpentine into Malcolm's face. She immediately dropped into a crouch just before he started shooting again. He shouted and stumbled backwards, wiping at his face and body as if she'd just thrown acid on him.

While he fumbled around, she opened her lighter and flicked the flint wheel. As a flame leapt to life, she lowered it to the path of turpentine she'd left on the floor. It instantly caught fire and raced across the room to the primer soaked stack of cloth and paper in the corner of the closet.

"What the fuck is this?" Malcolm was screaming. She took a deep breath and moved out of the doorway, holding the flame low to the floor still.

"Make one more fucking move, and I will light you on fire," she threatened, keeping the lighter over the trail of turpentine he'd left on the floor as he'd moved around. She was impressed with how tough she sounded.

Malcolm did as he was told. He squinted down at her through one good eye—his right eye wouldn't open all the way, and was already looking bruised and swollen. His gun was on the floor, he must have dropped it during his freak out.

"Wow. You know, Archer always said what a sweet girl you are, but considering the circumstances, I have to beg the differ," Mal chuckled, then he ran his hand over his face, still trying to wipe the solvent off his face.

"Archer is a big fat liar, remember?" she breathed, slowly standing upright. She kept the lighter open and burning, however.

"So what now? I don't like the idea of becoming the human flame," he sighed, watching her while she side stepped her way across the room to a door.

"I don't like the idea of getting shot," she replied, nodding at the gun he still had in one of his holsters.

"Mexican Standoff?"

She glanced at the storage room. There was a popping noise, quickly followed by a small explosion. Both of them ducked. The fire had reached the shelves and the cans were going to start going off like popcorn. Extremely dangerous, volatile popcorn.

"This whole place is going to go up like a tinder box," she warned him. "Let's just go our separate ways? You can go to Mexico or Europe or wherever, and Archer and I will go to New York or Siberia or wherever, and we'll never speak of this again."

"Sorry, sugar. That's not how this movie ends. Archer owes me for ruining my life, and I'm gonna take *your life* as payment," he told her, taking a menacing step forward.

There was another explosion from the storage room, enough to make Malcolm drop into a crouch. Flames flew into the work room and he hissed, crab walking backwards to get away.

Now, Jojo. GO!

She turned and sprinted out the door. She was in the same hallway she'd been in before and she kept going down it. Eventually it opened into another large space, but this one had a set of iron stairs against one wall. She quickly ran up them to a metal walkway that ran along the side of the building, just under the roof.

"Jodi!"

She screamed as a bullet pinged off the railing in front of her, but she didn't stop moving. She could hear Malcolm pounding up the stairs behind her, knew she didn't have much time.

Time for what—where are you going!? Great fucking plan!

The walkway went all the way back to the front of the building, and soon enough she was running over the exact same beam she'd been tied to, just moments ago. Malcolm was also on the walkway, back at the other end of the building, but she could hear his footsteps, knew he was racing towards her. She had to think of something, and she had to think of it *fast*.

She realized she was heading straight for the hole in the roof. If she could make it, she thought maybe could hoist herself onto a beam, then maybe run across the roof. Find a fire escape or something, maybe get away!

"*STOP!*"

The next bullet was much closer to her. Enough so that she listened to him and came to a stop. She fumbled with her lighter, struggling to open it, but then she was tackled from behind. She shrieked as they both fell down, then she cried out as she watched her lighter go flying through the air. She didn't get to see where it landed because Malcolm forcefully rolled her onto her back.

"Stupid bitch," he was growling, trying to shove his gun into her face. She screamed and grabbed his wrist, forcing it away from her as he fired off a round.

"No!" she was screaming, over and over again. "Please! No! Stop! *STOP IT!*"

She was literally fighting for her life. It sounded like the back half of the building was turning into a fireball, Malcolm continued pulling his trigger, and a loud rumbling noise was coming from outside, but she didn't pay attention to any of it. She focused every ounce of her energy and strength on keeping his gun away from her head.

Though that rumbling noise is getting louder and louder ...

There was a loud crash beneath them and at first, she thought it was the storage room finally blowing up. Both her and Malcolm shouted in surprise, then they both started screaming as the walkway fell away from underneath them.

She clawed at the metal, finally grabbed hold of a railing, then she held on for dear life. She coiled her arms around the thin metal beam and her legs around the one underneath her. Across from her, Malcolm was clinging to the edge of the walkway.

They were dangling away from the wall at an awkward angle. Something had knocked out a few supports beams, which had caused the walkway to collapse and rip away from the wall. It was slanting towards the ground, groaning and creaking as the back end clung to one last beam.

What the hell happened?

She glanced down at the ground and was shocked to see her car. Her ugly ass car, sitting in the middle of the warehouse. Someone had driven it straight through a wall and the vehicle must have spun out of control, leaving black tire marks on the ground as the back end had taken out the support beams.

The front end looked vaguely like an accordion, and the back panel was dented so badly, it was pressing against the back tire. Various liquids were spilling out from underneath the car, from both ends. The impact had also knocked open the trunk, and laying maybe thirty feet away from the car was a large body-shaped bundle of tarp.

Bernard Krakow, the man I just can't seem to shake.

"What do you think you're—*OH FUCK!*" Malcolm cut himself off as the walkway groaned and shuddered. Jo cried out as they dropped again. The loose end of the walkway hit the ground, sending a wave of vibrations up the railings and causing her to lose her grip.

She fell, screaming the whole way down, which turned out to only be about eight feet. She landed in a pile of garbage and leaves, twisting her ankle along the way. She tumbled onto her front, sprawled out just a couple feet away from the trunk of her car.

"Jo!"

She looked up just in time to see Archer leap out of her car.

"Look out," she yelled. "Malcolm is somewhere arou—"

A bullet ripped through Archer's arm and he hit the ground. She screamed again and went to crawl towards him, but two bullets made pockmarks on the ground in front of her and she quickly went the other way. She wound up on the other side of her car and she pressed her back against it.

"Are you okay!?" she shouted, breathing heavy.

"Peachy fucking keen!" Archer shouted back. "You?"

"I'm still pissed that you lied to me and hid a body in my trunk!"

"*Seriously!?*"

"Yes! But I'm even more happy that you came to save me!"

"When we get out of here," he yelled, sounding out of breath. There was a ripping noise followed by a string of curse words. "We are going to have a long talk about you not giving me such a hard time anymore."

"Jesus fucking christ, would you two like to get married before I kill you both!?" Malcolm shouted.

"Well, now that you mention it," Archer chuckled.

"He's covered in turpentine!" she yelled, turning around and standing on her knees. "My lighter is down here somewhere."

"Uh, I don't think we'll need it."

She immediately saw what Archer was talking about—the entire back wall was covered in flames. Her little storage room fire had grown quite a bit. Then she looked back to where she'd fallen and she was surprised to see Malcolm on his feet. He'd taken off his holster and his shirt, probably hoping to lessen his chance of turning into a fireball. He held his gun in his right hand and he was inching towards Archer, who was hiding behind a beam on the other side of the car.

"What's the plan, Archer!?" she yelled, then ducked when Malcolm turned and fired a couple shots at her.

"This was pretty much it! Back up is on the way," he shouted back.

"Typical Archer," Malcolm growled. "Half asses everything and just expects to get away with it. Not this time!"

More gun shots and she listened as bullets pinged off Archer's beam. Since Mal's attention was focused elsewhere, she took a chance and peeked back over the car. Archer's brother was stalking across the room slowly, holding his gun in both hands out in front of himself. With his arms up and away from his body, she could see his entire side, and she was a little shocked at what she saw.

A huge tattoo of a tree, identical to the one on Archer's side. They had matching tattoos. It actually made her sad. At one point, these brothers had loved each other. They must have, to have permanently marked their bodies.

How awful. A father gains a son, a boy gains a brother, and another boy completely loses his mind.

She was so lost in thought, she hadn't noticed what was going on. Malcolm was at the beam, his back pressed against it. His legs were apart, his weight on his right foot, and in a second, he would be pivoting in a circle, his gun leading the way.

"*Archer!*" Jo screamed, and she didn't even think about, she jumped to her feet.

Both men whipped their heads around to look at her, and Malcolm swung his gun around. She flinched and as Archer got to his feet, Malcolm pulled the trigger.

I'm dead. I'm dead, I'm dead, I died.

She hadn't realized she'd closed her eyes, but when she caught onto the fact that she wasn't actually dead, she opened them back up. Blinked down at herself, then at Mal. He was clenching his teeth together and stepping towards her, pulling the trigger over and over again. There was nothing, just a rapid fire clicking noise.

"You're out of bullets," she gasped. He groaned.

"Oh shi-"

Archer rammed into him from behind and they both slammed into the ground. Mal's gun went flying and then the two men were rolling around, throwing punches and kicking their legs.

Archer was the bigger of the two and quickly gained the upper hand. A solid right hook stunned Malcolm, and then Archer straddled him. He grabbed his older brother by the hair and slammed his head into the concrete, over and over again.

"Stupid ... mother ... fucker!" he growled, punctuating each word with a slam. "Fucking ... touched her ... mother ... fucking ..."

"Archer," Jo panted as she hobbled around the car.

"I ... always ... wanted a ... brother ..."

"*Archer.*"

"And you ... fucking ... *ruined it!*"

"*ARCHER!*" Jo screeched, and at the same time, a large portion of the back wall collapsed. She fell to the ground, grimacing as she banged her ankle on the way down.

"What!?" he snapped, finally looking up.

"I think he gets it," she breathed, gesturing to Malcolm. She wouldn't be surprised to find out he was in a coma. Or a vegetable. Or dead.

"Holy shit," Archer gasped, looking back down at his brother. "*Shit.* Yeah, I think he ... *fuck.* What a fucked up weekend."

"This whole place is coming down," Jo said, gripping onto the bumper of her car and using it to climb back to her feet. "We need to get out of here. The car is leaking gas, I can smell it everywhere."

"You're right. C'mon, we gotta pull him out," Archer said, standing up as well.

While Jo grabbed her backpack out of the backseat of the car, Archer grabbed his brother by the wrists and started dragging him out the exit. She started limping her way after them when there was another explosion. Much bigger than the others. She wondered what had been stored in the different rooms. She was knocked clean off her feet and she flew threw the doorway. Luckily the backpack broke her fall.

"Fuck, I am so over this goddamn weekend," she groaned, rolling around like a turtle on its back.

"Fuck! Oh, fuck, run, Jo! *Run!*"

She'd barely gotten back on her feet when Archer started yelling. She looked over at him and hissed through her teeth. Burning pieces of rubble were all around them, and some must have landed on Malcolm. One leg of his turpentine soaked pants had lit up in an instant, like a Roman candle. Archer was trying to drag him *and* beat out the flames, but wasn't having much success.

Worse than that, though, was the trail of flames racing their way back into the warehouse. They'd left a lovely path of turpentine along the ground, and it was all leading back to her car. Her car, which now had a large pool of gasoline under it.

"Oh, *fuck.*"

Before she could utter another swear, she was picked up from behind. Archer threw her over his shoulder like she was a sack of potatoes and he just started running. She wrapped her arms around her head and since she didn't know what else to do, she screamed.

They'd barely made it a couple feet when the gas tank must have caught on fire. The car exploded and the entire building rocked. Archer fell to his knees and Jo was thrown away from him. She landed in a patch of grass and she went to sit up, but then curled into the fetal position, trying to cover her most vital body parts as pieces of the building rained down on her.

I'm done. Just land the engine block on me, and let's call it a day.

"You're on fire," Archer's voice was near her. She pulled her arms away from her head, but he was already slapping and beating at her foot. By the time she sat up, the danger was gone. There was a black scorch mark on her right shoe, but he'd gotten to it before it could burn through to her skin.

She looked up to find his intense hazel eyes staring at her, and they sat that way for a minute. Just staring at each other. Then she opened her mouth.

"Well," she was gasping for air. "I guess that all went better than I thought it would."

Then she promptly burst out crying.

3:04 P.M.

DAY TWO

Archer had picked her up and carried her to a ditch that ran alongside the warehouse. Such a romantic. He sat her down and told her to stay there, out of the way. Then he'd gone back and found Malcolm. The other guy was still unconscious, but he wasn't on fire anymore, and he was breathing. Archer shoved him into the ditch, then he sat down next to her.

"Just give me a minute," he moaned, rubbing at his arm. He'd torn off the bottom part of his t-shirt and had wrapped it around the bullet wound in his bicep.

"What … the fuck …" Jo breathed, staring up at the sky. It was a clear day in California, only marred by the ugly black smoke that was curling into the air.

"We only have a couple minutes," Archer said, and when she glanced at him she saw that he was staring up, as well. "The fire department will be coming. The police. It's better if we're not here."

"They'll find my car," she said.

"Don't worry about it."

"And Krakow's body. And my car. In a burning warehouse. *My* car. All this running around, and for nothing. I'm going to get arrested anyway," she laughed.

"No, you're not. Don't worry about it."

She looked over at him again.

"Care to explain?" she asked. He put his hands behind his head and kept staring up.

"Remember how I said there are crooked cops?" he asked. She processed that for a moment, then laughed again.

"Your dad owns the cops," she filled in.

"Well, not *all* of them, but enough of them," he assured her.

They were silent for a long time. At some point, a few cars pulled into the lot behind them. Archer peeked over the edge of the ditch, then laid back down.

"My dad," he said. "Some of his men. They'll find us in a second."

"You lied to me for almost the whole time we've known each other," she blurted out in response. He sighed.

"Not the whole time."

"Okay. You lied to me the whole time we were actually friends," she corrected herself.

"I did. And I regret it more than anything I've ever done," he told her. She raised her eyebrows.

"More than selling coke?"

"Yup."

"More than killing Krakow?"

"Totally."

"That's good," she said, pushing herself up into a sitting position. "But not good enough."

"For what?"

"For me to forgive you."

"Are you serious? Jojo, I don't know if you were paying attention back there, but I just saved your life."

"Um, I'm the one who got loose and started a fire," she pointed out.

"I drove a car through a building! I got *shot*, for fuck's sake!" he argued, sitting up as well.

"All of which wouldn't have happened, if you'd just been honest from the beginning," she snapped.

"Oh, for the love of ... alright, fine! *Fine.* Then what will it take for you to forgive me!?" he demanded, glaring down at her.

Jo thought for a second, then she snapped her hand out and whacked him in the throat. He let out a surprised yelp, then pressed a hand to the wound, coughing and gagging.

"*Are you shitting me!?*" he hacked out.

"There, *now* I forgive you."

Before he could bitch some more, she leaned in fast and kissed him. They toppled over, Jo landing on top of him. He only hesitated a moment before kissing her back, forgetting all about his injured throat.

"When I thought he was going to shoot you," she breathed between kisses. "I couldn't ... I can't imagine my life without you, Archer."

"When he took you, I thought I was going to explode. *Die.* I just wanted to die," he whispered, his lips wandering along her jawline.

"I was so scared. I can't ... I don't know if I can handle this life," she warned him, wrapping her arms around his shoulders.

"You don't have to. Tell me what you want, and I'll do it for you," he said, hugging her close.

"Anything?"

"Name it. Want me to walk away from it all? I will. Want me to move to a new town and change my name? I will. Anything for you," he sighed into her neck.

She thought for a long time. Then she gently pushed him away and she sat up.

"I want you to answer a question," she finally replied.

"Okay," he said, sounding nervous.

"Why in god's name did you hide Krakow in *my* trunk!?" she

demanded. "I mean, wouldn't it have made more sense to stash him somewhere? Or steal a different car and put him in it? *Literally* anything else!?"

He surprised her by starting to laugh.

"All great ideas. And I would have done something else. I had even taken out my phone so I could call Mal, thinking he would help me hide the body without telling my dad," he told her.

"So what happened? What led to Krakow being in my car?"

"*You* happened."

"I ..." she was thrown for a loop. "Wait, what?"

"You popped up behind me, scared the shit out of me. I was standing there, my phone in one hand, Bernard Krakow dead at my feet, and you were just staring at me. At first I thought 'shit, this is it. She's never going to speak to me again', and I just stared back at you," he said. Jo thought for a moment, remembering what the bouncer from the nightclub had said. Remembered her friends teasing her.

"And then ...?" she prompted him, almost not wanting to hear it.

"And suddenly you were all over me. Practically jumped on me and sucked my tongue out of my mouth. You shoved your hand down my pants and rational thoughts stopped existing. I'd spent the last five years dreaming about you touching me. My brain short circuited and all I could think about was laying you out on the hood of your car and fucking your brains out."

"Classy."

"You were the one dry humping my leg. I managed to wrestle you into the back seat and you started taking your clothes off. It was insane. So I just turned around, grabbed the body, and threw it into the trunk."

"I'm gonna be sick."

"You asked. When I got back in the car, though, you were passed out cold. I couldn't just leave you there while I disposed of a body. So I drove us home and figured I could call my brother once we were there. But you woke up as I was parking and you were all over me again. What can I say? I thought I was gonna get laid by the girl I'd been in love with forever—*nothing* is as important as that, I don't care what anyone says. We got back to your apartment and you were pulling down my zipper with your teeth. How did you learn how to do that?"

"Your mom taught me."

"Well, I'm scarred for life now because before you got it all the way down, you leaned to the side and puked all over my leg. I dragged you into the bathroom and held your hair back for the next hour. Then I left you hugging the toilet so I could clean up the mess. I was a little drunk and so fucking tired. Adrenaline crash. I went home to change out of my puked on clothes, but wound up crashing out on my couch. Next thing I knew, you were banging on my door."

She took a deep breath.

"That is … without a doubt … the stupidest fucking story I have ever heard," she told him.

"I know, right?"

"You left a dead body in my trunk because you thought you were going to get laid?"

"Pretty much."

"You're a horrible, horrible person."

"Yeah, kinda."

She paused for a second.

"And you said you're in love with me," she pointed out. He swallowed thickly and nodded.

"I did. You said it, too," he reminded her. She nodded, as well.

"I must be in love with you. Completely, stupidly, suicidally in love," she replied, struggling to keep from crying.

"You think?" he asked, brushing his thumb down the side of her cheek. She laughed and nodded again, causing one tear to escape.

"Yeah. How else could you explain me putting up with this horrible fucking weekend? Any other girl would dump your ass," she told him.

"Can't dump me if we're not technically dating."

"Oh, technically, huh. Then I guess I can technically go out with the hot maintenance guy from our building."

Archer gripped her by the back of her neck and pulled her close again.

"Careful, or you'll wake up to another dead body in your trunk," he warned her, his lips brushing against hers.

"Too soon, Archer."

"Just giving a fair warning. Can I kiss you again?"

"Too soon, Arch-"

His tongue silenced her, and she didn't mind one little bit.

THOUSANDS OF HOURS LATER

Jo leaned back in her seat, propping her bare feet on the dash of the car.

"What, were you raised in a barn?"

Archer slapped her ankle, but she didn't move. She was playing a game on her phone, and she was about to level up.

"It's my car, I can do what I want in it. Don't bother me right now," she mumbled, squinting through her sunglasses as her fingers raced across her screen.

Suddenly, her phone was snatched out of her hand. She gasped and watched as Archer tossed it into the backseat. It fell to the floor with a thunk, then promptly slid under the driver's seat, completely out of reach.

"C'mon, Jojo, this is quality time we're spending here, and you're wasting it on your phone," he teased her as he put both hands back on the wheel, steering them around a gentle curve.

"Quality time? We've been driving forever, that's not quality time.

And honestly, I think it's okay for me to zone out on my phone for twenty minutes, seeing as how we spend every single today together."

It was true. Since that fateful Saturday morning when she'd found Bernard Krakow's body in her trunk, they hadn't been apart from each other for more than eight hours at time. And really, that was pushing it. He drove her bat shit insane about half the time, but usually around the six hour mark, she started missing him and worrying about him.

Archer had been telling the truth—it was amazing how far a little drug money went in covering up their weekend antics. She felt kind of guilty, but really, she hadn't done anything wrong. Well, not too much, at least. She didn't want to go to jail because Archer was an idiot and his brother was insane.

Santana Rodriguez made most everything go away. Her apartment fire was blamed on "faulty wiring"; the building management even offered her a settlement, but she felt too guilty to take it. She was just glad the bad guys had somehow managed to escape with their lives, and that no one was any the wiser about Archer's Molotov cocktail skills.

The warehouse had made her the most nervous. They'd been long gone from the burning warehouse before any officials had shown up, but even so. There was a lot of evidence left behind, all of which could easily link her to the crime scene. Not to mention the fact that her car was burning in the center of it all.

But it never came back to her. Bernard Krakow's body was never identified and her car was never traced back to her. The whole thing was blamed on a chemical fire, mostly likely caused by squatters and those damn ravers who kept using the place.

The rave was probably the best part about that whole weekend, really. Maybe we should go to another one …

"Helloooo," Archer's voice broke into her thoughts. "Earth to Jo. We're here."

She snapped to attention and looked around. They were back

at the Universal City Overlook, up on Mulholland Drive. Only this time it was broad daylight, and there were other people around. No twinkly lights to captivate her, but it was still a stunning view.

"Awww, here?" she sighed, slowly climbing out of the car. "That's sweet, Archer."

When she'd woken up that morning, he'd informed her they were going for a ride. He wouldn't tell her where to, just said she needed to get ready and get in the car. She hadn't bothered to ask any questions, had just done as asked.

That's just how it was between two people who'd been best friends for years, and had been dating and living together for the better part of one of them. She trusted him implicitly. He knew her better than anyone else on the planet, loved her and took care of her. Gave her a home and a whole new family.

Turned out dealing coke had never really been Archer's thing. *Shocker.* Before their crazy weekend, he'd already done a lot of questionable things that had made him uncomfortable. But shooting a man and dragging his body around for a weekend? It was too much.

On top of that, it had also been one of Jo's requests. She would love him and stick with him no matter what, but the drugs and the danger scared her. It hadn't taken any arguing or convincing—she told him she was scared, and he promised he'd be done with it. He didn't care if he had to go back to working in a garage or if he had to actually work construction, or even something worse.

His father had been pretty understanding. Archer was, after all, his favorite. And just like he'd said, Santana liked to spoil his children. He said he would never ask his son to do anything illegal ever again, on one condition. He had to move closer to his father.

Stupid question. Archer had barely told Jo and she'd already started packing what few belongings she still had—who in their right mind would turn down a free house in Malibu!? And since he didn't have a job, his father got one for him, as a manager for a foreign auto shop. That made it easier for Jo when she told her mother she was moving to somewhere so rich. She explained that Archer's new job had come with a rental as one of the perks.

Archer told his mom he'd won the lottery.

"I still can't believe your mom bought the lottery story," Jo chuckled as she moved around the car. He'd backed into the spot and she sat against the hood as she observed the view.

"Yeah. Her husband keeps hitting me up for money," he snorted, leaning next to her. She turned and smiled up at him.

"Thanks for bringing me here," she said. "But I have to ask—what's the occasion?"

"You don't know what today is?" he asked.

"Um … should I?"

He pressed a hand to his heart and feigned shock.

"I can't believe it. It's like our relationship means nothing to you."

She snorted and racked her brain. It had been a little over six months since the first time they'd slept together, and since he'd saved her life. A little over six months since he'd almost ruined it. Didn't really seem like an anniversary kind of date.

"Apparently whatever happened on today's date meant nothing to me. What was it?" she asked.

"It has been exactly two years since the first time I saw your boobs."

She burst out laughing and hit him in the arm.

"What? Two years? When? How?"

"We were at the beach, remember? Your top came off when you were coming out of the water."

"Oh my god," she gasped. "That's right! And there was that like French exchange group! A bunch of eighth graders. I thought I was going to get arrested."

"I'd always had a thing for you, but after that day, Jo … there was no other woman for me," he sighed. She hit him again.

"Such a romantic."

"I know."

"Pig."

They were silent for another moment, then she turned to face him.

"That's really why you brought me out here?" she checked. He laughed.

"No. Well, I mean, I realized what day it was, and that kind of inspired it. It's a little surreal, isn't it? You and me, together. After all the years and all the crazy shit. I still can't believe it. I just … I wanted to say thank you," he told her. She smiled at him.

"That's so sweet. You don't have to thank me."

"I do. You're the best time ever, the best in bed, the best … the best friend anyone could ever ask for. You put up with my shit and you make sure I eat right and you do that thing with your tongue that drives me insane. So thank you, and I'm sorry we didn't get together a lot sooner."

He leaned down and kissed her quickly.

"Well, you're welcome. And I'm sorry you were a drug dealing, lying, asshole who never had the balls to tell me how you felt."

He barked out a laugh.

"You're one to talk. You had a crush on me for way longer, and never said a word."

"I'm a delicate *lay-dee*, we don't just blurt things out like that."

"Jo, there is literally nothing lady like about you."

When Archer kissed her that time, there was nothing quick about it. He grabbed onto her hips and pulled her so their bodies were pressed together. She moaned against his tongue, but then when he started to slide his hands up her waist, she yelped in pain and pulled away.

"Ouch," she hissed, and he winced.

"Shit. Sorry, I keep forgetting. Is it okay?"

They both looked down while Archer gently lifted the bottom of her tank top and examined the right side of her rib cage. There, from just under her bra line and all the way to her hip, was a brand new tattoo. Her gift to Archer on his birthday—her *first ever* tattoo. It was a tree, done in heavy black ink. Identical to the one he had on his rib cage, and the one she now knew his father also had on his side.

Archer had gotten his tree tattoo just before moving to Van Nuys, and he'd always refused to tell her what it meant. After seeing it on his brother's rib cage, Jo had realized it must have been a family thing.

It was Archer's father, Santana, who'd explained what it meant. The body of the tattoo was for their family—family tree. The roots represented the new home Archer had found. After he'd come up with the design, all three of them had gone and gotten them together.

Turned out, though, only Archer and Santana had been getting them to represent familial bonds. The elder Rodriguez son had only gotten his to avoid being the odd one out.

Malcolm Rodriguez. He hadn't died in the warehouse explosion, amazingly enough. He'd suffered second and third degree burns down the right side of his body, the explosion had thrown him several yards from the warehouse, and Archer had beaten him into a week long coma.

But he'd survived. He was angry and possibly psychotic, but he was alive. Santana had gotten him the best medical care money could buy, and then when he'd been well enough to leave the hospital, Santana had essentially banished him. House arrest, at the family compound in Mexico.

Neither Archer nor Jo had any direct contact with him, but there were whispers. Staff were saying he was getting crazier by the day. Jo tried not to think about it, because she knew Malcolm's story would never end well.

I just hope however it ends up going, it doesn't involve me.

Since Archer had essentially lost a brother, Jo had offered to get the tattoo. After all, she and Archer had practically been family for even longer than him and Malcolm. She'd worried that maybe it would offend him, and she'd been prepared for him to say no. Maybe it was a boy thing, maybe it was a family-only-thing.

But silly her, of course he'd loved the idea. The day after making the offer, he'd dragged her to his tattoo artist. Several sessions later, and she was marked forever by him.

Please. That happened a long time ago.

"It's fine. Just a week or so more, and then you can rub your hands all over me again," she laughed, pushing her shirt back into place.

"A week?" he whined. "That's too long. I go through withdrawals when I'm not allowed to touch you wherever I want."

"Jeez. How are you gonna handle it if I ever decide to get the other side tattooed?" she asked. He raised an eyebrow when she reached out and moved his shirt out of the way so she could hook her fingers around the top of his pants.

"Thinking about another one already?"

"Sure. Maybe another matching one."

"Another one? You want the bow and arrow?" he asked, referring to the tattoo on the inside of his bicep. She shook her head and pulled him closer.

"Please. You know which one is my favorite," she teased, running her finger back and forth behind his button. He rolled his eyes.

"Oh jesus. I'm getting it removed," he swore. She laughed again and started pulling at his shirt, pushing it up his chest. He batted at her hands, trying to stop her.

"No. You can't, I love it."

"It's stupid."

"It's not stupid," she said, holding still.

She looked down at the tattoo that was just behind his fly. Scrolling letters spelling out a famous quote.

"It's completely fucking stupid, Jo."

"It's not," she argued. "You know why?"

"Enlighten me."

"Because you got this tattoo when you were black out drunk."

"Um, I think that might be the definition of stupid."

"No, because when you were blacked out and you wanted to get something permanently marked on your body, you got something that would always remind you of me," she pointed out, smiling big at him.

"That's very sweet. But I think I got it because I was wasted and you've made me watch that movie a million times."

"My point exactly."

"You're ridiculous. Fine, the tattoo is about you, and always has been. Happy?" he asked. She nodded.

"Ridiculously so."

"Good, because I have something I need to show you."

Archer's voice had grown serious, surprisingly her a little, and he turned away from her. She followed his gaze and saw that he was staring at the trunk.

"What is it?" she asked, a little nervous. She was pretty sure she had PTSD regarding all trunks.

"Scared?" he asked, taking the keys out of his pocket and sticking one in the lock.

"Terrified. Trunks and I don't get along so well," she replied.

"I promise, this body will be way easier to get rid of."

She'd been ready to laugh at his joke, but then he opened the trunk and all that came out of her mouth was a choking sound. Her eyes bulged as she took in the roughly adult body sized lump sitting in the middle of her trunk, all wrapped up in her favorite fuzzy blue throw blanket.

"What ... the fuck ..." she breathed, pressing her hand to her chest.

"I helped you when you came running to me with a body in your trunk," he reminded her. "No questions asked."

"Yeah, but you put that body there!" she growled through clenched teeth, slapping him in the chest repeatedly.

"Still. I helped, remember?"

"How could you do this? Archer, this is *my* car!"

"That *I* bought you, so really ..."

She shrieked and went from slapping to full on punching.

"You promised!" she started yelling. "You promised, no more drug bullshit!"

"Jo," he laughed, grabbing for her wrists.

"No more danger! Remember that!? You dickfuck!"

"*Dickfuck?* Is that even a word?"

"What is wrong with you!?"

"*Jo,*" he stressed her name as he finally got a hold of her flailing limbs. "Stop. Just hear me out."

"Hear you out? Oh, okay. Yes, please, tell me how your murdered this dude and stashed him in my trunk, *AGAIN!*" she shouted. There were several other groups of people at the lookout, and all of them turned to stare at the crazy screaming lady.

"Chill out!" he shouted back, then he abruptly let her go and reached into the trunk.

"What are you doing?" she asked, then gasped as he grabbed the edge of the blanket and started pulling "Don't do that! I don't want to see what ..." Her voice trailed off as the blanket unfurled, revealing its horrifying contents.

Pillows. Several pillows, arranged side to side. There was also a bottle of champagne, two mugs, and underneath it all, a pizza box.

"Seriously, Jo. Calm—you need to look the word up. Can you imagine if I had lost my shit when you showed me a body in your trunk? Not cool," he sighed, shaking his head back and forth. She glared and elbowed him in the stomach.

"What the fuck is all this? A joke?" she demanded.

"Yeah. Pretty funny, right?"

"*Wrong.* Not funny. Not funny at all."

"Oh. Too soon?"

"Yes, Archer. Too soon."

He laughed at her and bent into the trunk. A couple pushes and the pull of a lever later and the backseats were folded down. He arranged the blanket so it covered the bottom of the car, then he pushed the pillows back before climbing into the vehicle.

"What are you doing?" Jo asked. He fumbled around for a minute—he was such a big guy, he didn't fit at all. Even with his head resting on the back of the seats, his legs still stuck outside. He moved the pizza box so it was resting sideways next to him, then he gestured for her to join him.

"C'mon. It's a picnic," he said.

"Are you joking?"

"Get your ass in the car, Jo."

She frowned, but she did it. She gingerly crawled over the lip of the trunk and ducked as she moved further into the vehicle. It was awkward twisting and rolling around, but eventually she was laying down next to him. He smiled and put his hands behind his head.

"You know," she sighed, staring out at the clear blue sky. "This isn't so bad."

"Right?"

"But the joke wasn't. You ever do that again, and I'll mace you."

"Fair enough."

He popped the cork on the champagne and managed to pour some into the mugs. He handed her one and they sipped at the bubbly in silence for a couple minutes.

"This was your idea?" she asked after she'd finished her champagne and had set the cup aside. She turned onto her side and moved so she was resting her head on his bicep.

"Yeah," he replied, moving his legs around so he could kick off his shoes. They landed inside the trunk with a heavy thump.

"What brought all this on?"

"I told you, your boobs."

"Archer. Please. Be serious, just this once?" she asked, laying her hand flat on his stomach and brushing it back and forth. She could feel his abs jump and constrict under her fingers.

"I don't know," he finally answered. "I just … like I said, I wanted to say thank you. It may have had a really fucked up start, but this has been the best six months of my life. I honestly wouldn't change a thing that happened, because it all brought me closer to you."

"Awww, Archer," she sighed, curling her fingers and clutching at his t-shirt. "That's really sweet."

"You've always been the best part of my life. Now I get to say it out loud and show you."

"All thanks to a dead body in a trunk," she chuckled, gently pulling his t-shirt up his body.

"Yeah, good ol' Bernie. A hell of a weekend, huh?"

"Yeah. Archer?"

"Hmmm?"

"Stop talking now."

As she scratched her nails across his bare skin, he leaned down and kissed her hard. She would never get tired of the sensation. Archer touching her, kissing her. Turning her body into putty and setting it on fire. Giving her everything she never knew she was missing. She gasped into his mouth and wrapped her legs around one of his, seeking movement and friction.

"As much as I love this side of you," he panted, one his hands moving under the back of her shirt. "I have to give a warning—you're perilously close to getting fucked in public."

"Perilously close, huh," she breathed, then she shimmied out of her shirt. He groaned and one his hands immediately went to her breasts. "That just won't do."

"Goddamn, I am so in love with you," he chuckled before biting into her bottom lip. She sucked air through her teeth and pulled away.

"Not as much as I am with you. How long will the drive home take?" she asked, reaching down and tugging at his belt.

"Too long. Good thing I planned for this," he said, and she watched as he lifted his leg, struggling to use his toes to catch the strap that hung down from the trunk lid.

"You did?" she asked, then she laughed as he got hold of the strap and started pulling down the lid.

"Of course. Most people have a picnic on the grass, Jo. Why the fuck do you think I laid it out in the trunk?" he asked.

"Sick sense of humor?" she guessed.

"Well … yeah, that too," he replied, and with one final jerk of his leg, the trunk slammed shut.

Saturday morning in Los Angeles in July. The sun was shining, the birds were chirping, and everything seemed right with the world. Anyone who came to Universal City Overlook that day and saw the classic 1970 Chevelle SS parked there wouldn't have thought anything was strange about it.

They certainly never would've guessed there were two bodies in the trunk, doing their best to become one.

degradation

Available Now

Tatum plucked at her shirt in a nervous manner. She had tucked it into a tight pencil skirt and even put on a pair of sling back stilettos. If someone had personally requested her, she wanted to make an effort to look nice. She had blown out her hair and put curls in the ends, and toned down her make up. Even she had to admit it, she looked presentable.

For once.

Men in expensive business suits began to file into the conference room and she stood still, giving a polite smile to everyone who entered. A team of lawyers was meeting with their client. Six chairs were lined up on one side of a long table, with just a single chair on the other side.

Tate had been positioned at the back of the room, next to a sideboard filled with goodies and coffee and water. She fussed about, straightening napkins and setting up the glasses. When all six chairs were filled on the one side, she stared at their backs, wondering who the big shot was that got to stare them all down. The person who would be facing her. A door at the back of the room swung open and her breath caught in her threat.

Holy. Shit.

Jameson Kane strode into the room, only offering a curt smile to his lawyers. His eyes flashed to her for just a second, then he looked back. His smile became genuine and he tipped his head towards her, almost like a bow.

She gaped back at him, positive that her mouth was hanging open. What was he doing there!? Had he known she would be there? Had he been the one to request her? Impossible, he didn't know what temp agency she worked for—but what would be the chances? She hadn't seen him in seven years, and now twice in two days.

Tate felt like swallowing her tongue.

"Gentlemen," Jameson began, seating himself across from the lawyers. "Thanks for meeting with me today. Would anyone care for any coffee? Water? The lovely Ms. O'Shea will be helping us today." He gestured towards Tate, but no one turned around. Several people asked for coffee. Jameson asked for water, his smile still in place. It was almost a smirk. Like he knew something she didn't.

She began to grind her teeth.

She delivered everyone's drinks, then carried around a tray of snacks. No one took anything. She moved to the back of the room, refilled the water pitcher. Tidied up. Felt Jameson staring at her.

This is ridiculous. You're Tatum O'Shea. You eat boys for breakfast.

But thinking that made her remember when he had said something very similar to her, and she felt a blush creep up her cheeks.

She was pretty much ignored the whole time. They all argued back and forth about what business decisions Jameson should, or shouldn't, make. He was very keen on dismantling struggling companies and selling them off. They tried to curb his desires. His tax lawyer explained how his tax shelter in Hong Kong was doing. Another lawyer gave him a run down on property law in Switzerland. Tate tried to hide her yawns.

They took a five minute break after an hour had passed. Tate had her back to the room, rearranging some muffins on a tray, when she felt the hair on the back of her neck start to stand up. She turned around in slow motion, taking in Jameson as he walked up to her.

"Surprised?" he asked, smiling down at her.

"Very. Did you ask for me?" she questioned. He nodded.

"Yes. You ran away so quickly the other night. I wanted to get

226

reacquainted," he explained. She laughed.

"Maybe I didn't," she responded. He shrugged.

"That doesn't really matter to me. What are you doing tonight?" he asked. She was a little caught off guard.

"Are you asking me out, Kane?" she blurted out. He threw back his head and laughed.

"Oh god, still a little girl. *No.* I don't ask people out. I was asking what you were doing tonight," Jameson replied.

She willed away the blush she felt coming on. He still had the ability to make her feel so stupid. She had been through so much since him, come so far with her esteem and her life. It wasn't fair that he could still make her feel so small. She wanted to return the favor. She cleared her throat.

"I'm working."

"Where?"

"At a bar."

"What bar?"

"A bar you don't know."

"And tomorrow night?"

"Busy."

"And the night after that?"

"*Every* night after that," Tate informed him, crossing her arms. He narrowed his eyes, but continued smiling.

"Surely you can find some time to meet up with an old friend," he said. She shook her head.

"We were never friends, Kane," she pointed out. He laughed.

"Then what is it? Are you scared of me? Scared I'll eat you alive?" he asked. She stepped closer to him, refusing to be intimidated.

"I think *you're* the one who should be scared. You don't know me, Kane. You never did. *And you never will*," she whispered. Jameson leaned down so his lips were almost against her ear.

"I know what you feel like from the inside. That's good enough for me," he whispered back. Tate stepped away. She felt like she couldn't breathe. He did something to her insides.

"You, and a lot of other people. You're not as big a deal as you think," she taunted. It was a complete lie, but she had to get the upper hand back. He smirked at her.

"That sounds like a challenge to me. I have to defend my honor," he warned her. She snorted.

"Whatever. Point to the challenger then, *me*. Defend away," she responded, rolling her eyes.

He didn't respond, just continued smirking down at her. The lawyers began filing back into the room and Jameson took his position on the other side of the table. She wasn't really sure what their little spar had been about, or what had come out of it. She was just going to try to get through the rest of the conference, and then she would scurry away before he could talk to her again. She didn't want anything to do with Jameson Kane, or his—,

"Ms. O'Shea," his sharp voice interrupted her thoughts. Tate lifted her head.

"Yes, sir?" she asked, making sure to keep her voice soft and polite.

"Could you bring me some water, and something to eat," he asked, not even bothering to look at her as he flipped through a contract.

She loaded up a tray with his requests and made her way around the table. No one even looked at her, they just threw legal jargon around at each other—a language she didn't know. She stood next to Jameson and leaned forward, setting his water down and then going about arranging cheese and crackers on a plate for him. She was about halfway done when she felt it.

Are those ... his fingers!?

Tate froze for a second. His touch was light as he ran his fingers up and down between her legs. She glanced down at her knees and then glanced over at him. He was still looking down, but she could see him smirking. She tried to ignore him, tried to go back to setting up his food, but his hand went higher. Daring to brush up past her knees, well underneath her skirt. He couldn't get any farther, not unless he pushed up her skirt, or sunk down in his chair. She dumped the rest of the cheese on his plate and started to scoot away. She had just gotten back to her station when she heard a thunking noise, followed by groans.

"No worries. Ms. O'Shea! So sorry, could you get this?" Jameson's voice was bored sounding.

She turned around and saw that he had knocked over his water glass. He was blotting at the liquid as it spread across the table. The lawyers were all holding their papers aloft, grumbling back and forth.

Tate groaned and grabbed a towel before striding back to the table. She glared at him the whole way, but he still refused to look at her. She started as far away from him as she could get, mopping everything up, but eventually she had to almost lean across him to reach the mess. She stood on her toes, stretching across the table top.

As she had assumed it would, his hand found its way back to her legs. Only this time he wasn't shy, and her position allowed for a lot of access. His hand shot straight up the back of her skirt, his fingertips brushing against the lace of her panties.

She swallowed a squeak and glanced around. If any of the other gentlemen lifted their heads, they would have been able to see their client with half of his arm up his assistant's skirt, plain as day. He managed to run his finger under the hem of her underwear, down the left side of her butt cheek, before she pulled away. She stomped back to the food station, throwing the towel down with such violence, she knocked over a stack of sugar cubes.

When she turned around, Jameson was finally looking at her. She plunked her fists on her hips, staring straight back. His smirk was in place—as she had expected it would be—and he held up a finger, pointing it straight up. *One.* Then he pointed at himself. One point. *Tied.* He thought they were playing a game. She hadn't wanted to play games with him, but she hated to lose at *anything*, and she never wanted to lose to a man like Jameson Kane.

An idea flitted across her mind. Tate wanted to make him as uncomfortable as he had just made her feel. She coolly raised an eyebrow and then took her time looking around the room. The lawyers all still had their backs to her—not one of them had turned around the entire time she'd been there. Blinds had been drawn over every window, no one could see in the office, but she knew the door wasn't locked. Anyone could walk into the room. She took a deep breath. It didn't matter anyway, what was the worst that could happen? She would get fired? It was a temp job, that Jameson had requested her for—he didn't even work there. Did she really care what happened?

She dragged her stare back to meet his and then ran her hands down the sides of her skirt. He raised an eyebrow as well, his eyes following her hands. When she got to the hem of the skirt, she pressed her palms flat and began to slowly, *achingly*, slide the material up her legs. Now both his eyebrows were raised. He flicked his gaze to her face, then went right back to her skirt. Higher, up past her knees. To the middle of her thighs. Higher still. If anyone turned around, they would be very surprised at what they saw. One more inch, and her skirt would be moot. Jameson's stare was practically burning holes through her.

Taking short, quick, breaths through her nose, Tate slid her hands around to her butt. She wiggled the material up higher back there, careful to keep the front low enough to hide her whole business, and was able to hook her fingers into her underwear. She didn't even think about what she was doing, couldn't take her eyes off of Jameson, as she slid her underwear over her butt and down her hips. As the lace slid to her ankles, she pushed her skirt back into place. Then she stepped out of the panties and bent over, picking them up. When she stood upright, she let the lace dangle from her hand while she held up one finger. Point.

Winning.

Jameson nodded his head at her, obviously conceding to her

victory, then returned his attention to the papers in front of him. Tate let out a breath that she hadn't even realized she was holding, and turned around, bracing her hands against the table. She leaned forward and took deep breaths. She had just started to gain some ground on slowing her heart rate, when a throat cleared.

"What is that, Ms. O'Shea?" Jameson called out from behind her. She spun around, balling up her underwear in her fist.

"Excuse me, sir?" she asked.

"That," he continued, gesturing with his pen at her. "In your hands. You have something for me. Bring it here."

Now everyone turned towards her. Tate held herself as still as possible, her hands clasped together in front of her legs, hiding the underwear between her fingers. All eyes were on her. Jameson smirked at her and leaned back in his chair. She took a shaky breath.

"I don't know what—,"

"Bring it here, Ms. O'Shea, *now*," he ordered, tapping the table top with his pen. She glared at him.

Fuck this.

She turned around and pulled one of the silver trays in front of her. She laid her panties out neatly on top, making sure the material was smooth and flat. She was very thankful that she had gone all out and worn her good, expensive, *"I'm-successful-and-career-oriented!"*, underwear. She balanced the tray on top of her fingertips and spun around, striding towards their table, a big smile on her face.

"For you, Mr. Kane," she said in a breathy voice, then dropped the tray in front of him. It clattered loudly and spun around a little before coming to a rest, the panties sliding off to one side.

As she walked away, she could hear some gasps. A couple laughs. A very familiar chuckle. When she got to the door, she pulled it open before turning back to the room. A couple of the lawyers were gawking at her, and the rest were laughing, gesturing to the display she had just put on; Jameson was looking straight at her, his smirk in place. She blew him a kiss and then stomped out the door.

A Twin Estates Novel Excerpt

NEIGHBORS

Available Now

"I've seen you around the buildings, and then I was on this dating website, and I saw your profile."

Oh. Jesus. Katya was really going to murder her roommate. It was one thing to have a bit of fun and put some naughty stuff up on a website, but when it brought random strange men to where she lived, it was going too far.

"Ooohhh, yeeeaaahh. *That* website," she grumbled, finally kneeling down to pick up her bag.

"Yeah. I gotta say, I've noticed you for a while, and I always thought you were …"

"Were what?" she asked, glancing up at him. He shrugged.

"I don't know. Just … I read that profile, and I had to meet that woman."

Katya wasn't sure what to make of his statement—she was a little insulted that the woman he'd seen around the building hadn't been interesting enough to meet. But she was also a little flattered—and, admittedly, excited—that he'd sought out the woman from the profile.

"So if you hadn't seen my profile, you would never have introduced yourself?" she double checked. Liam chuckled and rubbed at the back of his neck, looking a little sheepish.

"Honestly? No. I mean, don't get me wrong, you seemed like a really sweet girl, and you're gorgeous, but I'm not exactly a sweet guy. I didn't want to waste your time, or freak you out," he said.

"Freak me out?"

"Yeah."

"How? What do you mean?"

"Well, like I assumed you were a Sunday school teacher or something," he explained. "I own and operate a club downtown. The two don't exactly match."

"Sunday school teacher? Why?" she was a little surprised, then was even more so when she watched his gaze blatantly travel up and down her body.

"My other guess was librarian. You just always seemed … sweet. Innocent," he said.

Sweet and innocent. Translation: **boring**. *Tori was right. I'm dull, and it took a made up online profile to get a guy to notice me.*

Katya should've been angry at him. For judging her before he'd met her, solely based on her outward appearance. For perpetuating the stereotype that a woman had to be overtly sexy in order to be interesting. For only giving her the time of day because of some ridiculous website.

But she was actually angry at *herself*. She felt like a prisoner of her own inhibitions, her own naïveté. She was angry that deep down, she *wanted* to be an overtly sexual woman, the kind that could draw men in with a single glance.

She wanted to be that woman from her profile bio.

She just didn't know how, and before her anger could boil over, all her carefully built manners and over the top etiquette cooled her off. She managed a tight lipped smile for him.

"Well, I'm sorry to disappoint you, but I didn't write that bio," she told him the truth.

"You didn't?"

"Nope. My roommate did."

"Ah. Roommate. So I take it you don't do strip-aerobics," he said with a chuckle. She shook her head.

"I didn't even know that was a real thing."

He burst out laughing.

"Gotcha. So the whole sweet and innocent thing, that *is* the real you."

She opened her mouth, then froze. Was that the real her? Or was that just who she'd convinced herself she needed to be? She was so sick and tired of everyone assuming she was this insipid goody-two-shoes. Tori telling her to get a life. This stranger assuming she was a librarian. It wasn't fair. She could be just as wild, just as fun-loving as the next person. All she needed was the chance.

Take a chance ...

"Just because I don't walk around in a thong bikini doesn't mean I'm all innocence," she replied. He cocked up an eyebrow.

"I dunno. A baker, huh? You pretty much look like angel food cake to me," he teased her. She glared at him.

"Was this your big plan? Stalk me down in my building and interrogate me? Is this how you ask out all your dates?" she demanded.

"Who said I was gonna ask you out on a date?" he replied.

"Oh, please. You didn't come over here to ask me about my strip-aerobics class, and we both know it," she said, proud of herself for the quick and snappy come back.

"Touché. I was going to invite you to my club," he said. She took a deep breath and for a split second, thought about how early she had to get up for work. Thought about the design she had to work on for a client. Thought about her big plans for the evening—reinforcing all the buttons on her dress shirts.

"I'm free after eight o'clock," she blurted out. He laughed at her again, and she couldn't help but notice that he had a great laugh, and an even better smile. She'd known him for all of two seconds, but she was willing to bet "fun-loving" was his middle name. The man was made to smile.

"Whoa there, angel cake, I don't think this is such a good idea," he said, holding up a hand.

"Why not? I love to dance."

"It's not that kind of club."

"What? Is it like a book club?"

He laughed again, but she hadn't been joking. She figured he didn't need to know that and she managed to laugh as well.

"Look, you seem like a nice girl. I'm sure you get asked on lots of dates, and if I was a tax attorney, or an insurance salesman, I'd for sure want to go out with you, but I don't want to make you uncomfortable," he told her. She rolled her eyes.

"If anyone here is a '*nice girl*', it's you—I've made all the moves so far. If you don't want to go out, just say so, and I can move onto the next guy, and you can go to your little club house thingy," she said.

This was so far out of her comfort zone, she wasn't sure she was still the same Katya anymore. Her Eros profile had come to life and body snatched her. The words coming out of her mouth, the tone of her voice, were completely foreign to her. Yesterday, Katya would have gotten embarrassed. Blushed at the way he talked about her, apologized for taking up his time—even though he'd been the one to stop her.

This new-Katya, though, refused to be embarrassed. He had come there for a reason, to ask *her* out, so she had nothing to be sorry about, and hell, maybe she would move onto another man. She'd certainly gotten a lot of offers from the website. She squared her shoulders and looked him straight in the eyes, praying her bravado held out for a few more minutes.

"Club house thingy, huh," he mumbled, his eyes wandering over her form again.

"Are we done? I have some messages to catch up on," she said, then she went to step around him. He reached out and grabbed her arm.

"Alright, alright, calm down. You want to see my club?" he asked. She noticed he kept putting emphasis on that word, *club*.

"I don't know, now. You've made it weird. Am I going to show up and it's some football club? A One Direction fan club? I'm not so into those things," she said.

"How about a sex club? You into that?"

She almost swallowed her tongue. A sex club? He owned and operated a *sex club*? Did those even exist in real life? And the way he'd said it. A perfect stranger, talking about a sex club with her. In broad daylight.

Maybe I never really woke up this morning and this is all a dream.

"I'm sorry," she cleared her throat. "Are you saying you want to take me to a sex club?"

"Yes."

"Is that where you take all your first dates?" she asked, still thinking he might be joking.

"No. Usually I keep it a secret. Freaks most girls out—just like I thought it would you, until I saw that Eros profile," he explained.

"So let me see if I have this straight. Whatever you saw on my profile made you think I'd be interested in going to a sex club with you," she spelled it all out.

"Yeah. Clearly, I was mistaken. It was nice meeting you, Katya."

She was having a moment. A tidal pull on her conscience. This was a bad idea on an epic level. Going to a sex club with a man she'd just met? That's how women ended up on Dateline. Not to mention the fact that Katya simply didn't do things like that—she was more of a museum or opera house kind of girl.

But new-Katya, the woman from the profile, she bristled against old-Katya. Got mad at the way this handsome stranger was looking at her, as if she couldn't possibly be brave enough to try something new and daring. Something sexy and a little dangerous.

"Nine o'clock," she blurted out.

"Excuse me?"

"I'll need more time," she explained. "I can meet you down here at nine o'clock."

"C'mon now, this isn't like truth or dare. No points for trying, it's okay. We can just pretend this didn't happen, go back to avoiding eye contact when we pass each other on the sidewalk," he suggested.

"Awww, see? You're such a good little girl, trying to look out for me," she spoke to him in a baby-voice. His smile finally reappeared and she had to will away the blush she felt creeping up her neck.

"Alright, angel cake. Let's see how far you'll take this cute little act. Nine o'clock," he said, then he finally let her go. She nodded her head.

"I'll be down here," she assured him, then she started for the elevator.

"Oh! And a suggestion," he shouted after her. She turned as she stepped onto the lift and saw that his grin was stretching from ear to ear.

"Yes?"

"Don't change your clothing. What you're wearing is *perfect.*"

ABOUT THE AUTHOR

Crazy woman living in an undisclosed location in Alaska (where the need for a creative mind is a necessity!), I have been writing since …, forever? Yeah, that sounds about right. I have been told that I remind people of Lucille Ball - I also see shades of Jennifer Saunders, and Denis Leary. So basically, I laugh a lot, I'm clumsy a lot, and I say the F-word A LOT.

I like dogs more than I like most people, and I don't trust anyone who doesn't drink. No, I do not live in an igloo, and no, the sun does not set for six months out of the year, there's your Alaska lesson for the day. I have mermaid hair - both a curse and a blessing - and most of the time I talk so fast, even I can't understand me.

Yeah. I think that about sums me up.

Made in the USA
Columbia, SC
30 May 2017